WHAT LIES BENEATH

An absolutely addictive crime thriller with a huge twist

BILL KITSON

THIS IS A REVISED EDITION OF A BOOK FIRST
PUBLISHED AS "DEPTH OF DESPAIR"

Revised edition 2019
Joffe Books, London

First published as "DEPTH OF DESPAIR" in 2009
© Bill Kitson

Please join our mailing list for free Kindle crime thriller, detective, mystery books and new releases.
www.joffebooks.com

ISBN: 978-1-78931-210-2

FOREWORD

'No one would really choose this as a way of life,' she says. 'No one. I am glad to be able to send money home. My family are very poor. Sometimes,' she covered her face with one hand, 'it is as if your soul is getting hurt.'

'Lolli' — Reported in the Daily Mirror 24 January 2006

ACKNOWLEDGMENTS

I am grateful to the following people who have given me information and advice in the preparation of *What Lies Beneath*.

To Tatiana Mechklovska, who provided valuable background and Russian translations; Dr Dave McGorman, for advice on water temperatures and diving techniques; Pat Almond and Kathleen Dabb, my readers and critics; Joan, for pointing me in the right direction and not allowing me to give up; Val, for countless hours of meticulous editing.

DEDICATION

For Val
Wife, lover, best friend, critic and editor.

PROLOGUE

Bosnia 1996

The house was in the middle of a war zone. The roof was perforated by shell holes, the walls pock-marked by bullet scars.

It was a far from safe refuge but for the woman and child there was no alternative. They ducked through the gaping doorway ahead of a curtain of machine gun fire that traced a fresh pattern on to the brickwork close to where they'd been running.

They passed the remnant of the door hanging in splinters. Their footsteps crunched as they hurried down a hallway, stepping carefully over broken glass, chipped masonry and plaster.

The house smelt abominably of stale urine and worse, the sweet cloying stench of rotting corpses. A smell that was too familiar. They found a body in the first room. It was an unrecognizable travesty of what was once a human being. What remained had provided a feast for too many predators. Neither mother nor daughter showed surprise, let alone shock.

In the second room they found three more bodies, bloated and bloodstained. As they peered in, the room's other occupants scurried hither and thither, their meal disturbed by the intrusion. The child clutched at her mother's arm. Death held little terror but rats were different.

Their only choice was to go upstairs. They'd be more vulnerable but it would be safer from intruders. At the head of the stairway they found one room relatively unscathed. It contained nothing but a bed and a cupboard. They sat on the bed and waited. Waited and prayed.

They'd been there a few minutes when they heard someone enter the house. They listened as the newcomer trod the path they had. They clung together in fear as the footsteps approached.

They saw the shadow first. Then the man appeared. Friend or enemy? They were unsure until they saw the uniform, recognized the emblem and relaxed.

'Thank God,' the mother said. 'Now we're safe.' She smiled. She was still smiling when the bullet entered her brain. The child began to scream. She screamed at the blood that spattered her face, her hands and dress. She screamed for the murder of her mother and she screamed in fear for her life.

The killer looked at the child. She'd be ten perhaps eleven years old. A pretty little thing, but looks were unimportant for his purpose. 'I'm not going to shoot you.' She didn't understand. No words in any language would have comforted her.

He approached, unzipping his trousers. The child began to scream with renewed vigour. He clamped one hand across her mouth and with the other began ripping the clothing from her slender body.

He pushed the naked child on to the bed and straddled her, too preoccupied to notice the figure in the doorway. An hour later he collected every scrap of combustible material and lit a bonfire to destroy the house, his victims and all evidence of his crimes.

The man in peacekeeper's uniform walked away.

Two weeks later as he was leaving his quarters he heard a voice. 'Good evening; I'd like a word.'

He turned. He didn't recognize the voice or its owner. 'What can I do for you?' He looked at the insignia. 'Captain...?'

The man was leaning against the wall, smoking a cigarette. He gestured towards the makeshift hospital. 'I guess you must be pretty busy?'

'Yes I am. Is there some point to this?'

'A shame that. Being so busy I mean, not having time to relax. I bet you can't remember the last time you watched a video?'

'No, but I still don't see—?'

'You look like someone who'd enjoy a video. I've got one for you. It's so recent it hasn't been released yet. You really should see it. It's one I shot right here.' The officer gestured towards the town. 'I reckon you'd enjoy it. After all, you're starring in it.'

CHAPTER ONE

2007

Cauldmoor hadn't always been deserted. Once there'd been a community there. A community whose isolation bonded them. Theirs had been a peaceful existence working lead and other ores, tending sheep or growing what they could in the bitter soil. They battled constantly against nature. The disaster that wiped them out was man made. Even in their isolation they'd heard of the men who'd come from over the sea. Brutal men who slaughtered to gain control of vast swathes of land. The invaders arrived in the middle of a spring morning when the sun was nearing its height.

It was after that the rumours began to circulate. Rumours that became the legend of Cauldmoor. It was said that cries could be heard, carried throughout the valley on the ever present wind.

The causeway became known as The Grieving Stones and the hitherto unnamed lakes were called Lamentation Tarn and Desolation Tarn.

Legends didn't worry the angler as he arrived at the tarn, took his gear and walked to the lake. He unlocked the boathouse, climbed into a boat and rowed out to the middle.

He dropped anchor, chose a fly and commenced casting. It was 7 a.m. Faint sounds seeped through the air. The hiss of the wind channelled by the hills, the call of a curlew, the bleating of sheep. For the most part, however, the silence was absolute.

The fish weren't rising. It was an hour before he felt his line go taut. Long before it broke surface he realized it wasn't a fish. A fish would have writhed and struggled. There was no resistance. Just a dead weight.

He stared in horror at the obscenity on the end of his line. As he told a friend in the pub that night, 'There I was. Alone in the middle of the tarn. Miles from anywhere. And there was this bloody skull grinning back at me.'

Detective Inspector Mike Nash stared out from the veranda of the bothy. Like the rest of the low building, it was painted with creosote to counteract the weather. Inside, the gas heaters were on full blast but the room was still cold. It would be cramped but it would have to do as an incident room. At least a few people might warm the place up a bit. If anything could be warmed up in such a desolate place. He shivered, only partly from the raw wind that whipped round the building. He burrowed deeper inside his waxed coat.

They'd been there an hour. Three of them plus a couple of uniforms. Now they'd to wait for the divers. They were taking their time. Not that Nash could blame them. 'Rather them than me.' He was unaware he'd voiced his thoughts. The woman alongside him stirred, 'What? Who do you mean?'

Nash looked at his assistant. He pondered the twist of fate that had brought this handsome young woman from Belarus to England, to Yorkshire and finally into a career in the police.

'What did you mean, "rather them than me"?'

'Talking to myself, was I? Can't say I'm surprised in this godforsaken spot. I was thinking about the divers.'

Sergeant Clara Mironova stared at the dark waters of the tarn and shivered. 'I get your point. What do you think of this place?'

'I'd rather not think about it. There's something eerie about it. I can't rid myself of a feeling of depression.'

Mironova looked at her boss with concern. He looked tired. The last case they'd worked on together had affected him badly. Hardly surprising with the outcome. She thought of Stella Pearson. Nash and Stella had been an item until Stella was injured, paralyzed by wounds intended for Nash. She could only guess at the guilt he felt. She also knew how ill he'd been before he transferred from the Met. Was this a symptom of that illness? Or an example of the way Nash reacted to his surroundings. It was a strange ability. Or was it more of a curse than a blessing? She knew he was prone to nightmares about the cases he worked on. Perhaps she was the lucky one. When she slept it was dreamless. On the whole, she thought, she was better off. 'All we have is a skull, Mike,' she said, half teasing him.

'True and that might not tell us anything. Is Mexican Pete on his way?' Like everyone else Nash referred to the pathologist by his nickname. Fortunately, Professor Ramirez either hadn't heard it or didn't know the Ballad of Eskimo Nell. Or possibly both.

'He's got lectures all morning. He'll be here at lunchtime. He asked for directions.'

'Hell, Clara, that's a long conversation for Mexican Pete.'

'I think he was trying to chat me up. Is Superintendent Pratt coming?'

'He's not planning to. Just said we're to keep him up to speed. What did you get out of the angler?'

'Nothing useful. He was fishing for an hour, felt the resistance and pulled in the skull. Seemed peeved because it's the last day of the season and he's been cheated of his fishing.'

'What did you tell him?'

'I said think yourself lucky. You could have been on the other end of the line. That silenced him.'

'I'll bet. Listen, I'm going for a walk up the valley. I want to have a look round and see if I can get my circulation going. You hang on here in case the Rubber Johnnies arrive.'

'I'll see if Viv's got the kettle on. This bothy's quite comfortable in a fashion. No electric, of course, but once Viv worked out how to turn the bottled gas on it started to warm up a bit.'

As she watched Nash walk towards the ridge separating the lakes, DC Pearce joined her on the balcony. He glanced over towards their boss. 'Trouble?'

Clara nodded.

'What is it?'

'I reckon he feels guilty about Stella.'

'That's ridiculous,' Pearce interjected.

'Maybe, but Mike thinks he's responsible for her being in a wheelchair.'

'If it hadn't been for Mike and you, Stella and the others would be dead.'

'I know that and you know it. And in his more rational moments Mike knows it. But when he's got that depression on it's a different matter.'

'No one's to blame except that damned psychopath. We never know how hostage situations will end.' Viv paused and watched Nash heading up the slope. 'Don't suppose it helped that Mike was giving Stella one.'

'Put with your usual delicacy. But you're right, and it proves something else. The victims of violence aren't always those who die. Sometimes survivors suffer even more.'

Nash fastened his coat up to the neck. He'd put his gloves on and pulled his flat cap down firmly before setting off, walking as briskly as he could. It took twenty minutes to reach the top of the ridge. He stared to the west where Desolation Tarn lay dark and uninviting, then back towards Lamentation Tarn with its grisly secret. Nash still felt cold. But this was a coldness that struck from within. He shivered and looked around.

As the wind strengthened, Nash heard a faint keening sound. It was like a cry of distress. Of pain beyond endurance. The moaning appeared part of the wind and yet separate.

The day darkened and Nash shivered again. Louder, harsher and shriller the sound came.

There was mist writhing around now as the wind caused it to eddy. Nash stared about. He could almost imagine there were shapes within the gloom. Figures moving in the distance. Then the mist was gone, the shapes vanished. The threnody ceased. It had only been a fleeting impression. But it was enough to send a cold chill down his spine.

Nash came briskly down the hillside, his walk only marginally short of panic. He neared the bothy and saw the diving team struggling down Misery Near with their equipment. Theirs was an unenviable task. There was no certainty the angler could pinpoint the place he'd been fishing. And the 'Rubber Johnnies' would be working in dark, cold water. At this altitude and at this time of year they'd have little more than twenty or thirty minutes under water. The soil on the moor was peat. It would darken the water, defying even their powerful torches. They would have to work by touch. Nash shivered anew at the prospect.

Pearce had brewed tea. 'I need you to fetch supplies from Bishopton.' Nash told him. 'Whilst you're there contact the secretary of the angling club. I want him here.'

Mironova and Pearce exchanged glances. 'Does that mean you're treating this as a suspicious death?'

'No, Clara, I'm treating it as murder.'

'Why?' Pearce asked.

'That tarn is half a mile long and a quarter of a mile wide. Tell me how anyone got into the middle unless someone dumped them?'

'What about suicide?' Pearce asked.

'How? To get into the middle of the tarn would have required a boat. What would have happened to the boat afterwards?'

'Could the body have floated there?' Clara asked.

'I don't think there's enough current to move a body, even that of a girl. Besides, how did they get here in the first place? It's twenty miles from the nearest town, ten from the nearest village. Are you asking me to believe a girl hiked here? That she got overcome by depression? That she swam out into the middle of a tarn that would be bloody cold even in summer? That having avoided hypothermia she drowned herself? Or that somebody drove her here so she could kill herself? It doesn't add up.'

Pearce missed Nash's last few words because of the sudden roar made by the diving team's outboard. All three glanced round. The divers were ready to start, checking with the angler where he'd been fishing.

When Pearce had gone and the divers were chugging out into the lake, Mironova turned to Nash. 'You kept saying "she". How do you know it's a girl?'

He shrugged. 'Guesswork I suppose. But from the size and shape of the skull I reckon it was probably a girl.'

Mironova stared at him suspiciously. 'What happened when you went up the valley? You looked as if you'd seen a ghost.'

'Nothing.' His tone was unconvincing.

Clara shrugged, 'No doubt you'll tell me in your own time.'

Pearce returned an hour later bringing pies, sandwiches and milk, coffee and tea bags. He arrived at the same time as Ramirez and charmed the pathologist into carrying bottled water to the bothy.

Nash greeted Ramirez. 'The divers have recovered most of the skeleton, with the exception of one arm and hand.'

A cry from the lake suggested they'd been successful. When the dinghy reached the shore the divers removed the forearm and hand from its covering and placed it with the rest of the skeleton on the unzipped body bag. They started gathering their equipment as Ramirez examined the remains. After a moment he glanced towards the divers, 'If I was you I'd tell them not to leave yet.'

'Why Professor?'

'Because this hand and arm do not belong to this skeleton. Not unless the woman had an unusual deformity. Like two left hands.'

The secretary of the angling club was a fussy middle-aged man. He seemed to take it personally that a body had been found in Lamentation Tarn. When Nash suggested they were looking for two bodies he went pale and swayed a little before recovering his composure. When Nash asked who had a key to the boathouse or the padlocks securing the dinghies, he appeared to think it was an accusation against his members.

'Tell me,' Nash took the secretary by the elbow and turned him to face the tarn, 'how do you think those bodies got there?'

'Are you certain they were put there? Couldn't it have been an accident?'

Nash shook his head. 'I'm afraid not.'

The angler swallowed. 'That means—'

'It means they were murdered.'

His face registered horror. 'Do you suspect one of us?'

Nash ignored the question. 'Whoever dumped the bodies had to use a dinghy. Unless you know of anyone else who has a boat? Who owns the land?'

'It belongs to Bishopton Estate, although they have nothing to do with the management. Their only involvement is to collect rent. But as far as the land's concerned your best contact is Simon Wardle. He rents the pasture-land. Those are his sheep grazing on Misery Near.'

'Where will we find him?'

'His farm is the other side of Bishop's Cross off the Helmsdale road, a few miles past the village. A big place on the left. Wardle's family have owned it for generations. He has cattle and pig units there, keeps his sheep over this side. Be careful how you tackle Simon. He hasn't much love for officialdom.'

Nash waited, certain there was more. 'It goes back to the foot and mouth epidemic. Wardle wasn't intending to be a farmer. He was a professional soldier but his father had a heart attack after their livestock was destroyed. Wardle resigned his commission and returned to help out until his father was fit. But that didn't happen. The old man was in Netherdale hospital for six weeks before he died. Simon's mother followed six months later.'

'That's sad. I can see Wardle would be sensitive. How old is he?'

'In his late thirties. He's a real loner and if you're planning to visit him, watch out. He's got a sophisticated security system backed up by ferocious guard dogs.'

'Is he married?'

'No, he reckons he's too busy. To be fair he's done really well. Rumour was, the losses were so bad the farm was on the brink of having to be sold, but Simon turned it round. Like I say, it's only rumour, but he persuaded the bank to let him run with a huge overdraft until the compensation kicked in. Since then he's never looked back but I think the scars are still there.'

Nash looked across at Mironova. 'If he's single perhaps I'd better send my sergeant.'

Mironova got up to leave, 'If I find out he's gay I'll come back for Viv.'

'Returning to the matter of those keys. I need a list of your current members and any who have resigned or died. Say within the last ten years.'

'It'll take a lot of work.'

'Then the sooner you start the quicker it'll be done. I'll get my constable to collect the list tomorrow morning, right?'

He nodded, recognizing the inevitable.

'One more thing; can you make a note of any members who might have lost their keys during that time? If they asked for a replacement set, for example.'

The autumn afternoon was well advanced when the diving team recorded further success. The detectives emerged from

11

the shelter of the bothy to supervise the handling of the latest find. The second set of remains was as skeletal as the first. As Nash rounded the tarpaulin shielding the corpses he wondered why they'd bothered erecting it. There were no passers by to be shocked or to ogle or take photos. The screen didn't even act as a windbreak.

'What do you reckon, Professor?'

The pathologist looked up in obvious irritation. 'I think the sooner I get them to the mortuary and can examine them without the risk of hypothermia the better,' he snapped. 'But I don't suppose that's what you're waiting to hear. Give me ten minutes and I'll join you inside.' He nodded towards Pearce, 'That'll be long enough for you to get coffee on.'

Nash and Pearce returned to the bothy. The wind had strengthened, the chill factor increased. When Ramirez joined them he was almost blue with cold. He wrapped his fingers gratefully round the mug. 'Both victims are female, no more than thirty years old.'

'How do you know?' Pearce was intrigued.

'Because the flesh has been destroyed I was able to examine their spines. In neither case was there deterioration nor wear and tear in the discs as you'd find in an older person.'

'Not mother and daughter then?' Nash asked.

'I'd need DNA confirmation to be certain, but it's unlikely.'

'Any chance of establishing the cause of death?'

'I can tell you exactly.'

'Already?' Pearce exclaimed.

Ramirez permitted himself a wintry smile. He held out his mug, 'Refill, please,' he demanded. 'They were both shot in the back of the head where it joins the neck. Probably from above when they were kneeling. The reason I know,' he explained before Pearce could ask, 'is because the bullet, or bullets that killed them damaged the vertebra. That's probably why the skull became detached when your angler hooked it.'

'Mr Wardle?'

The loudspeaker echoed eerily as the disembodied voice replied. 'Who is it?'

'Detective Sergeant Mironova, Helmsdale CID. I need to ask you some questions.'

'What about?'

'If you let me in, I'll explain.'

'No. If you want me to let you in, you'll explain first. If I judge it to be important then you can come in.'

Mironova looked round the deserted windswept farmyard with exasperation. The lack of welcome had been apparent from the moment she'd pulled up. 'Howlingales Farm'. The name couldn't have been more appropriate. The notice fixed to the gatepost read, 'Strictly No Admission Without Authority. No Representatives Without Appointment'. Alongside this notice was another. Below the picture of two Dobermans the caption read, 'Guard Dogs Running Free'. Further down was the chilling addendum, 'You Have Been Warned!'

'It's in connection with two skeletons we've recovered from Lamentation Tarn. We understand you rent grazing land there. You may have seen something significant.'

There was a pause. 'Wait two minutes.'

Mironova reckoned it was nearer five before the intercom buzzed. 'When you hear the door click, come in. Walk down the hall, past the stairs and go into the room on your left. Don't go into any of the rooms on your right, not if you value your safety.'

She heard the electronic lock disengage and pushed the door. As she walked down the hall she heard ferocious baying sounds from her right. She increased her pace as she passed the staircase and reached the room as directed. The man looked up from his computer. He was quite good looking, slim and tall, and seated at a large old-fashioned desk containing a very up-to-date PC. It wasn't exactly how Clara had expected to see the farmer but then nothing about this visit had been like her expectations. He scowled at her furiously. 'Mironova? What part of Helmsdale's that from?'

She smiled. 'It isn't from Helmsdale, it's from Belarus.'

'Bugger me,' he exclaimed. 'It's a hell of a way to go home to Minsk after a day's work.'

It was Mironova's turn to be surprised. 'You know Minsk?'

Wardle smiled patronizingly. 'A farmer would know about a country whose exports include tractors and fertilizer. Well, are you coming in or are you going to stand there all day?' When she entered the office she was able to see Wardle more clearly. 'Tell me what you want to know.'

Clara explained about the bodies. She was slightly surprised by Wardle's calm acceptance. She commented on this. Wardle was devoid of humour. 'Nothing you've found surprises me. I go there to check my sheep. As soon as I get out of the Land Rover I want to be away. The place depresses me. To be perfectly honest, it scares me as well. That might sound ridiculous from someone who served in two war zones but this is different. I'm glad when it's time to leave, I can tell you. Don't you think it's significant there's been no attempt to build there? That valley looks beautiful on a warm day when the sun shines and the heather's blooming. Yet you never get picnickers or walkers up there. I'll tell you something. I've known that place and hated it all my life. My father used to take me when I was a kid,' Wardle grimaced. 'On a farm everyone has to help. Even then Cauldmoor frightened me like no other place has since. I thought I'd seen the back of it and didn't miss it.'

'Why? Do you think the valley's haunted or something?' Clara half smiled.

'I'm not sure I believe in things like that. And if you don't mind, I'd rather not dwell on the idea. I've to be up there at night during lambing and if I thought there were ghosts roaming around I'd not stand it five minutes. All I'll say is I'm not happy being there alone. Especially not at night.'

'Have you had any strange experiences up there? Anything you can't understand or explain? Heard or seen anything unusual?'

Wardle stared long and hard. When he spoke it was as if the words were being forced from him. 'Every spring I'm there a lot. Some of my ewes get tupped early so I'm on with lambing from the beginning of January. Some years we don't get much snow but there are always bloody sharp frosts. I have to rely on my own resources. The vet can't get out in time, and besides which I've no way of calling him. There's no phone signal this side of Bishop's Cross. Three, maybe four winters ago I was out there a few weeks earlier than normal. It was a clap-cold night. One of those when the stars are out and that means a keen frost. I drove on to Misery Near where the ewes were penned. I left the Land Rover engine running. There was no moon so I was using the headlights as well as my torch. I didn't fancy running the battery down and finishing up stuck there or walking ten miles for help.'

Wardle paused and looked at Clara. 'I didn't park too close to the pens in case I frightened the ewes. They're skittish enough at the best of times. I checked them and saw none was ready. I was about to go back to the Land Rover when I heard a sound. It was silent out there, even the wind wasn't howling. The breeze was coming off Stark Ghyll side, that's across Lamentation Tarn, so it would carry any sound towards me.'

'What did you hear?'

'I'm not sure. I know what it sounded like. Whether I'm right's another matter.'

'Go on,' Mironova encouraged him.

'I thought it was a splash. As if something really heavy had dropped into the tarn. I could have been wrong. I didn't hang around to investigate. I dismissed it at the time because I didn't want to believe it. I didn't want to be up there on my own. I fancied the idea of someone else being there even less.'

Superintendent Pratt looked at Nash with interested speculation. They were sitting in Pratt's office at Netherdale where Nash had called in to update his superior. 'You went there to recover a body and by the end of the day you've recovered two. Now you want authority for the diving team to look for more. Isn't two enough?'

Nash smiled. 'It is and it isn't, Tom. Given that we know two young women have been murdered, I'd be happy if that were the end of it. But I'm not sure it is.'

'Why?'

'It's a hunch, no more.'

'I'm sorry, Mike. I can't justify a diving crew's expenses. Not for the time it would take to search that lake. Bring me something substantial and I'll authorize it. But not on the strength of a hunch. What plans have you regarding the bodies you've recovered?'

'There's very little we can do yet. Most of our hopes are pinned on the post-mortems. We're facing a long, hard slog to get anywhere. Identification will rely on dental records or DNA. We can check all women who've gone missing within the timescale, but only when we know what that is.'

'When will we know?'

'When I hear from Mexican Pete. He said something on the phone that gave a clue. He reckoned they'd been down there several years.'

'Did he explain why?'

'He said the ambient temperature of the water at the depth the divers reported would be very low. That plus the concentration of peat as the predominant soil substance would tend to act as preservatives. He said it would only be natural predation that could have speeded up the deterioration.'

'What did he mean by that scientific mumbo-jumbo?'

Nash smiled grimly. 'He said there would have been less decay if the fish and other creatures had refrained from dining on the corpses.'

Pratt, hardened as he was, turned pale. 'I'm so glad I asked. On second thoughts, I prefer the scientific version.'

'He did give one piece of positive news, though. He reckoned he might be able to tell us something about the weapon.'

'Have you any other ideas?'

'I'm waiting until Mironova reports her conversation with the farmer. Then I reckon we'll search the area round the tarn. It's a long shot but we've two unidentified corpses. Someone snuffed the life out of them in cold blood.'

'It's making you angry.'

'Yeah, sometimes murder is just sad, because much of the violence is avoidable. Domestic quarrels that have got out of hand, violent acts committed in the heat of the moment. It's when I see crimes like these, committed against defenceless women that I get angry.'

'Those are two big assumptions you've made. I mean that the women were defenceless and were killed in cold blood. You got any facts to back them up?'

'Not really, apart from the fact that they were shot in the back of the neck; classic execution technique.'

Back in Helmsdale Nash stared sightlessly at the wall, his thoughts far away. Clara stood in the doorway watching him. She'd seen Nash drift off into a semi-catatonic state before when he was trying to work out how a crime had been committed. Was he visualizing a crime scene or something else? Recently, she'd often seen him like this, even when there was no crime to solve. It had happened far too often. Clara thought the time was right for her to confront the situation head on.

'What's up, Mike, you trying to work out what happened at the tarn?'

Nash shook his head. 'I called at the clinic when I was in Netherdale. I'm surrounded by crime and its after-effects. Not just at work, when I leave here I take it with me.'

'That sounds as if the job's sickening you. You're not thinking of chucking it in, surely?'

'No, I suppose I'm just a bit down. To start with, Cauldmoor spooked me. The thought of those girls executed and dumped in that bloody lake made things worse. Then I went to see Stella.'

'How is she?'

'There's no improvement. I think she's beginning to lose heart. She won't tell me what her consultant says. She won't allow me to talk to him. She won't even let me go with her when she sees him.'

'Isn't the physiotherapy doing any good? I thought the prognosis was hopeful; the specialists were confident she'd walk again sooner or later?'

'It's certainly not sooner, and I'm beginning to think it won't be later. I reckon she's half way to being institutionalized.'

'How do you mean?'

'She's convinced she'll be tied to that wheelchair for life. I think she's starting to give up, subconsciously I mean. She'd never admit it.'

'Isn't there anything you can do?'

'No, that's the trouble. It makes me feel bloody helpless.'

'Really? Or do you still feel guilty that she's in a wheelchair whilst you're leading a normal life?'

'That too. I can't rid myself of the notion that if she hadn't got involved with me she wouldn't be in the state she's in.'

'That's ridiculous.' Clara's tone was sharp, dismissive. 'For one thing, Stella was involved before you met her. Whatever you'd done, she'd still have been taken hostage. So get rid of these crazy guilt notions. Stella would be the first to say it. You saved her life. Why beat yourself up because that life isn't normal yet. That won't help her.' Clara paused to let her words sink in. 'Would it do any good if I went to visit her?'

'I don't know, Clara, but I don't suppose it would do any harm.'

'I will when I get a minute. Speaking of visits, do you want to hear how I went on at Howlingales Farm?'

'Oh yes,' Nash forced his mind back to business. 'What did you make of Wardle?'

'He's okay, I think. Not quite what I was expecting. He's paranoid about security and scary about Cauldmoor. He's well

18

educated and down to earth,' she paused and added. 'It makes what he told me all the more remarkable.'

She went on to relate Wardle's tale.

'Three or four years ago, are you sure?'

'It'd have to be,' Clara reminded him. 'Remember what the guy from the angling club said about Wardle leaving the army. That was only five or six years ago.'

'True,' Nash conceded. 'Well, that's something. But I don't think it's enough to convince Pratt.'

Mironova looked puzzled.

'I was trying to persuade Tom to authorize another search by the Rubber Johnnies but he won't okay it without proof.'

'Why do you want to do that?'

'Because I think there may be more bodies at the bottom of Lamentation Tarn.'

CHAPTER TWO

'Let's start with the location,' Nash said. The three were seated in the CID office at Helmsdale. The premises were purpose-built and contained all three emergency services. As yet, the team was still settling in.

'The tarn is so remote we can discount eyewitnesses, even if we knew when the victims were murdered. Those bodies have been in the water so long there seems little point in examining the area. Nevertheless, we have to, if only to avoid the charge of negligence.'

'Have we any idea how long they've been there?' Pearce asked.

'Not yet. Unless we turn up something in our search, any information about the victims will depend on the autopsy and Ramirez's analysis. I'm scheduled to meet him later.'

'What do you want Viv and me to do?' Mironova seemed anxious for action.

'Organize the search party and collect the information from the angling club secretary. If you've time, start trawling the computer for young women under the age of thirty-five reported missing over the last ten years. Concentrate on the search party and the angling club first. Identification is going to be slow, so if we discover some clue at the tarn it could be invaluable. Not that I'm counting on it. I'll want every member of that club interviewed and their keys accounted for. Someone had access to those boats. Another thing. When I was at the bothy I picked up a fishing log for the current season. It records the date, the catch and who was fishing. There's a column devoted to guests. Find out the club policy on visitors and how strictly they enforce it. I want to know about everyone who's visited the tarn.'

'What's your thinking, Mike?' Pearce asked.

'It's so remote. It makes me wonder how the killer selected it. It's not as if it's Windermere or Loch Ness. You won't find it marked on any maps. As well as interviewing the club members, I think we should talk to all the guests we can.'

'That should keep us out of mischief,' Mironova muttered.

Sitting at his desk in Sarajevo, Janko Vatovec regarded the figures on the screen with satisfaction. Figures were a source of delight to him. He regarded them as the life-blood of his business, and for Janko, life itself was a business. Janko was born in Slovenia, raised in poverty by a mother who fed him when she was sober and when she could afford to. His father departed when Janko was ten, but he left a lasting impression. One characterized by physical and sexual abuse.

Janko learned early that people were of little importance. Their value lay only in what they could contribute to his prosperity. This enabled him to cast aside troublesome burdens such as family ties and scruples. In their place were the twin goals of power and wealth.

Seeking these, Janko entered the conflict between the warring factions of the former Republic of Yugoslavia. Not as a combatant but as a supplier. Janko didn't ask which side the buyers of his military hardware represented. He merely counted the money and examined each banknote before he released the munitions. He asked no questions. If the arms were used to kill old or defenceless people, mothers or babies, it was of no concern to Janko. His wasn't the finger on the trigger.

He'd been annoyed when the war ended. But he found that those who enforced the peace represented an even greater source of income. It didn't take him long to spot a niche in the market. It was the supply of a commodity required in peace and war alike. He had a willing, eager customer base and a vast supply of raw material. Moreover, it was an operation he could run on a hands-on basis, with a little assistance from a few associates.

It was hardly surprising he was pleased by the figures.

Lulu was afraid. Unhappy and afraid. She could barely remember a time before the fear and unhappiness. Added to this deep well of misery, Lulu bore a sense of shame and self-loathing. These were part of her daily life, as was the violence and abuse from which it stemmed. So much a part that she'd almost come to accept them.

Almost, but not quite, for there still remained a tiny grain of something she might have called hope had it been stronger, or spirit, had she been free to express it.

It remained locked deep inside. It survived despite the abuse. She was only thirteen when it started. It came when three strangers entered her village in Moldavia and approached her parents. They said they'd heard good things of the couple's eldest daughter. Their employer was a senior figure in the establishment, based in the capital, who required domestic servants. They would pay Lulu a handsome salary. They would provide her parents with money. Her parents were overjoyed. Lulu's future was secure, and they would have one less mouth to feed, one less body to clothe.

Two years later that mouth was fed only the basic necessities and that body was clothed in garments totally unsuitable for a fifteen year old.

Lulu's body showed the malnutrition and abuse she'd suffered. Her illusion of a well-paid job, supporting her parents and siblings, had been shattered the night she'd been taken from her home. She'd been heartbroken at leaving, but proud to help them, proud she'd been chosen for such high honour. The shattering of the illusion began before the car had gone five miles from the village. The driver stopped the car and the passenger from the front joined his companion in the back, one on either side of Lulu. As the driver continued towards their destination the others took turns to rape her. After a while the car stopped so the driver could change places with one of the others.

Lulu didn't know if she reached the capital. Her pain and anguish was continuous. Terror at what would happen to her, the unmitigating shame and knowing she would never be able to face her family again. After the journey she was dragged into a building and locked in a dark, windowless room. The only light switch was outside the door. Sometimes it was flicked on so Lulu could eat the meagre food provided. More often it was switched on so someone could look at her through the inspection flap. Later a stranger, sometimes alone, often accompanied, would enter and the nightmare would begin again. A nightmare that would go on for what seemed endless hours. In which Lulu was repeatedly raped, sodomised and forced to have oral sex with strangers.

Disorientation and violent sexual abuse continued for weeks. She was even forbidden to use her own name as part of the subjugation process and had to suffer the corruption of it her captors foisted upon her. So Ludmilla became Lulu and Lulu became their property. An asset that would earn them money.

Lulu was a prize asset but her homeland was not the best place to exploit it. They had ceased to think of her as her; she'd become 'it'. Lulu was auctioned off through the wonders of the internet and transported overseas. She was sold on and her new owners were quick to realize a profit on their investment. Despite all she'd suffered, Lulu was still a good-looking young girl.

Lulu knew nothing of this. All she knew was her tormentors had changed. Her slavery was as complete as before. Even worse, she didn't speak their language and they couldn't understand hers. They managed to communicate their desires in other ways.

Lulu was held prisoner in a room containing only a bed. She was allowed out under guard, to cook and clean for her captors. That was how Lulu spent her daytime. At night at least one of the men would want sex, usually more than one, often whilst the others watched and commented. Lulu didn't understand the words. The meaning was unmistakeable. Their desire for her seemed inexhaustible.

Lulu's hope grew day by day, like a fragile seedling in a frosty climate, its hold on life precarious. She didn't know where she was but at last she had something she'd not had since her captivity began. Lulu had a plan. She planned to escape. She knew how she was going to do it. She also knew what she was about to do was a terrible thing, but terrible things had been done to her. She knew she ran the risk of even more dreadful retribution. She didn't care. Nothing could be worse than what she'd endured.

Nash was speaking to Ramirez. 'Considering the state of the bodies, the place they were found and the length of time since they were dumped, I don't think we've a cat in hell's chance of identification unless you can come up with anything. I hope you can give us some sort of a lead. We're going to be reliant on you.'

'I realize that. I might be able to tell you a little, or again I might be able to tell you a lot. What you really want to know is the extent of what my examination will reveal. Right?'

'I've never seen a case where deterioration is so complete. It's a bit like being called in to investigate the murder of one of the pharaohs.'

'I think you'll find the remains of the pharaohs would be in better condition than those in the mortuary drawers,' Ramirez told him dryly. 'But I get your point. This is a far from normal enquiry. If we get lucky I could tell you their names, addresses and dates of birth. That relies on us getting a match from their dental records. For that we need them to have been British citizens who had regular dental treatment.

'Failing that, given time I should be able to tell you their age, give or take a year or two. Where they come from, their ethnicity and any diseases they contracted. If your enquiries turn up someone who may be related to them I could either prove or disprove that also.'

Nash stared at the pathologist in surprise. 'Are you joking?'

Ramirez smiled and shook his head. 'I rarely joke about work. Let me explain. X-rays can show evidence of medical conditions such as stress fractures or broken bones that have healed after setting. There's a standard procedure that can determine age. It's particularly effective in pre-adults and up to the age of thirty, so we're lucky they were young. We can also gauge conditions like anaemia or periostitis, that's inflammation of the periosteum and soft tissue surrounding the bone. That's usually associated with traumatic infection. That might mean injuries, more commonly of the sort associated with a physically demanding occupation. Iron deficiency, anaemia, is symptomatic of malnutrition and a high pathogen load, i.e. bacteria or viruses that can cause diseases. All of which is routine.

'The most spectacular results stem from advances in DNA analysis. We can identify genetic characteristics and associate them with specific locations. The genetic signature from different regions is distinct. Although each individual's DNA is unique, every locality has a broadly similar gene pool. That means we can trace someone's origin to a specific region and with the advance of a new technique called "familial DNA" we can identify enough similarities to place someone within a family.'

Ramirez tilted his chair back so he was balanced on the back legs. He gripped the edge of his desk with one hand. 'Of course, the jewel in the DNA crown is the ability to identify someone's genetic forbears via mitochondrial DNA.'

He smiled at Nash's look of bewilderment. 'Mitochondrial DNA is passed from a mother to her offspring. It's indestructible. If you provide me with a tiny scrap of mitochondrial DNA from your pharaoh, for example, I could tell you,' Ramirez kept his face straight, 'who his mummy was.'

'I thought you didn't joke about your work?'

'I couldn't resist that. What I'm saying is by using mitochondrial DNA we could give as positive an identification of the victims as if someone had looked at them an hour after they died.'

Nash nodded, 'The problem is going to be finding someone to provide a cross-sample.'

'I understand that. Of course it takes a long time. You have to grow the strands that form the DNA chain.'

'Where's Clara?' Mike asked.

'Gone to collect the angling club membership list. How did your meeting go?'

'Pretty well. Ramirez reckons the skeletons will tell us a lot about the victims, where they were from and how they died. The only drawback is it's going to take time. I don't suppose a few weeks will be critical.'

'The press have got hold of the story. The *Netherdale Gazette*'s headline this evening is "Angler's Grim Catch". Their reporter was on earlier asking for a quote.'

'What did you tell him?'

'I said I could confirm both victims were definitely dead.' Pearce grinned. 'Then I told him, "pick the bones out of that".'

Nash winced. 'I've noticed you've started making lousy puns. I'm afraid it's infectious. Even Mexican Pete's doing it.'

He looked round as Mironova walked in. She waved a sheaf of papers. 'I've got the details of the members of the angling club, plus the retired ones and, those who resigned. All the keys have been returned. They have quite a neat system. You pay a joining fee, £500 at present. If you leave, that gets paid back but only after you've returned any club property. That includes the keys to the bothy, the boathouse and the boats.'

'That's not much help,' Nash objected. 'They could have been copied.'

'That would only work for a year. The locks are changed before each season. Members only get their new keys once they've paid their subscription.'

'That's helpful. Do you know how long the club's been going?'

'About sixty years. Before the war, Bishopton Estate kept the fishing for themselves. However, the father and eldest son were killed in the war. The estate passed to the younger son and he'd no interest in either the estate or fishing. Several local anglers got wind of it and approached the estate manager. A lease was agreed and Bishopton Angling Club was formed. Angling's become so popular the club's gone from strength to strength. That's why they're strict on controlling guests. If someone's name isn't in the guest books it means they haven't been to the tarn. The penalty for not recording all the information is expulsion.'

'We ought to interview the landowner or whoever's in charge.'

'I reckon the estate manager would be the best bet. The owner is well over ninety and absolutely loopy fruit. That means—'

'Thanks, Clara, I know what that means.'

'The secretary told me there are no direct descendants and when the old lady pops her clogs—'

'I know what that means too.'

'—the estate will pass to another branch of the family. Apparently, it's of great concern to the anglers. They're worried a new owner might want to fish the tarn and the club would lose the rights. There are only two seasons left on the lease. They're praying the old lady stays alive long enough for them to renew.'

'Thanks, Clara,' Mike said. 'I'm off now. I'll pop in the library on my way home; see what I can find out about the area.'

Nash called at the off-licence first and selected a couple of bottles of his favourite wine. Back at his flat the meal he'd left in the slow cooker would be ready when he was. He uncorked one of the bottles and took a leisurely shower. He settled down to read the library book written by a local historian. He was disturbed by the phone. It was Clara to confirm the search party had been organized for the morning. 'Good, you can pick me up en route.'

'I assume from that you're about to open a bottle of wine?'

'Wrong, I've already opened it.'

Clara groaned in mock despair. 'How did you go on with your research?'

'I was right about Cauldmoor. It does have an evil reputation. I'll tell you the details tomorrow.' He laughed wickedly, 'When we're there and you can soak up the atmosphere.'

'Thanks a bundle. Just don't soak up too much atmosphere tonight and don't give yourself nightmares either.'

'No, Mother,' he mocked.

Despite Clara's warnings, by the time he'd finished reading, the first bottle was almost empty. Without conscious thought he'd opened the second. By the time he was ready for bed that too was half empty. He tried to remember whether or not he'd taken his tablets. To be on the safe side he took two, washing them down with the last few drops of wine in his glass. Nash was in bed by eleven o'clock. In the early hours he began to dream.

He was standing on a ridge overlooking water. Mist swirled round him. Mist, or was it smoke? He could hear screams, wailing, unanswered cries swirling round and round in his head. He saw flames rising and writhing, but there was no heat. He tried to leave, but was drawn, compelled, to walk towards the carnage beyond the fire. He fought against it, terror gripping him.

Burning timber, burning clothing, burning flesh, burning hair, burning, burning, everything burning.

He lay trembling, knew he'd been dreaming. A nightmare so realistic that the horror remained until morning.

Nash stared out from the bothy as daylight crept reluctantly over the tarn. A stiff breeze was blowing, ruffling the surface of the water into white-capped wavelets. Nash shivered, not from cold but from the sense of foreboding that had dogged him since his first visit.

Mironova came out to join him and passed him a mug. He nodded his thanks and continued to watch as members of the search party made their way down Misery Near and crossed The Grieving Stones towards Lamentation Tarn.

'What's wrong, Mike?'

'Wrong,' he said with an effort. 'How do you mean?'

'You look as if you've had little more than five minutes sleep,' she smiled. 'If things were different I'd suspect you'd been shagging all night, but you've hardly spoken a word since I picked you up, and now you're here you've spent all your time staring into the distance. It doesn't take a genius to work out something's wrong. Is it a hangover?'

He told her what he'd learned of the history of Cauldmoor.

'There was a settlement here in Saxon times but the inhabitants were massacred. The piece I read described how the Vikings slaughtered them. The men were killed first. Then the women and children were raped and murdered. In the middle of it the long hut caught fire and everyone perished. The rumour is this place is haunted. None of the locals will venture near.'

'That explains a lot,' Clara said. 'I mean what Wardle told me. This place is beautiful so how come it isn't the most popular picnic spot in the area? How come nobody's built here? You'd have buyers queuing up, normally.'

'Agreed, then to cap it off I had a bloody awful dream.'

'I'm not surprised, having read that lot. I hope this was a one-off and that you're not starting to have nightmares again. You haven't got Stella at home to watch over you.'

'It worries me too. I wish I knew how to stop them but I'm scared to talk to the medics. The last thing I need is them saying I'm not fit. I've been there once and I don't want to go back.'

'If it's starting to affect your health you might think differently.'

Pearce joined them on the veranda. 'Everyone's here, Mike. Do you want a word before we start?'

'I'd better. Gather them round the front.'

Nash looked at the assembled officers. 'You understand the problem we've got. The victims have been in the water so long identification will be next to impossible unless we get really lucky. We need anything that might help us, might give us some idea as to who these young women were, where they came from, how they came to this desolate spot and were killed. What you're looking for is anything that doesn't belong here. Anything. No matter how insignificant or irrelevant it might seem. Anything that might have been left by the victims or whoever murdered them.'

The search took all morning and into the afternoon. The team was split into two sections. One, led by Pearce, quartered the slopes of Misery Near before moving on to The Grieving Stones. The other concentrated on the area immediately surrounding the tarn. The teams moved slowly, inching their way with painstaking care from the far distance towards the bothy.

Nash stood watching as the operation drew to a close. He felt a sense of disappointment. He'd hoped the day would have produced some result. He'd no idea why he expected this, a hunch, sixth sense, whatever. A weak autumn sun filtered down the valley providing light but no warmth. The wind had stiffened and swung to blow cold from the north. 'Make a note, Clara. Sometime this week we ought to interview house owners on the road between here and Bishop's Cross. I know there's only a handful, and I realize it's long odds against them remembering strange vehicles but we must still do it. Whoever killed those girls had to use that road to get here.'

The teams gathered in front of the bothy. Nash could sense their dejection. Their leader, a sergeant from Netherdale, reported the failure then excused himself. He disappeared to answer a call of nature. He returned a couple of minutes later; his despondent air gone, signalling to Nash and Mironova.

They followed as he led them round the building and pointed along the back wall. The bothy had been sighted by digging a cleft out of the hill where it sloped down to the tarn. Where the hillside met the building a protective wall of heavy, ancient railway sleepers had been sunk into the ground to prevent a landslip pushing the bothy into the tarn.

The sergeant marched to the far end of the building and pointed. They could just make out something protruding slightly from between the sleepers. Only the tip of the object was visible. 'I was about to er... water my horse,' the sergeant said. 'I looked down and saw this. It was wedged between the sleepers and the building. I bent down and pulled it out a bit, then I thought I'd better call you.'

Nash donned his gloves and began to ease the object from its hiding place. He gazed at it in complete, speechless amazement. He looked at Mironova, who seemed equally dumbfounded. The 'object' was about twelve inches tall. Two bright, beady eyes stared back at Nash from alongside a black-tipped muzzle. The rest of the body was bright blue. Nash was staring at a particularly handsome teddy bear.

'How did that get here?' Mironova exclaimed.

'Put it in an evidence bag. It may have no relevance but we ought to follow it up,' he passed the toy to Mironova. 'Thanks, Sergeant.

'I want that bear forensically examined. Then I want it checked by an expert. I have a feeling that bear can tell us a lot.'

When they returned to Helmsdale, Pearce called through Nash's office door, 'Mexican Pete's on the phone, and he sounds agitated.'

'I've completed my preliminary examination. My report will be with you in a couple of days. I've sent samples off for analysis and most of what the bodies have to tell us will be as a result of those tests. However, I did discover one significant fact during my examination of skeleton B. I had occasion to move the pelvic bone and I noticed a minute bone on the table below it. A very tiny bone.'

'A piece that had broken off the skeleton?' Nash asked.

'No, you misunderstand me. I didn't say it's a piece of bone. It's a tiny bone. Complete, but in miniature.'

'I'm sorry. I fail to see the point.'

'It's a foetal bone. It didn't belong to skeleton B at all. Or rather it did and it didn't. The bone came from a developing foetus. Skeleton B was pregnant.'

That evening Nash finished the red wine and followed it with a couple of scotches. He realized he was drinking too much but he also knew the reason. It was the thought of what those young girls might have endured before they were thrown like garbage into the icy water. Pratt had forbidden further expense for the divers to search the remainder of Lamentation Tarn but Mike believed there were still more horrors below those dark waters. He shuddered as a fresh thought came to him. If the Tarn hadn't yielded all its secrets what more were there? Not only there but in neighbouring Desolation Tarn? Nash tried to push the thoughts away but they refused to leave. He almost forgot his medication and had to get out of bed to retrieve the tablets from the kitchen. He returned to bed for what would be another unsettled night's sleep.

Nash stared at the uneven ground. There was a building. His sleeping self was disembodied as he watched. Cold, stinging, sleety rain blurred his vision, hurting his eyes. He saw a crouched figure at the end of the building. Was it a woman, a child? Nash wasn't sure. He sensed fear, but fear of what? The figure was holding something. He peered harder through the mist of fine rain. The only colour to brighten the drabness was a patch of red. Why red? Nash couldn't make it out. A bullet wound? He could hear weeping. Was she speaking to someone? Where, who? Although he heard words, he couldn't understand them. Everything was strange, jumbled, but he sensed love as well as fear. She seemed to cradle something. He tried to move forward, tried to speak, but as he did so she disappeared.

Nash's dream ended and he awoke.

CHAPTER THREE

Two months later

Lulu was ready. Day after day, week after week she'd watched and waited for each opportunity, each moment her captors' attention was distracted. The process was agonizingly slow and she lived in constant fear of her plan falling apart. This didn't add to her distress, but that was because her ordeal was already beyond endurable.

At last everything was set. Lulu had the plan, now she had the opportunity. She had the means and above all the motive. Her only concern was if she'd have the resolution. What she intended was a sin and a crime. Lulu pondered this, feeling her resolve weakening. Then she remembered what had been done to her, each sordid and degrading act, and her courage returned. All doubt vanished and her resolve hardened.

As she worked under the relentless supervision of the most sadistic of her guards she was terrified that some last-minute hitch would throw her plan into disarray. Time crawled by until the man signalled to Lulu to start preparing the evening meal. He held up three fingers to signify for how many. Lulu nodded and turned away. She smiled grimly.

Perhaps the gesture was an omen. The sign he'd just made denoted victory in Lulu's country.

The men gathered at the table and Lulu began to serve. She waited in a corner until they'd finished. As they ate, apprehension and agitation grew as the time for her escape bid came closer. There was much conversation as they lingered over the dish. Finally, the leader signalled her to clear and make way for the dessert.

She placed the dishes of aromatic confectionary in front of them, passed the tiny cups of thick, dark coffee and walked over to the sideboard. She glanced back. They were already tucking into the dessert, one had almost finished. Lulu put out the small glasses to hold the liquor that signalled the end of every meal. She took a bottle from the cupboard and filled their glasses, taking care not to spill any of the precious, colourless liquid.

They called for the drinks and Lulu set them down swiftly on the table. Tradition called for the fiery liquid to be downed in one gulp without the slightest hesitation. All three snatched at the glasses and did this unflinchingly.

Lulu was so petrified she could barely look. Fiery the liquid certainly was, although not as they anticipated. They rose to their feet, hands clutching, scrabbling at their throats with choking, incomprehensible sounds. Gasping, eyes bulging, faces reddening and convulsed. They turned towards Lulu. They realized what they'd drunk. The knowledge came too late.

Like synchronized swimmers they raised themselves on tiptoe as the agony became intolerable, then collapsed to the floor writhing in agony. Lulu stood watching as hope began to replace fear. The tremors of her tormentors lessened and she moved across the room.

Carrying a carving knife from the dresser and without displaying any emotion, she went to each in turn. With a skill born of too much practice she unzipped their trousers and pulled them down. Wielding the knife, clumsily at first but with increasing dexterity she operated on the second and third of her victims. Although they were far beyond speech, unable to cry out, the violent thrashing of their bodies showed Lulu they were not yet insensitive to pain. She smiled angelically and on impulse went through to the kitchen and returned with a lemon. She sliced it in three with the bloodied knife and rubbed, then squeezed the lemon over each wound site in turn. Her smile becoming beatific as she saw the increased agony the astringent liquid produced. As a final gesture, almost an afterthought, Lulu emptied the salt cellar over the wounds then rubbed it in with the sole of her shoe. She gathered up the sets of genitals and thrust them into each man's mouth, taking care that none should get his own.

Removing a bunch of keys from the jacket of one of the dying men she hurried through to the kitchen and tossed the knife on to the draining board. She ran upstairs to her room and stripped off the blood-soaked clothes. In the bathroom she quickly cleaned herself. Dressed again, she unlocked the back door, opened it and stepped out. Despite the time she'd been held prisoner she'd never seen outside the building and had no idea where she was. The curtains of each room had been kept closed so Lulu could not see out; others could not look in. Shivering in the unaccustomed cold she turned to lock the door. A rickety gate set in the stone wall of the yard screeched, causing her to wince. She peered out into a narrow alley lined with houses identical to the one she'd left.

Lulu felt a moment of panic. She'd escaped her vile prison but had committed three murders. She was free from the nightmare she'd endured for so long but was now faced with an appalling dilemma. Where should she go, what should she do? She didn't even know what country she was in.

Lulu steeled herself and walked to the main road. Here she could see more activity. She watched in terror as the headlights of a vehicle came towards her. The car was on the wrong side of the road. Worse still another car was approaching from the opposite direction. Lulu closed her eyes, waiting for the inevitable crashing, rending sound of metal on metal as the two vehicles collided. Nothing happened, her eyes opened again. The cars had passed one another. What stunned her was that both drivers had stuck to the wrong side of the road. Both had been driving on the left.

Smolensk is a bustling city in western Russia, capital of the Smolensk Oblast, or administrative division. It is a beautiful city with a distinguished and heroic history of resistance against invasion. The city is dominated by the magnificent Assumption Cathedral and has many other fine buildings. In common with most cities housing a thriving industrial community not all the structures are beautiful; some areas are run down and less than handsome.

One such building was shabby and anonymous in a row of three-storey, equally unattractive ones. Built a long time ago, the building hadn't aged well. Years of neglect had followed its construction, and it showed.

The house had been quiet all day with none of the usual callers, all male, that visited the place whatever the hour. Two large vans drew up at the front whilst a further two arrived at the rear. No sooner had they halted than a black saloon car with darkened windows stopped in front of the house.

The rear doors of all four vans opened simultaneously. A team of uniformed policemen emerged and formed a cordon around the house, obviously following a well-rehearsed manoeuvre. The occupant of the car, a woman of between thirty and thirty-five years of age climbed out immediately the officers were deployed. She spoke to one of her companions, her tone clearly an order. The man spoke into his radio and officers began attacking both entrances with door enforcers. When the doors gave way they poured inside.

The woman lit a cigarette and leaned against the car, watching and waiting. Eventually an officer emerged. He approached her and saluted. He spoke rapidly, nervously. 'We were too late Commander. Every room is empty. However, it's obvious what they were used for.'

The woman showed no emotion. She jerked her head and the officer followed her into the house. Larger rooms had been subdivided to create smaller units. Each contained only a chair, a bed, a small wardrobe and a mirror. Every bed had an iron frame. Each had a set of chains dangling from the wall behind it. The worst aspect of the brothel was the smell. Every room stank with the unmistakeable sour odours of stale sweat and semen.

After the first floor the woman had seen enough. She pointed towards the stairs. Before climbing back into the car she paused to address the local commander. 'Stay here,' she ordered. 'Make arrangements with the Fire Department. As soon as they get here, torch the building.'

'You can't do that,' he protested.

She looked at him, her face expressionless, but a chill in her eyes. 'This building is being used for criminal activities. Therefore it is forfeit. I shall pass here in two hours. If it isn't already burning I shall set the fire myself.' She turned away, adding, 'and you will be looking for work.'

She climbed into the car. 'You know where to go.'

The driver swung the car out into the street. 'What went wrong?'

'I'm afraid our friend has been supplementing his income. I worry about what we'll find.'

'Do you think there'll be a backlash?'

The woman shrugged. 'I don't know and I don't care. I've been given the task of destroying these bastards. Our actions have been approved by Moscow. Let the criminals complain.'

It was a fifteen-minute drive to their destination. As the car came to a halt at the kerbside the woman said, 'As I suspected, we are too late.' She pointed ahead. Lying in the gutter was a human head. It had been severed from the body with great skill. She recognized the head immediately. It was that of a Ukrainian girl who'd escaped from the brothel. She'd been courageous enough to tell the police of the place, how she'd been subjected to three years of enforced prostitution there. Now she was dead. Slaughtered for betraying her captors and as a message to others. She'd been two months away from her fifteenth birthday.

The woman climbed wearily from the car. She glanced up and down the street. It was deserted, much as she'd expected. Nobody would have seen or heard anything. She knew that from bitter experience. 'Get on to the DNSI' (Investigation cell duty officer). Order him to send a unit here. Then ring the EKU (Directorate of Criminal Expertise) and tell them I'll be on my way in shortly.' She lit a cigarette and continued. 'Explain what happened. Tell them the man we suspected has given himself away. He was the only one apart from us who knew where the girl was.'

As the phone calls were made she waited, staring bleakly at the dead girl's head. She straightened and threw her cigarette into the gutter where it smouldered in a pool of blood. 'Is the local commander coming?' she asked. Her driver nodded. 'The minute he gets here, slap the handcuffs on him, stick him in the back of the car and we'll set off for the Bolshoi Dom ('Big House', St Petersburg Police Headquarters), okay.'

The exhaustive enquiries into members and guests of Bishopton Angling Club had taken several weeks and produced nothing. Nash was on the phone to Tom Pratt. 'The problem is we've no idea what we're looking for. Two girls were murdered and thrown into that tarn years ago, but apart from that and the fact that one of them was pregnant we know no more than we did on the first day. Investigating a case with so little evidence is bloody frustrating and we're still waiting for the final reports from Mexican Pete.'

Mironova entered his office with a visitor. 'Mike, let me introduce you to our local toy expert.'

'DI Mike Nash,' Mike shook hands with the frail-looking, middle aged man. 'I'm pleased to meet you. I assume you've come to tell us something about our teddy bear?'

'Indeed I have, Mr Nash.' He pushed his glasses back on to the bridge of his nose and took some papers from a document case. 'And a very interesting bear he is.'

He glanced down at the topmost sheet. 'I'd a long job searching for this little fellow's make. The problem is there are so many mass-produced bears it's not easy to keep track of them. This isn't one of them though. This chap is very special. I thought so when Sergeant Mironova brought him to my shop. I didn't like to say as much until I was sure of my facts but once I'd checked out the materials used I knew we were dealing with something out of the ordinary.'

'I thought a teddy bear was just a teddy bear,' Nash confessed. 'I didn't think there was anything different about this one.'

A pained expression crossed the expert's face. 'Ever since they were first made,' he told them severely, 'there's been a mystique about teddy bears no other toy can match. Take Steiff bears for example. Steiff is the German manufacturer who invented the bear with jointed limbs. They can fetch really big prices at auction.' He paused before continuing, 'As for this one, he is distinctive and unique. I had a clue from both the material and appearance. It was made with special fabrics and threads. Obviously handmade. Above all there was the appearance. It differs from European and American bears. I got the idea he might be Russian so I got in touch with the Vakhtanoff Doll Gallery in Moscow. They're the foremost experts on dolls and bears. They were able to supply me with the name of the maker,' he paused triumphantly and added, 'as well as the name of the bear.'

'The bear has a name?' Mironova asked.

'Indeed he has.' He was clearly enjoying himself. 'Allow me to introduce him. This is Mitya. Mitya is a diminutive form of the name Dmitriy. Mitya was made by a lady who has a high reputation for quality. She's been making dolls for three or four years I believe.'

He stopped, although it was clear he had more to tell. 'The gallery told me she doesn't produce many so they would try to track the owner of Mitya.' He paused before delivering his bombshell. 'Within forty-eight hours I had a return phone call. Not from the maker or the Gallery, but from this person.' He fumbled a piece of paper across the desk. 'She wanted to know why I was enquiring about that bear. The phone number is that of the EKU, the Directorate of Criminal Expertise, part of the MVD. She said it was similar to the FBI in America.'

When Mironova returned from showing him out Nash was on the phone. 'Thanks, Professor, that's all I needed to know. I'll see you next Friday.'

He put the phone down. 'Why on earth would the Russian police be interested in that bear?' she asked.

'Search me. Perhaps he's on their bear most-wanted list. I suppose I'll have to ring them, although it has nothing to do with our two skeletons.'

'How do you know?'

'It doesn't tie in date-wise. Ramirez says the shortest time those skeletons could have been in the water is seven or eight years. This bear is less than five years old.'

'So you're discounting the bear?'

'I didn't say that. I still want to know how a handmade teddy bear found its way from Russia to one of the most remote parts of North Yorkshire.' Nash glanced down at the paper. 'It's to be hoped Commander Dacic can tell me, because it's got me baffled.'

'I wish to know,' the English was accent-free, 'why you're enquiring about the teddy bear?'

'It was found in a remote area and seemed to have been hidden deliberately. In the circumstances, we were curious to find out how the bear ended up here.'

'Please explain. What circumstances?'

'The bear was found close to a small tarn in a very isolated area where two skeletons had been discovered.'

'Tarn?'

'Sorry, tarn is a mountain lake. Very small, usually remote.'

'Thank you. These skeletons, they were recovered from the tarn?'

'Correct, they'd been there a long time.'

'Please tell me more about the skeletons?'

'I don't know much more, Commander.' Nash admitted. 'We believe the skeletons had been in the water somewhere in the region of ten years. According to our pathologist they were young girls of about sixteen. One of them was pregnant when she was killed. They were shot in the back of the head. When we found out how short a time the bear-maker had been in business we discounted it from our enquiries. It still begs the question of how the bear found its way to such a place, though,' Nash paused and added. 'Now perhaps you'll tell me what your interest is in the bear?'

'It's part of an ongoing enquiry my department is making,' the woman stated flatly. 'Please fax me copies of all the relevant papers. Here's the number,' she recited a fax number.

Her arrogant tone was too much. 'I'm afraid I can't do that without more information.'

'It's concerned with a continuing enquiry.' Dacic's tone was one of irritation. 'I'm unable to say more. Kindly send that information.'

'If you refuse to divulge any of the facts, there's little point in retaining your number.' As he spoke Nash crumpled the paper near enough to the receiver for the sound to be heard at the other end. He then replaced the handset.

'That's interesting.' Mironova had been standing alongside Nash's desk throughout. She pointed to one of the notes Nash had made. 'The name Dacic, that isn't Russian.'

Nash looked up. 'Where's it from?'

'One of the Slav states,' Mironova told him. 'My father could tell you for certain, but if I had to guess I'd say Serbia or Croatia. Serbia most probably.'

'Your point being?'

'If she's a Slav as well as a woman, she must be very highly thought of to have risen to the rank of commander within the Russian police. They're renowned for being both xenophobic and sexist.'

'All of which gets us no further forward,' Nash commented gloomily. He smoothed out the paper containing the fax number and placed it into the file.

Janko Vatovec was way beyond anger. He glared at his subordinate. 'You mean to tell me,' he hissed, 'that one of our houses has been burned down, our contact in the police arrested and one of our assets disposed of. All because of some woman from St Petersburg? Who is this bitch, Wonder Woman?'

'She's a commander in the EKU,' his underling replied miserably. 'Her name's Zena Dacic.'

Vatovec stood up abruptly. 'Snow Woman!' He exclaimed harshly. 'Shit! That's all we need. If that bitch is on our tails then we're in trouble. No wonder they burned the house down if that cow's in charge.'

He began pacing the floor. 'You've not heard of her, have you?' His deputy shook his head. 'Zena means "snow woman" in Croat. It's wrong though. Dacic is colder than snow, she's pure ice. She was the one who broke up the Minsk trafficking ring. The two leaders were shot, supposedly whilst trying to escape.' Vatovec laughed, a laugh that was totally devoid of humour. 'Escaping, my arse! They were both shot twice.' He leaned over his assistant. 'The first shot blew their balls off. The second was through the temple. Rumour has it Dacic fired the first shots herself. Then she left them in a locked room, handcuffed and with one round apiece in their pistols. When the pain got unbearable they topped themselves. That's the evil cow who's turned her attention on us.'

'What will you do?'

'There are two choices. We either fold up or take her on.'

'Take her on, what does that mean?'

'It means we have her terminated.' Vatovec smiled, another mirthless gesture. 'The Minsk operation wasn't part of the Federation. We are. That gives us a distinct advantage. Dacic has never taken on the Federation before. I don't think they'll be happy to learn she's interfering in their operations.

I've been paying into Federation funds for years and I've never claimed anything in return. Now I realize what a shrewd investment it was. I have to make one phone call and the Snow Woman will be melted like that.' Vatovec flicked his fingers.

Vatovec broke off as the phone rang. His face darkened with fury as he listened. 'The bitch has hit us again, and it's worse this time. Another house burned down. If someone's squealing I'll circumcise the bastard from his crotch up to his neck.'

'What's happened this time?'

'The Bulgarian police raided our house in Vidin. They closed it down, arrested everyone inside and carted them away. When our man came back next morning the fire department was hosing down the remains. She's destroyed two of my properties in forty-eight hours. He had a word with one of the firemen. They got a call from the police who told them it was a disused building and they were going to use it as a way of testing emergency responses. The fireman also told him that although the local police were giving the orders there was a woman on the scene as well. She was about thirty years old, copper-coloured hair and spent the time leaning against her limo smoking cigarettes. That sounds like Dacic to me. Now do you understand how dangerous this bitch is? Now do you understand why I call her an evil cow? Why she must be eliminated?'

The four detectives sat round the table in Helmsdale CID office. Superintendent Pratt had driven over to join Nash, Sergeant Mironova and DC Pearce for the briefing. The main item on the agenda being Ramirez's findings. The December afternoon was well advanced by the time Nash had returned with the file, but the first snow of the winter added a little brightness as the flakes drifted lazily past the window.

'We know how little we have to go on, even less now our little bear has been cleared of any involvement in the murders. So I'll give you a rundown on Mexican Pete's results and see if it gives anyone a bright idea.'

Nash glanced down. 'We know the first of the skeletons, skeleton A, is that of a young girl of no more than seventeen. Skeleton B is probably at least a year younger. We also know skeleton B was at least five months pregnant. So in addition to the murders we can be sure that at least one other crime was committed, that of unlawful sexual intercourse, if not rape. Whether the girl's pregnancy was the motive for her murder or not we don't know, but I'll return to both these points later.

'On the dental records, these do not match any patient treated within the NHS. From what we'll hear shortly that's hardly surprising.

'Analysis of the skeletons revealed malnutrition over a long period. There was also evidence of localized trauma in certain areas of the body, consistent with beatings or physical abuse. There was significant deformity to the pubic bone in both cases. The malformation suggests a high level of sexual activity that occurred whilst the bones were still relatively soft. The assumption Ramirez draws is that both girls had been engaged in child prostitution.'

Nash's face was grim, his eyes as bleak as the weather. 'Ramirez concludes that this sexual activity must have commenced at least four years before the girls were killed, otherwise the bones would not have been soft enough to register the deformity. That means,' he said heavily, 'they had become, willingly or otherwise, prostitutes before they reached the age of twelve.'

The silence reflected the horror of what they were hearing. Nash waited a few moments before continuing. 'Finally, Ramirez has now received the laboratory analysis on the DNA removed from the skeletons. The mitochondrial DNA suggests both girls came from the same region. The genetic structure of their DNA is consistent with the gene pool covering Eastern Europe.'

Nash waited for this to sink in. 'That's all Ramirez had to report. I don't know how it reads to you but I'm beginning to see a pattern. I find it highly significant that the two dead girls hail from Eastern Europe and that we've found a Russian toy close to the scene. Admittedly our little friend isn't directly associated with the murders but the link can't be ignored. Particularly given the acute interest shown by the Russian Federal Police.'

Superintendent Pratt leaned forward, resting his forearm on the table. 'How do you interpret all this?'

Nash rolled his biro to and fro. 'I think we're faced with an appalling crime, Tom. I think it's a crime none of us has ever encountered. Maybe we thought our patch was safe from this sort of obscenity. We were wrong. My belief is these poor girls were victims of sex traffickers. I think they were smuggled into the country to service the perverted needs of paedophiles. My guess is that when they became pregnant they were got rid of. The ultimate in a disposable society.'

'What about the bear? How does that fit in?' Mironova asked.

Nash's expression became grimmer. 'I think Mitya belonged to another of the traffickers' victims. I think the bear belonged to a child who has been reported missing more recently, hence the Russian police interest.'

'Do you realize what you're implying?' Pratt asked.

'I do. I think the bear was concealed as a last act of defiance. By a girl who knew or guessed what was going to happen and left the only clue she could in the hope that someone would interpret it. If you remember, I said two months ago I believed there to be more bodies at the bottom of Lamentation Tarn.'

'I also remember saying if you bring me evidence I'll authorize another search. I think I've heard enough.'

'Thank you,' Nash said quietly. 'There are a few more points to settle, however.'

'Such as?' Pratt asked.

'First, there's the question of whether we should involve MCU?'

'The Major Crimes Unit is certainly the right vehicle for international crime; however, I think it's a bit early to be involving them. We only have Ramirez's report to give us an international connection. The bear signifies nothing at present. No, we'll leave MCU out of it for the time being. We can always review the situation later.'

'We also have to consider the request from St Petersburg for information about the facts surrounding the case.'

'No bloody way,' Pratt growled. 'If they want facts from us they'll have to come up with a few themselves. Let them stew.'

'Fine by me,' Nash grinned.

Tom Pratt got to his feet. 'Unless there's something urgent, I'm off. I'm away as from tomorrow so I want to get back to Netherdale before the roads get too bad. Much as I like the three of you I'm not sure I want to spend the night with you.' He paused before correcting himself. 'Well, two of you at least.'

Pearce left shortly after the Superintendent, leaving Nash and Clara reviewing developments. She noticed Nash was a little preoccupied and thought she knew the cause. 'How's Stella?' She asked. 'You went to visit her last weekend, didn't you?'

'Just the same, really; she doesn't seem to be making any progress.'

Clara nodded. 'I agree. I went again yesterday evening.'

Nash stared at his sergeant in surprise. 'That was kind. What did you think?'

'I think you're right when you said she's lost the will to fight. I think she needs something to motivate her. The trouble is finding the right button to press.'

'I know. I've been trying to think up ways for long enough.'

'I had an idea that might help. Why not bring in a specialist?'

'I told you, she won't allow me to talk to her consultant.'

'I wasn't meaning the neurosurgeon. I think you should talk to a psychologist.'

Nash smiled fleetingly. 'For Stella or me?'

Clara grinned. 'Both of you. Although you might be past help.'

'Thank you kindly.'

'My idea was for you to think about something I heard of called distraction therapy. It involves getting the patient to concentrate so hard on something else they forget what's really wrong. Apparently it's been used extensively on pain management with a lot of success.'

'What problem do you suggest I set for Stella?'

'Well, there's always you.'

'You never miss the chance to insult me. Now you're suggesting I'm a problem, are you?'

'Definitely,' Clara grinned. 'You're a problem for any woman who gets close to you. What I meant was if you were to go see her and tell her about everything that's worrying you, it might take her mind off her own problems.'

'I'd feel lousy dumping all that on her.'

'No you wouldn't. Let's face it, you used to talk to her about cases. It might get her fighting again.'

The security guard at Good Buys supermarket, Netherdale branch, was bored. The morning trade was slack. He saw the girl enter, saw her hesitant look round before venturing further inside. At first he'd taken her for a young mother from Carthill council estate, then realized she was far too young. She was dressed inappropriately for the weather. The mini dress with high hemline and plunging neck was too flimsy, covered too little. Her shoes, flashy enough in a tawdry sort of way, were far from new. She looked, the guard thought, 'foreign, in need of a good wash, and a proper little tart'. He decided to follow her. He watched as she wandered up and down the aisles staring at the food. She looked lost, confused. 'Probably drugged up,' he thought. She reached out and slipped a chocolate bar into the pocket of her dress, then another before heading for the exit. That was when he signalled a female employee to help him tackle the shoplifter.

Commander Dacic read the text. It was brutally short. It read, 'Contract placed. Target; you. Hit tomorrow a.m.' There was no signature.

She picked up the phone. 'We have a problem.'

Early the following morning the man was in position. The window in the apartment he'd chosen was directly opposite Police Headquarters and gave him an excellent line of fire. He'd hit the tenant over the head and hauled her into the bedroom, then placed a pillow over her face until she stopped squirming. It was a pleasant apartment. The old lady had kept it really nice. The new occupants would appreciate that.

His Kalashnikov was set up on a tripod. He went through to the kitchen and brewed coffee. Having finished his drink he glanced at his watch. Time for action. The street was deserted. He set up a photo of his target against the window frame, admiring her good looks, the well-stacked figure, the gleaming auburn hair. At times his job was hard. It was never easy killing a lovely woman, but money was money and there were plenty more beautiful women.

He saw a long, black limousine pull up in front of the Police Headquarters. It's squat, dated shape proclaimed it to be a Zil, the model favoured by Russian government officials. This would be the one that was to collect Commander Dacic. His job was to ensure she didn't reach the car. He checked the Kalashnikov. When he turned back to the window he blinked for a moment in surprise. The Zil limousine had been joined by two more.

A few minutes later the double doors of the Police Headquarters swung open and the woman strode out dressed in uniform. He recognized the auburn hair below the peaked cap and started to sight the Kalashnikov.

Almost at once he was distracted by movement in his peripheral vision. He straightened and stared in disbelief. He looked again. Another Commander Dacic with the same auburn hair had emerged. As he stared, mouth agape, a third Commander Dacic exited the headquarters. The trio stood like mannequins on a catwalk.

He was still gazing at them when a voice alongside him brought his wandering wits back into focus. 'Dobera Den,' (Good day,) Zena Dacic murmured. 'Please raise your hands high above your head.'

Zena's voice was persuasive to the point of seductive when she wanted but what really convinced him was the small, extremely ugly Makarov semi-automatic pistol she was holding against his temple. That ensured his unquestioning obedience.

CHAPTER FOUR

Lulu should have been frightened. But she was beyond fear, at least the fear the staff of Good Buys Supermarkets was trying to instil. They weren't to know she didn't understand their threats. More to the point, her ignorance rendered her unaware and unafraid of the consequences of her theft.

Even if she'd known, Lulu wouldn't have been concerned. Lulu was an illegal immigrant, without passport or any identification. Within the past twenty-four hours she'd murdered three men. A charge of shoplifting would have frightened many youngsters. It would have hardly raised Lulu's heart rate.

Unable to get any response, the manager rang the police. As the only female available, Mironova agreed to accompany the constable responding to the call.

'I haven't been able to get a word from her,' the manager said irritably. Lulu sat motionless. She stared at a point between the uniformed policeman and a stack of boxes.

'I'll see if she'll talk to me,' Clara said. 'The warrant card might help.'

She placed herself in front of the girl and tapped her on the shoulder. 'Look at me.'

The girl looked up. Whether in response to Clara's touch or her words, the detective couldn't be sure. 'I'm a police officer.' She displayed her warrant card. 'Understand?' The girl's face registered no emotion. 'Do you understand?' She repeated. Again there was no sign the girl had heard or comprehended. Clara looked up and nodded to the uniformed policeman who advanced with a pair of handcuffs. 'We'll need statements from all of you. You in particular,' she glanced at the guard.

Back at the station Mironova looked at the young prisoner, a faint stirring of something approaching recognition troubling her. It wasn't that she knew the girl, but there was something vaguely familiar about her. A familiarity based on Mironova's past. Something in the cast of her features suggested an origin far from Yorkshire. After several minutes a mental image drifted before Clara. One from her childhood before her family left Belarus. She'd seen girls with similar features. That was a ludicrous notion, she told herself.

Clara pulled a chair up and sat facing the prisoner. 'Zdravstuj' (Hello), she began. 'Menia zvat Clara' (My name is Clara). 'Ja prishla chtob pomoch tebe' (I've come to help you). 'Kak tebia zovut?' (What's your name?).

There was no doubting the reaction. As Clara began speaking, the girl stared wide-eyed at her. Then she burst into tears. Through her loud, hiccupping sobs Clara heard her whisper, 'Ludmilla, my name is Ludmilla.'

The youngster was sitting, shoulders hunched, her expression a combination of misery and fear. Whatever the tale, Clara thought, it wasn't going to be good news. 'What should I call you?' Mironova began. 'Do you prefer "Luda", or "Milla"?'

'Milla,' the muttered response containing a wistful yearning. 'I used to be called Milla at home.'

'Where was that, Milla? Tell me about yourself? Tell me your name and where you're from. Tell me how you got here and how you came to be caught shoplifting in a supermarket in northern England.'

Milla stared at Clara. Her expression one of bewilderment, 'England,' she repeated, 'I am in England?'

'Of course. Don't tell me you didn't know?'

Milla shook her head. She appeared dumbfounded. Clara waited and for a moment it seemed as if Milla was about to speak, then she appeared to think better of it. Despite Clara pressing her, she refused to add any more. To every one of Clara's questions Milla gave the same, single uncompromising 'niet' (no) in reply.

The abortive interview lasted half an hour before it was interrupted. The uniformed officer signalled Clara from the doorway. He muttered something. Milla stared straight ahead unmoved.

Clara wasn't sure why she translated. 'Milla,' she told the youngster. 'I have to leave you. The bodies of three men have been found and I must go to investigate.'

There was no lack of emotion, no stolid resistance this time. Every vestige of colour drained from Milla's face and her eyes widened in horror.

There were three officers at the house. 'What's been done so far?' Mironova asked.

'Nothing, apart from securing the crime scene.'

'You're certain it's a crime scene?'

The officer's smile had no humour in it. 'I found three dead men in the dining room. I'm not sure how they were killed but what was done to them leaves no room for doubt. I only hope for their sake they were dead before and not after.'

'What do you mean?'

The constable glared at her, his irritation apparent. 'Their dicks and bollocks were slashed off and stuffed into their mouths.'

Mironova swallowed and took a moment before continuing. 'Who found the bodies?'

'The postman. He'd a letter that was too big for the box. He knocked on the door and it swung open. He looked inside. He could see into the dining room. He saw the legs and feet of one of the men and went to investigate. The pool of vomit is his.'

'Okay. I'll take it from here. You keep the neighbours and press at bay. I need to get hold of Inspector Nash. You get on to the station, ask them to organize SOCO.'

Wearing white suits and overshoes, shower caps and latex gloves, the three detectives had a sexless uniformity. Nash led the way into the dining room. Curiosity overcame their natural revulsion at the sight that awaited them.

Clara and Pearce gasped aloud. The stench of blood and the stink given off as the victims' bowels voided on death was overwhelming, nauseously repulsive.

Mironova fixed her eyes on Nash, who spent a couple of minutes assessing the room, ignoring the bodies.

There was little of value in there. The carpet was worn but not threadbare, the furniture shabbily utilitarian, probably bought second-hand. There were a couple of shot glasses on the table, one of them on its side. A third was on the floor near the corpses. Nash advanced towards the table, treading a serpentine path to avoid the blood which had soaked in massive patches into the meagre pile of the carpet.

He bent over the upright glass on the table and sniffed, recoiling instantly from the sharp, acrid smell. He looked closely at the corpses. Standing deep in concentration he studied each in turn. They were of similar age and appearance. Possibly in their early forties, their olive complexions suggesting a warmer climate than Netherdale. He transferred his gaze to the table and the few items on it, before looking at the corpses again.

Eventually he turned to the others. 'I'd say these are revenge killings. The killer used household bleach to poison or disable these men. The genitals were cut off before death as they lay choking in agony, their throats and digestive tracts burning from the corrosive substance they'd ingested. Unconsciousness would probably have taken some time, but I'm sure Mexican Pete will tell us more. The bleach would probably have killed them in any case but the murderer wasn't about to take that chance. The neat bleach had to be substituted for something they would down in one gulp.' Nash pointed towards the bottle on the sideboard. 'That looks favourite.'

They glanced at the bottle but the only one able to read the label was Clara.

She nodded agreement. 'That's Raki,' she told them. 'Product of one of the Slav states, Montenegro or somewhere like that.'

Nash nodded. 'The removal of the genitals not only ensured the death of the victims, it provided a message. Rejection of what the genitals represent and hatred and contempt for the men themselves. The mutilation suggests revenge for some act or acts of extreme sexual violence. That's the key to the murders.' Nash gestured to the floor behind him. 'The men lying there are criminals. They've violated someone, man or woman, in a way that provoked this retribution. They're abusers. The manner of their killing is the ultimate in abuse.'

Pearce spoke, his tone awed. 'Did you deduce all that from looking at the bodies?'

'From the bodies and the crime scene. The killer wasn't satisfied with administering a virulently corrosive poison. He or she went way beyond that.' He pointed to the pieces of lemon and the salt cellar. 'The killer ensured the victims suffered the highest level of pain.' Nash paused.

'We'll have a look round before SOCO get here. It won't take all of us.' Nash turned to Pearce. 'Go chat to the neighbours. See what you can find out about the people who lived here. Get on to the council. See what they can tell us about their tenants.'

The kitchen provided further evidence of the horrific nature of the crime. The carving knife tossed carelessly on to the draining board, its blade festooned with shreds of skin and fleshy tissue was enough to turn the strongest stomach, and theirs were already churning.

The next room was obviously used as a lounge. In one corner was a plasma TV complete with DVD and VCR players. The rest of the furniture was a couple of cheap settees and a coffee table.

Nash went upstairs. The first door led to a double bedroom. He paused on the threshold, assimilating the scene. The room was set out like a dormitory, with three single beds in a row down one wall. Opposite them was a double wardrobe, the doors of which were open. Beneath the window was a chest of drawers, all open, their contents spilled across the nearest bed. Every item of furniture was cheap and far from new. Nash stared for a long time before walking across to the drawers. He signalled to Clara and pointed to a single fawn sock lying on the carpet. 'Search that pile of clothing on the bed and see if you can find a companion to this.' The sock had a distinctive diamond pattern in pale green. 'While you're doing that I'll have a look in the other rooms.'

The next room was slightly smaller and set out in identical fashion but with only two beds. Only one of which was made up. Neither wardrobe nor drawers seemed to have been disturbed. Nash opened each drawer in turn. Although the contents appeared intact, Nash saw unmistakable signs that someone had moved them. Why?

The third door was slightly ajar. Nash examined the stout bolt and sturdy padlock on the outside, his eyes hot with anger. He looked inside at the single item of furniture, a double bed. He'd suspected what the room would reveal and his heart went out, not to the trio of men lying dead, but to the victim they'd abused. If ever there was a case of justifiable homicide, Nash thought, this was it.

Mironova joined him. 'There's no other sock with that pattern. Are we looking for a one-legged murderer?'

Nash shook his head. He stepped round the bed and twitched the curtains back from the window. It had been boarded over. He turned to face her, his expression bleak. He beckoned her. 'Tell me what you can smell?' His tone as forbidding as the look on his face.

She sniffed; the sour aroma faintly disgusting, vaguely familiar. 'Yes, I know what that is.'

'This room holds the key to the motive. If I'm right, the men went to great lengths to ensure their prisoner didn't escape and that they weren't seen. I believe the person held in this room was their sex slave. This was where he or she was abused until they seized the chance to exact revenge and make their escape. This is where the real crime in this house took place.'

'Mike, look at this.' Clara pointed to a dirty cardboard box protruding from under the bed. 'Are those bloodstains?' She slid the box out, to reveal a badly stained dress thrown on top of the other contents.

'At least we know we're looking for a woman.'

The final room was a bathroom and toilet combined. On the floor lay a discarded towel. It had never been clean but now it was badly stained. The soap and wash basin were covered in brown flecks. 'Okay, leave all that for SOCO. One last thing, we need to go through every room, all the drawers and cupboards and look for any papers or documents.' Nash turned and led the way back to the bedrooms.

As they were completing this task, with not a single sheet of paper to show for their effort, Nash's mobile rang.

'Nash, where are you?' The caller sounded far from happy.

'Who is this?'

'Saunders, who the hell do you think? Have you forgotten you were supposed to be meeting us this morning? I've had to drive five bloody miles to make this call!'

'Damn! I'm sorry. I got called to Netherdale. There's been a triple murder. Look, Johnny, I'm nearly finished here. Can you make a start? I'll join you as fast as I can.'

'Don't leave it too long. Remember, we don't get many hours of daylight at this time of year.'

Nash turned to Mironova. 'I've to get over to Cauldmoor. I'd forgotten we'd scheduled the Rubber Johnnies to resume their search of the tarn today. That was Saunders spitting blood because I'm not there. Can you hold the fort? With luck, I'll be back before dark.'

'I need a word first. It's no big thing but I've got a problem with a shoplifter. She was caught red-handed, arrested and cautioned but no matter what I ask she won't talk.'

'Get her a solicitor and tell him to persuade her to cooperate, otherwise we'll throw the book at her.'

'I'd have done that,' Clara said. 'The only problem is finding a solicitor who speaks Russian.'

Nash stopped suddenly and turned back. 'What?'

Clara explained her abortive attempt to interview the girl. 'All I got from her was her first name, Ludmilla, Milla for short. She's from somewhere in the old Soviet Bloc but she won't say where.'

'Describe her.'

'No more than fourteen or fifteen, looks half starved. Dressed like a cheap whore and absolutely terrified about something. It isn't the shoplifting though; she doesn't seem the least bit worried about that.'

Nash was silent for a few seconds. 'Leave her for the moment. Stay here and wait for SOCO. I'm taking Viv with me then I'm coming straight back. I'll give you a call when I'm on my way and meet you at Netherdale station. I want a word with this young lady.'

He noticed the surprise in Mironova's face. 'Think about it, Clara. We've two unidentified skeletons at Lamentation Tarn, supposedly of Eastern European origin. A Russian teddy bear. A trio of dead men, whose appearance suggests Slav or Baltic origins, and now a Russian child shoplifter. Unless we've been twinned with Vladivostok, there's got to be a connection.'

As they drove towards Cauldmoor, Pearce told him what little he'd discovered about the tenants. 'The neighbours know next to nothing. They've only seen men coming and going. Reckon there are about five or six living there. Foreigners, asylum seekers they think. That's all they know, or are prepared to say. They're no trouble, keep to themselves, don't make any noise. Nobody knows what they do for a living but they come and go at odd hours. That contrasts with the council's information. The Housing Department told me the house had been let to an elderly couple from Slovenia. Rent's paid promptly in cash and they've had no complaints.'

As Nash and Pearce walked down Misery Near they could see the diving team had already met with success. A green tarpaulin sheet had been spread on the ground close to the bothy. On it were two smaller sheets. Saunders met them by the lake, his face grim confirmation of what they'd already guessed. 'Your hunch was right. We've recovered two already and they've just located a third. They're in no better condition than the two you've already got.'

'I'm going to have to get back. Pearce will stay with you whilst I raise Ramirez and get some uniforms here.'

Once Nash had driven beyond Bishop's Cross he pulled over to phone. 'When you've finished at the house, can you get out to Lamentation Tarn?'

Mexican Pete sighed, 'You're becoming a one-man cottage industry. Even Burke and Hare in their prime didn't manage six corpses in one day.'

When Nash returned to Netherdale they entered the interview room. He sat down opposite the girl and studied her. He absorbed a dreadful sense of suffering, a desolation of the soul this girl exuded. He almost wept, so strong was the despair in her aura.

Eventually she looked up. Nash smiled and leaned forward, his eyes fixed on hers. 'Say to Milla,' he instructed Mironova without taking his gaze from the girl, 'that I understand everything, that I don't blame her for what she did. Tell her I can only guess at what she must have suffered at the hands of those filthy beasts. Nobody will want to see her punished because she killed them. They deserved to die and if killing them was the only way she could escape, I think she did the right thing. Tell her I am ashamed, as a man, for what she had to endure.'

Mironova began translating. At the first words Milla's eyes widened. All the time Nash held her gaze with his. She began to cry. Her heartbroken, racking sobs were a torment for the detectives.

Nash added, 'Tell Milla we'll help her. Tell her she'll be safe. We'll protect her. Tell her the ordeal is over.'

Slowly and painfully Milla's tale was told. The horror of it almost overwhelmed her audience. She wouldn't reveal her full name or where she came from. Was this guilt or shame? 'A village in Moldavia,' was all Milla would say. 'A village I once called home.' A fresh bout of tears overwhelmed her. When she recovered there was an abyss of sadness in her voice. 'A home I can never return to. My parents believe I have gone to be successful. The truth would shame them beyond belief. I must bear the responsibility alone. What will happen to me? Will I be executed?' It was a moment before her meaning became clear. 'Certainly not,' Nash told her, his tone forcible. 'We don't have the death penalty in England. Besides, no jury would convict you of murder after what you've gone through. At the worst you might have to stay in a special place for young offenders but only for a short time. If I have my way you'll not even have to face that.'

When the interview ended the detectives were traumatized by the revelations. They left Milla tucking in with relish to the meal Nash had sent out for. He was marvelling at the resilience of youth when Clara asked, 'Do you think she'll be deported?'

'I'll make sure she gets every help to avoid that. A lot depends on us. We have to catch the bastards responsible. I mean the ones who brought her here and subjected her to such cruelty. If we can do that and Milla testifies, it'll be very favourable for her. Particularly if we stress how she'd be in danger should she be returned to her own country. Which she would be if the traffickers were at large.'

'What do we do next?'

'It's time to get MCU involved. We've five victims from the tarn and God knows how many more elsewhere. Tomorrow I intend to make a couple of phone calls that might help push our enquiries along.'

*

That evening as Nash ate his meal he remembered Milla as he'd left her. Her enjoyment of the food was the most optimistic part of a long and depressing day.

The only other positive note had been provided by DI Saunders. He reported that the diving team had completed their search and he was confident there were no further bodies in the lake. 'Thank God for small mercies,' Nash had replied.

It was only later that he was to regret that easy optimism.

Pearce returned late in the afternoon with confirmation of the pathologist's findings. 'Three more females, all young and each of them had been in the water a considerable number of years,' he summed up.

Recalling this, Nash thought of the Russian teddy bear. It seemed none of the five victims was linked to the toy, so what had happened to its owner?

Vatovec was in a foul mood. The burning of two of his most lucrative brothels and the arrest of his informer, together with the bungled assassination were major reverses. The possibility that the Snow Woman would pay even greater attention to his operation was cause for concern. He was not in the most receptive frame of mind to hear more bad news.

When his deputy came into his office it was obvious he wasn't about to tell Janko he'd won the lottery. 'What now?' Vatovec snapped.

'I've had word from England. Three of our operatives in the north have been murdered. Their girl must have killed them. There was no sign of her. The fourth man returned, found the corpses and nearly shit himself.'

The deputy paused. 'He stripped the house of all documents and his clothing, did a runner before the police arrived.'

'Good thinking. How were they killed?'

'She poisoned them, sliced their pricks and balls off and stuffed them in their mouths.'

Janko was hardened to almost all forms of atrocity. Even he paled at this description. 'Hell! Which girl was it?'

'One of the Moldavians we took a couple of years ago. We sold her to the Serbs.'

'I take it there's nothing to link her to us?'

'Only if she or the survivor talks. He's a gibbering wreck by all accounts.'

'We can't afford him gibbering to the police. I'll have him eliminated and the girl as well. I only hope the police haven't picked her up already.'

CHAPTER FIVE

Next day, Nash discussed matters with the chief constable. He needed sanction for the proposed course of action. The chief constable expressed her approval. Soon after, he met with Mironova and Pearce. 'We've decided to call in MCU and I also intend to speak to that Russian policewoman.'

He was interrupted when the phone rang. 'I have Chief Superintendent Armistead on the phone.'

Nash had never heard of Armistead but instructed the operator to put him through. 'DI Nash, Armistead here, Major Crimes Unit.'

'I was about to ring you.'

'Really?' the word conveyed disbelief. 'We've had a complaint about you.' The tone was frosty. 'We've been running a joint operation with our colleagues in St Petersburg. That's in Russia,' Armistead added pompously.

'I know,' Nash's interruption was deceptively gentle. 'I visited The Hermitage a few years ago.'

'What's that got to do with it,' Armistead snapped.

'The Hermitage Museum. It's in St Petersburg.'

'It appears that when Commander Dacic asked for information regarding two murders committed in your area you were less than cooperative.'

The man's supercilious tone and arrogant attitude irritated Nash. 'Correction,' he said. 'It wasn't Commander Dacic who was seeking information and it wasn't about the murders. You should get your facts straight. I enquired about a teddy bear and she seemed to regard the transfer of information as a one-way street. However, matters have moved on. We've recovered three more bodies from the same location yesterday. The first two were of Eastern European origin; we'll know in time if the same is true of the remainder. In addition, we've a young Moldavian girl in custody in connection with the death of three men whose appearance suggests them to be Slav or Baltic.'

'Hell's bloody bells!' Armistead's composure was blown apart by Nash's revelations. 'What's going on?'

'I rather hope you or Commander Dacic might shed some light on it. I've my own theory, which I'd share in exchange for some cooperation. My next call was going to be St Petersburg.'

'Don't worry about that. I'll speak to her and arrange for her to ring you. I'll call you back. I'll also get one of my most senior officers to you ASAP.'

Armistead left Nash in no doubt that his co-operation with Commander Dacic was essential. Nash replied, 'I'll be as helpful as you want but not if I'm being shafted. Either I get the co-operation I require or when your officers arrive here they'll get sent back where they came from.'

'You can't do that.' Armistead's breath whistled alarmingly. He recovered his composure. 'You've gone too far, Nash. I intend to speak to your chief constable and report what you've just said.'

Nash's tone was sweetness itself. 'Didn't I make it clear? Those are the chief constable's instructions.'

Five minutes later Armistead was back on the line. Although it was clear he and Nash were never going to be soul mates he was courtesy itself and promised the full cooperation of both MCU and the Russian authorities.

Nash told his team the gist of the conversation. 'Perhaps we have been twinned with Vladivostok after all,' Mironova observed wryly.

Nash scratched his head. 'I hope the Dacic woman proves more helpful than last time.' He didn't sound optimistic.

Nash still had doubts on hearing Commander Dacic's opening words.

'Please fax all the relevant documents to me,' she told him. 'Superintendent Armistead assures me you'll do this. That way I can study them as I travel to England. In return, I'll bring with me all our information. I'll brief you in full when I arrive in three days' time.'

'It'll take a few hours to assemble the paperwork but I'll fax it as soon as I can.' Nash was now relaxed. 'Has Armistead brought you up to date?'

'I'm not certain how these things work in your country, but I guess Armistead is an administrator, not an investigator?'

'I think that's safe to assume.'

There was no doubting the laughter in Dacic's voice. 'I asked him about Yorkshire. He said, "It's a sleepy region containing mostly agriculture and quiet market towns." I'm looking forward to seeing Yorkshire, for it doesn't seem quiet or sleepy to me.'

'Perhaps that shows how serious the problem is.'

'But perhaps Armistead was right in one thing. He said you're an exceptionally talented detective. I'm looking forward to meeting you and working together.'

Nash stared at the phone after Dacic rang off. And perhaps that cuts two ways, he thought. He called Clara into his office and updated her. 'You'll have to stall anyone who wants me tomorrow. I'm having a day off. There's not much more we can do until everyone's on board.'

'Anything interesting in mind?'

'I'm going to visit Stella.'

'Any improvement?'

Nash shrugged.

'Speaking of Commander Dacic, Viv had an idea. He suggested looking her up on the internet. If she's as prominent as we think there ought to be some mention of her.'

'Might be worth a try.'

The escalation had far-reaching effects. Pratt was summoned back from holiday and Armistead rang to advise he'd be visiting Netherdale to greet Commander Dacic. In addition, two of his officers would be coming to liaise with their Yorkshire colleagues and the Russian.

When Pratt arrived back, he received a call from Nash. 'Good holiday, Tom?'

'It was until the Chief's secretary rang. The wife went off the deep end when I told her I'd been called back. I explained the force would be paying the travel expenses but it didn't pacify her. I wasn't too bothered myself. There's only so much sangria and weak lager one man can drink. Besides, if I'd had to sit through another evening of third-rate entertainment interspersed with bingo I'd have headed for the airport off my own bat. Anyway, you'd better bring me up to speed with what's happened. Apart from your election as the patron saint of North Yorkshire Guild of Funeral Directors, that is.'

'Don't you start! I'm having enough trouble with Mexican Pete. He's developed a dodgy sense of humour. Every time I ring him he asks, "How many this time?" The joke's starting to wear thin.'

After he'd been updated Tom commented, 'It's clear this thing's much bigger than a couple of isolated incidents. It makes you wonder how big the problem really is. It's obvious both MCU and the Russians are treating it as a matter of extreme concern.'

Clara handed Nash a message, a phone number on a slip of paper. He read the name alongside it, 'That's the psychiatrist I want to consult about Stella. I'll ring her now.'

'Mr Nash, I can see this poses a problem but without conducting an assessment of the patient I can't advise you. Any recommendation I made without having seen Miss Pearson could be fatally flawed.'

'That complicates matters because interviewing Stella would give the game away.'

'We seem to be at an impasse then.'

Nash had a thought. 'Unless you could use the pretext that you'd been asked to talk to all my friends and colleagues, because my bosses are worried about me?'

'I could do that, but at some stage I'll want to interview you.'

'Is that necessary?'

'For my own satisfaction, yes. I'd be interested to meet the owner of such a devious mind.'

DCS Armistead was big viewed from any angle. He was well in excess of six feet tall. This helped keep his girth in proportion. To use the local expression he was built 'like a brick shithouse'. His frame dwarfed even that of Tom Pratt.

His companion was by contrast slim to the point of being slender, with small, almost fragile hands and feet. She was in her early thirties, extremely pretty, with dark hair, brown eyes and an olive complexion.

Nash eyed her appreciatively. He assumed her to be Armistead's secretary until the MCU chief introduced her as DCI Jackie Fleming. After the introductions, Nash briefed the MCU officers.

Armistead watched him with an expressionless gaze throughout. 'You've made a good start. You and your team have done well. I'm impressed with the grasp you have on the case. It's only a beginning, though. Part of my brief is to sum up the strengths and weaknesses of the task force set up to handle the case. Although I'll be overseeing the course of the investigation and liaising with police forces both here and on the Continent, I'm happy to leave the operational side in your hands. I've had a word with Pratt on the subject. Your team has a fine reputation. What you're faced with is an enormous challenge. DCI Fleming will be here to assist you. You'll also be joined by DS Thomas. He's on his way to Heathrow to meet Commander Dacic. I suggest we leave the finer points until after her report tomorrow. Once you hear it you'll appreciate what we're up against.'

That evening Nash read the information Pearce had printed off. Commander Dacic, it seemed, was even higher profile than they'd suspected. The article suggested she was highly thought of in governmental circles. Nash sipped his wine as he stared at her photograph. Although the grainy image was far from clear there was no doubt the commander was an attractive-looking woman. He turned the page and found another news item, to which Pearce had stapled a note. 'When I searched the name, this came up. I'm not sure if there's a connection but thought you'd want to see it. Viv.'

NEWS REPORT: NOVEMBER. 1995

THREE-YEAR HUNT FOR MISSING OFFICIAL ENDS. IFOR TROOPS GRIM DISCOVERY.

Sarajevo, Bosnia.

Last week, troops of the IFOR (Implementation Force) of peacekeepers searching for victims of the recent conflict, found a shallow grave in woodland close to Sarajevo which resolved a three-year-old mystery. It contained the corpses of three men. Forensic experts confirmed they were those of a former Communist regional governor and his two bodyguards. They went missing in 1992 shortly after Bosnia gained independence. All three had been shot at close range, probably within days of their disappearance. The IFOR area commander told reporters that tests had yielded a vital clue as to the possible killer. 'Hair samples from the clothing of two of the victims has been analysed and the results show it belonged to a female. This evidence will be passed to local police. How energetically they pursue the matter, given the unsavoury character of the deceased, is another matter.'

Local legend has already invested the area with a sinister reputation. It results from an incident in 1982. A local man, Bogdan Dacic, was discovered hanging from the same tree underneath which the bodies of the officials were found. It is believed he committed suicide following the death of his elder daughter who had earlier been abducted. His body was found by his younger daughter.

Nash closed the file. It was obvious Viv had printed the article because of the name, but was there a connection with Commander Dacic? Memory returned in a mental flashback. He pictured himself, as a much younger Detective Sergeant at Scotland Yard. That news item had caused some speculation. An older colleague had commented, 'That'll be a revenge killing.'

'How do you mean?' Nash had asked.

'Stands to reason,' the DI told him. 'After all those years of repression there must be lots of people with an axe to grind. Who knows what sort of atrocities those blokes committed. Think yourself lucky you live in a democratic society, young Mike.'

Had it been revenge? If so, the motive seemed obvious. But was Commander Dacic related to the suicide victim? Was she perhaps the younger daughter referred to in the news item?

Nash gave up the puzzle and decided on an early night. He reached across the breakfast bar for his tablets and swilled the medication down with the last of his wine. As he drank, his mind was full of the events of the day. He'd barely fallen asleep when the dream began.

There was a tree, or were there more? He could see two figures. He walked towards them, heard a woman's voice, harsh with emotion, anger, fury and a deadly menace. The words sounded vaguely familiar but Nash couldn't understand. She appeared young, with dark auburn hair. She might be attractive but the emotion on her face marred her looks. Nash was afraid. He thought she had a weapon, but he couldn't be sure. The other figure could have been a man. He stood with an abject air of acceptance.

Nash wanted to intervene. He tried to move forward but was now rooted to the spot. They continued speaking; Nash felt a sense of distaste. He wanted to ask what was happening but the girl suddenly took a pace forward, the menace obvious. This time the man snarled a reply defiantly. This was no innocent victim. Without hesitation, the young woman stepped close to the man.

Nash watched the scene being played out in slow motion. It was a gun. He saw her finger curl round the trigger, saw the rush of expelling gases forcing the bullet down the barrel. He heard the loud report echoing through what had now suddenly become a forest and saw the bullet exiting the side of the man's head accompanied by a red and grey stream of pulp that had been his brain. Nash watched in sick horror as the man crumpled and fell, not to the floor of the forest but beyond, down and down.

Nash stared straight into the girl's eyes. She blinked as if she was aware of his presence. The impression was so vivid he recoiled as if she was going to shoot him. She seemed to gaze at him for a long moment, shrugged, then turned away. Nash watched her go. He glanced down at where her victim had fallen. The forest floor was carpeted with pine needles, beech mast and dead leaves. Of the victims there was no sign.

Next morning, Nash sensed an air of expectancy among his colleagues as they waited for the MCU detectives and the Russian. He told Clara about reading the news item and the resultant nightmare. 'I'm not sure if the name's a coincidence or if there's more to it.'

Clara thought it over. 'Dacic is a fairly common name.'

The meeting was scheduled to begin at 9 a.m. At 8.55 the door swung open and Armistead entered, followed by DCI Fleming and a male officer. Armistead introduced him. 'This is DS Thomas. Commander Dacic has been delayed while she takes a phone call from her director.'

Tom Pratt had barely begun introducing his officers when the door opened to admit a young woman with striking good looks. She could have been anything from twenty-five to thirty-five years old. She wore a light-grey business suit and white blouse which served to enhance the effect of her lustrous auburn hair. Clara watched as the woman strode confidently into the room. Ever keen to see Nash's reaction to a good looking woman, Clara's gaze shifted to her boss. Nash was staring at the Russian as she advanced to greet the rest of the party. His face was drained of colour. He was clinging to the edge of the table, his knuckles white. Clara stared; this was an effect she'd never witnessed before. 'Mike, you OK?' she whispered. There was no answer.

The Russian sat at one end of the table with Armistead and Pratt at the other. Nash was next to Commander Dacic, with DCI Fleming opposite him. From her position alongside Fleming, Mironova was able to concentrate on Dacic's address whilst keeping an eye on her boss. Nash's attention was not divided; throughout the meeting he kept his gaze unwaveringly on the Russian. He'd recovered a little colour but still looked shaken. Whatever the reason it had not been a two-way effect. Dacic gave no sign of recognition, no indication that meeting Nash was more than a professional encounter. So what had caused such a devastating effect?

'I'd like to start by telling you about myself,' Dacic began. 'Then I'll give a detailed report.'

She held up a folder, 'This will help to explain the reason for my being here. My department has put together a fact sheet. These will be available for you to refer to,' she looked up and smiled. 'Don't worry; they are in English, not Russian,' she smiled at Clara. 'Although that wouldn't be a challenge for one of you.

'My name is Snjezana Dacic. Not easy for the English tongue, I know. Please call me Zena. It means "Snow Woman" in Croatia where I was born thirty-three years ago. My parents,' she paused and then corrected herself, 'my mother moved to live in St Petersburg when I was nine years old.'

Mironova saw Zena's eyes darken as if at some bad memory. 'Now to the case details. As Inspector Nash has worked out, we believe the skeletons taken from your lake are victims of human trafficking. Following the disbanding of the old Republic, this evil business has become prevalent throughout Europe and beyond. This was not seen as a problem in Britain until recently.' Dacic paused to let the implication of this sink in. 'The excellent work by Inspector Nash and his team has given us chance to combat this evil.

'Please study the sheets you'll be handed later, particularly if your resolve weakens. I'm afraid much of what's in here isn't for those with queasy stomachs. Now, allow me to give you some facts.' She opened a file and glanced at it.

'In some countries the percentage of women from Russia and other Eastern European states working in the sex trade is so great that prostitutes are referred as "Natashas". Trade in women's flesh is lucrative and low risk compared to the supply of drugs or firearms. These are frowned on in most societies; however, prostitution is tolerated, encouraged, and in some countries legal.

'When *perestroika* came, it gave an opportunity for traffickers to smuggle women across borders,' Dacic paused. 'Willing or not. Statistics might help illustrate what we're fighting. In Germany, recent investigations revealed almost 90 per cent of all prostitutes were from Eastern Europe. A separate enquiry showed that over half a million have been smuggled to the West over an eight-year period from Ukraine alone.

'One of our difficulties is persuading people to believe prostitutes do not earn large sums of money.' Zena looked up, 'It is not like the film *Pretty Woman*. Women are tempted from poverty, betrayed by promises of work. Or they are kidnapped. I'll illustrate with three examples. Believe me, I could bring three hundred or three thousand just as easily.'

She turned the page and studied it. 'An eighteen-year-old girl replied to a newspaper advertisement for a training course in Germany. To reach there she travelled on a false passport. When she arrived she was told the school had closed and that she must continue on to Belgium, where she would find work as a waitress. In Brussels she was told she owed $10,000 and to repay this she must work as a prostitute. Her passport was taken. She was threatened, beaten and repeatedly raped. When she escaped she was arrested because she had no papers. Only when a medical examination revealed evidence of torture was she believed.' Dacic added softly. 'There were more than one hundred cigarette burns on her body.

'Another girl was twenty-one when she was recruited by, I regret to say a woman, who said her daughter was working in Greece and earning good money. When the girl arrived in Greece her passport was taken and she was locked in a room in a brothel, guarded by two fierce dogs. She was visited every night by men demanding sex. This lasted every night from 9 p.m. to 6 a.m. She escaped. When she arrived back in Ukraine she had only $55.

'Another,' the Commander turned a further page, 'is from the poorest region of Ukraine. She was told that rich families in United Arab Emirates were looking for housemaids. Her passport was also taken and she was sold to a brothel keeper for $7,000. She was made to work as a prostitute to repay the purchase price and her travel costs. She escaped and went to the police for help.' Dacic ended, 'She was arrested and sentenced to three years in prison for prostitution.'

She sipped her water. 'I'm quoting these examples for you to understand the size of the problem and the ruthlessness of the traffickers. There is even more wickedness, believe me. We have evidence that when women have earned enough to leave, their pimps tip off corrupt police officials. The women are deported and the pimps keep the money.

'Recruitment is done by misleading advertisements. They offer high wages for unskilled work as waitresses, domestic servants, nannies, dancers or hostesses. Other advertisements take the form of "marriage agencies". Inspection of newspapers in Ukraine and Russia found up to twenty such advertisements in every issue.

'So far, there have been few cases of this abuse in your country,' Dacic smiled grimly. 'But let's not be complacent. With the large influx of foreigners, asylum seekers etcetera, this form of activity is increasing. I'll give you one example of how much this business is worth. A doctor from Ukraine set up a brothel in Essex employing non-English-speaking girls. She was in business only eight months. In that time she made a profit of more than £130,000. That was several years ago,' Zena told them. 'I can confirm prices have not reduced.'

Someone, Mironova thought it was DS Thomas, whistled in surprise.

There was a knock at the door. 'That'll be the coffee.' Tom Pratt signalled the break in proceedings. By the look of Dacic's audience, it had come none too soon.

Zena reminded them when they resumed, 'I quoted those examples purely to give you an idea of the size of the problem and the character of those involved. I'm sad to say you haven't heard the worst. The criminals are always looking for new ways to make money. They found that if a man will pay for the service of prostitute, some will pay even more to have sex with a child.

'It didn't matter how they acquired them. Using offers of adoption, by paying poor families or simply kidnapping. They supply young girls and boys across borders to be imprisoned in special establishments. They are raped, sodomized and forced into indescribable sexual acts by anyone prepared to pay. Many acts are filmed and appear for sale on the internet or in videos. They are bought by other perverts and the criminals make even more profit.

'It's impossible to estimate the number whose childhood has been ruined, whose chance of a decent life is over before it began. All we can do is try to stop this evil and punish the criminals.' Dacic turned to Nash. 'We believe your assessment of the motive for the murder of the bodies in the lake is correct. If a young girl becomes pregnant there will be no abortion. The criminals will simply order her killed. If a girl or boy becomes infected, particularly with HIV, they are disposed of. They've ceased to be an asset. They're a liability. The cost of a bullet is small. It's crimes like these that my department was set up to investigate. Our director has authority from the highest level of government. The phone call I received before this meeting was to pass on a message of encouragement from the President of Russia.

'So far, we've had some success, but we've a long way to go to identify the people controlling this operation. We need all possible help. Your investigation is vital. I can think of no more wicked crime than the abuse of children.'

*

After Dacic conducted a question and answer session, they broke for lunch. Armistead had booked a table at The Golden Bear. As they were crossing the market place, Mironova manoeuvred herself alongside Nash, 'Are you all right, Mike?'

He looked at her warily. 'Why shouldn't I be?'

'From the look on your face when the Commander entered the room I thought you'd seen a ghost.'

Nash stopped. He looked round to make sure there was no one within earshot. 'That was pretty much it. You remember the dream I had last night?'

'In a forest with a young woman shooting a man?'

'The woman looked exactly like Zena Dacic.'

'But you'd never met her. You've only spoken on the phone.'

'No, I hadn't met her. But the last thing I got from Viv was that collection of facts about Dacic from the internet.'

Armistead opened the afternoon session, which was spent examining evidence and planning strategy. He announced that he would be returning to London that evening. 'DCI Fleming and DS Thomas will also be travelling south. They've to give evidence at the trial of a terrorist suspect. They should be back in a few days.'

Nash responded on behalf of the local force. 'Tomorrow will be taken up with the post-mortems on the three latest victims. Whilst we're at the mortuary we should see if Zena recognizes any of the men killed at the Carthill house. I also thought Zena would want to talk to the girl.'

'That's true,' Dacic agreed eagerly. 'The sooner the better. Next day, if Mikhail would be so good,' she smiled at Nash, 'I wish to visit this tarn.'

CHAPTER SIX

Ramirez had completed his examination. Any significant findings would have to wait until laboratory testing provided genetic evidence. For the moment he was able to confirm only that there was deformation of the pubic bones. 'This suggests a similar history of abuse. I'd be surprised if the profile of these victims didn't match the earlier ones. The cause of death is the same, right down to the calibre of the bullet which is 0.22.'

'I'd like Commander Dacic to view the bodies of the men killed at Carthill.'

Ramirez led them to the body cabinet. 'The killer did not place the men's own genitalia in their mouths. Each received a set belonging to one of the others.'

'A gesture of contempt?' Nash suggested.

Zena stared at the corpse. 'Hatred and rejection also,' she added. 'I don't recognize this one. The man who found the bodies is a mailman, I believe?'

'It was a postman who reported the deaths,' Nash contradicted. 'But he wasn't the first to find them.'

'Why do you say that?'

Mironova was also taken aback by Nash's statement.

'When we searched the house, four of the five beds were made up. That suggests there were four inhabitants plus

Milla. Before we arrived someone removed every document from the house. There wasn't even a utility bill or a rent statement.

'It was also obvious the wardrobe and drawers had been rifled and some clothing removed.'

Zena stared at him with growing respect. 'How do you know?'

'We found a single sock with a very distinctive pattern.'

Zena smiled at him. 'You see things others miss.'

'Sometimes I get lucky,' Nash returned Zena's smile with a warm look.

Mironova thought, 'Here we go again.'

'You don't have to be so modest, Mikhail,' Zena's tone was caressing enough to confirm Clara's suspicions. 'Wasn't it a famous golfer who said, "the more I practice, the luckier I get"?'

'Hell's bells,' Mironova thought. 'I've heard of some strange places to start a flirtation but the middle of a mortuary beats all.'

Mexican Pete obviously had similar ideas, for he coughed none too discreetly. 'When you're ready, perhaps you wouldn't mind examining the other corpses? Some of us have work to do.'

Clara noticed Nash's colour was a little heightened and Zena's was also a shade deeper than previously.

Neither of the other men was known to the Russian. On their return to Netherdale police station Zena suggested that she share the DNA evidence she'd brought from St Petersburg with them. 'We have classifications within the general gene pool and by close examination it may be possible to narrow down the origin of the victims. Is it possible some of your team could assist? The strands in each DNA ladder have to be examined in entirety. With more eyes the job will be faster.'

'I'll ask Superintendent Pratt. This is his jurisdiction. My responsibility is limited to Helmsdale and only Clara and DS Pearce work directly with me. I'm sure it'll be okay.'

'Perhaps you'll play me the tape of your interview with the girl

before I speak to her.' Zena listened to the recording in silence. 'Poor child,' she said as Clara switched the machine off. 'Milla's first luck was when she fell into your hands. Many officers would have treated her only as a killer, not a victim. It seems to me she has retained her spirit, which is remarkable after such an ordeal.'

Milla was being held in a children's unit. Nash listened to Clara's translation of Zena's questions and Milla's responses. He watched the Russian woman and the young girl in turn. It was clear from Milla's body language that Zena had put her at ease. Nothing in the conversation seemed to shake her composure. When Zena stood up to signify the end of the meeting Nash said, 'Ask Milla if she'd like some different clothes.'

Milla was dressed in the outfit she'd been wearing when arrested. She flushed bright scarlet when Nash's question was translated and he saw her eyes were bright with tears. Tears of shame and anger he supposed. He'd left gratitude out of the equation. Milla accompanied her joyful acceptance by seizing his hand and shaking it vigorously. 'I take it the answer's yes,' Nash laughed. He retained his hold on Milla's hand and looked the youngster in the eye. 'Tell Milla you'll take her to the shops tomorrow to buy what she wants. I'll pay, but don't tell her that. Ask her if she likes ice cream and take her to Sandoni's on the High Street. Tell her it's the best ice cream in the world.'

'St Nicholas arrives in a police car, not on a sleigh,' Zena teased him as they left the youngster. 'Mikhail, that was a very nice thing you did. I think there is more to you than just a good detective.'

'I was thinking the same about you, Zena. That there is more to you than meets the eye, much more.'

Mironova was due in court next morning so Nash collected Zena to take her to Cauldmoor. Once they'd passed Bishop's Cross and were heading for the high moorland Zena said, 'I understand what you meant when you said how remote this place is. But you forgot to mention how dreary.'

'It gets lonelier and drearier the closer we get.'

The moor was covered in a mist so heavy and clinging Nash was obliged to turn on his wipers and fog lights. They pulled up alongside the gate leading to Misery Near. News of the discovery of three more skeletons had reached the press but they'd relied on archive photographs rather than sending photographers. Nor were there any members of the public about.

Lamentation Tarn glittered dully with dark malevolence. The Grieving Stones reflected what little light there was from the wetness of their weathered surface. Across the tarn, the bothy hunched miserably against the hillside, its dark timbers barely visible through the gloom.

Zena shivered superstitiously as she stared at the dank, mist-laden scene. 'This is an evil place,' she murmured. 'Let's go to look at this aptly named tarn before my resolve vanishes in the fog.'

Nash led the way in silence. He was about to unlock the bothy door when Zena said, 'Wait please, Mikhail. I want to see where you found the bear.'

He showed her the narrow gap behind the bothy. 'It was a day much like this when she came here, although the rain was heavier. I think she knew what they were going to do so she hid the bear. A forlorn hope that someone would investigate. A message in a bottle, I suppose you'd call it.' He looked at Zena, 'Do you have a photograph?'

Dacic stared at Nash as if he'd gone crazy. It was a while before she spoke. 'How do you know all that?' She demanded.

'Show me the photograph. If I'm right, I'll tell you.'

Dacic shrugged. 'This had better be good.'

She unzipped her document case and pulled out a photo. Nash gazed at it intently, 'Yes, that's her.'

'Tell me.'

'After we found the toy I was puzzled. I realized the bear couldn't belong to either of the girls whose bodies we'd recovered. I wondered how that bear had got here. That night I dreamed I saw someone standing here. It was like today with mist and rain all round. She was terrified, weeping and talking to Mitya, her last, her only friend in the world. Then she hid him and the dream ended. I woke up.'

Zena stared at him with open-mouthed incredulity. She spluttered indignantly, 'What madness is this? You can't have such dreams. This is the road to insanity. How do you know this is the girl?'

'I just do.' Nash stared at Zena for so long that she stirred uneasily.

'Nash, please explain, what is the meaning of all this?'

He noted she'd reverted to using his surname. 'I'll tell you about a different dream, about men in a forest. Ones shot in cold blood.' Nash pulled the newspaper clipping from his pocket and held it up. 'You shot them didn't you?' Zena's eyes widened with shock. 'Was it because of your sister? Is that why you killed them? In revenge for what they did? Is that why you're fighting this crusade so ferociously?'

Nash watched her carefully. He saw her eyes glaze over and steadied her as she swayed. He led her to the bothy door. 'Rest on the couch until you feel better. I'll brew some tea. You'll have to drink it without milk.'

He moved to the kitchen area, grateful there was still some bottled water. He thought, 'What the hell am I doing? Why did I say all that? Maybe these nightmares are a form of madness. What did Zena call it, road to insanity?' He heard her stirring slightly.

Nash walked over and sat down alongside her. 'Feeling better? I didn't mean to frighten you but I didn't know how else to prove my point.'

She stared at him, her dark eyes moist. 'I don't understand. How do you know? Who told you?'

Nash reached out and touched her arm. 'No one told me anything. As I said, I have dreams.' He sighed and put his head in his hands.

'Are you psychic?'

Nash shook his head. 'No,' he continued gloomily, 'I'm not psychic. I'm not sure what I am. I don't understand these nightmares or where they come from.'

'You have many?'

'Not many. Only when I'm stressed.'

'I can't believe you dream these things. If it helps solve crime that would be good, but I guess it's more of a curse than a blessing.'

Nash tried to explain. 'I've no idea how it happens. After I'd held the bear and thought about the owner the dream came to me. Later, I read about you and saw the article about your father. I'd read the case years ago so I suppose the rest was inevitable.'

He shrugged, 'I dreamed about you before we met. Although, of course, I didn't know it was you. All I'd seen was a photo downloaded from the internet. When you walked in the office, it was a total shock.'

Zena was watching him closely. 'I remember it every morning when I awake; every evening before I go to sleep. I was six years old, my sister was eleven. Two men came, servants of the local party chief. This was before the end of the old system; men such as him were more powerful than the Tsars. It was known he liked little girls but there was nothing anyone could do. We were alone in our house. She saw the men and made me hide. She may have been trying to protect me. I don't know.

'I came out of my hiding place when I heard her screams. I saw them putting her in the car. I remember screaming at them to stop but they took no notice.

'It was three months before she was found. She was wandering the streets of the nearest town. Starving and with only the remnants of the clothes she was wearing when she was taken. They hadn't even the decency to bring her home.

'My father and mother were distraught. We nursed her back to health but her mind was gone. My job was to sit with her when Mother and Father were out. I remember her staring through the window with empty eyes. I told her jokes and stories and she stared through that hole in the wall as if I wasn't there. One day she vanished. She walked five miles to the nearest railroad, laid down on the lines and waited. It was her twelfth birthday. After the funeral my father said he was going for a walk. When he hadn't returned, Mother sent me to look for him. I found him.' Zena's face was red and distorted. Tears flowed unchecked, unnoticed. 'At first I didn't realize what was hanging from the oak tree. Then I saw it was a body. There was only a light breeze. It moved the leaves and swung the body towards me. That's when I saw it was Papa. I found the note at the base of the tree. He left it for mother and me. He pleaded for our forgiveness. He couldn't live with the shame of being unable to protect his daughter.'

Zena paused and wiped her eyes angrily, as if ashamed at her display of weakness. Nash put his arm round her shoulder. She leaned her head against him. 'As soon as we could, Mother and I went to St Petersburg where she had family. She died of a heart attack when I was eleven. I was placed in a state orphanage. When I was fourteen a boy from the orphanage tried to rape me. I stuck a knife in him.' Zena smiled a watery smile. 'A bit like Milla, I suppose. I put him in hospital. The policeman in charge of the case was sympathetic and friendly, not dirty friendly,' she added hastily seeing the look on Nash's face. 'I mean, he wasn't trying to get into my knickers.'

Nash laughed aloud and Zena grinned. 'I told him everything. My whole story, not just of the rape. He suggested when I grew up I should join the police force. He said the best way to fight back was by locking criminals away, not sticking them with knives. The old order was collapsing then, so I took his advice and entered the force after I left university. I worked hard and started to do well but I couldn't be satisfied until I'd settled matters with those monsters. Through them I lost my sister, my father and my mother.

'I found them round the time of the Kosovo conflict when the region was in turmoil. They were selling armaments to both sides. I hijacked all three at gunpoint and made them drive to the forest. I made them dig a grave at the foot of the tree where father hanged himself. I shot the two henchmen. Then I turned to their boss. He'd already shit himself. I explained why he was going to die. He begged and pleaded for his miserable life. I enjoyed that, enjoyed it even more when he pissed his pants. I think his terror caused me more satisfaction than killing him.'

Zena paused, her eyes on Nash. 'Didn't you mention tea?'

'I'll get you it in a moment. Go on.'

'I filled the grave in. I remember singing and laughing as I did this. Something I hadn't done for many years.'

She saw Nash's expression and asked, 'How did you dream such a thing?'

'I honestly don't know, Zena,' Nash replied. 'I can't explain it.'

'I find it hard to grasp.'

'I don't understand it myself. Half the time I think I'm going round the twist.'

'What does that mean? Going around the twist? I thought it was a dance?'

'It means going mad. Going insane, if you prefer.'

Zena placed her hand on Nash's and caressed it. Nash found the gesture highly erotic. He looked away. How successful he'd been at hiding his arousal, he wasn't sure, for Zena stopped stroking him and changed the subject. 'Where do we go from here, Mikhail? It seems you have knowledge that wraps us close together.'

'That's another question I can't answer.'

When Zena had recovered her composure they left the bothy. She looked back at Lamentation Tarn and shivered. 'I was right. This is an evil place. I wonder how those poor girls finished up here. I shrink from considering what dreadful stories their ghosts could tell us.'

'I think there are some things it is better we don't know. All else apart, I think I've had enough nightmares. I certainly don't want any on that subject.'

'I think we should forget this case until we've slept. Today has been too distressing for me to take any more. Tomorrow we'll examine the case of the girl who owned the bear. From what the pathologist told you, hers couldn't be one of bodies. Yet it's obvious she's been there at some time. So we're left with the mystery of what happened to her.'

'As you suggest, we'll look into that tomorrow.'

When Nash dropped her back at her hotel, Zena, who had been silent throughout the journey, turned to Nash. 'This has been a strange day,' she said. 'I can't understand what's happened.' She smiled. 'One thing's sure, Mikhail. Although I can't understand it, I'm glad you dreamed of me.'

CHAPTER SEVEN

The intruder worked slowly and methodically; there was no need for haste. He was unlikely to be disturbed. The occupant of the flat wasn't going to raise the alarm. Wasn't going to raise anything anymore.

He examined the bedroom critically. A sudden bleeping sound startled him. He spun round, eyes searching the room for the source. A red light flashed. It was a pager on the bedside table. His breathing inside the protective mask sounded loud once the bleep stopped. The mask covered his face from nose to chin, the air tube trailing over his shoulder to the tank on his back. When he was sure the room was entirely to his satisfaction he crossed to the gas fire and turned on the gas. He left the bedroom and closed the door firmly. He collected his equipment and replaced it in a large duffel bag. He set aside a length of coiled rope, closed the bag, and tied one end of the rope round its handles.

The next part was the trickiest. Entering the place had been easy. Exiting it so as to give the appearance he'd never been there was totally different. He lowered the holdall out of the window into the garden below. When the tension slackened he tossed out the rope.

He eased himself carefully through the window. A second later he was outside, hanging perilously by one hand as he endeavoured to grasp the frame with the other. He achieved a hold and swivelled to face the room he'd left, pausing to regain both composure and breath. Using his right hand he brought the window pane towards the frame. He knew he'd have to remove his glove for the next bit and hoped he'd manage it without leaving a fingerprint.

After several attempts he got the lever to engage against the button on the sill. To all intents and purposes the window was closed. As he wriggled his right hand through the narrow gap his left hand slipped and he was forced to cling on to the frame.

He thought of rubbing the frame to remove the prints but realized a patch of clean paintwork would look suspicious. He took a deep breath and launched himself out, down and to his left, dropping fifteen feet with the skill and grace of a trained athlete or paratrooper.

His knees buckled on impact, cushioning the effect of the drop, and his hands went out to further soften his landing. He retrieved the bag, coiled the rope, removed his mask and the tank from his back, placed them inside the bag and zipped it up. He slung the bag over his shoulder and glanced around. He could just make out the outline of shrubs and bushes. The night was cold with no moon. No one had witnessed his arrival. No one would witness his departure. He reached his car, placed the bag inside and closed the door quietly. He started the engine and drove away.

Three hours work, virtually no risk and minimal effort. He thought briefly of his fingerprints on the window frame, but even that failed to trouble him. Hopefully, those investigating the scene would take it at face value.

If his fingerprints were discovered, identification of them would serve only to confuse.

Pearce was detailed to continue the DNA sifting, a laborious process, whilst Mironova, free after giving evidence against a drug dealer, collected Zena from The Golden Bear.

'How did yesterday's visit go?'

'It was a strange and disturbing day. Nash is an unusual person.'

Clara glanced swiftly at her. 'You've noticed. What did he do, or was it something he said?'

'He told me something that shocked me.'

'He can be disconcertingly accurate. It must be odd to witness it for the first time. It's as if he's read your mind.'

'I still wonder if I dreamt it.'

'I've seen something like this before. We were investigating a series of apparently unconnected killings a year ago. Mike began having nightmares. Although he didn't understand them at the time, when more facts emerged they helped him solve the case.'

Their talk was interrupted by a cordon of flashing lights in the distance. Like all the vehicles in front, they had to take a diversion.

Helmsdale police station yard was deserted. They shared the premises with the fire brigade and ambulance service. Inside the building the 'Marie Celeste' atmosphere prevailed. It was with some relief that they spotted a harassed young constable in a ground floor office attempting to answer three phones at once. 'What's going on?' Mironova demanded when he eventually finished.

'You name it, it's happened. There's been a major RTA between here and Netherdale. An oil tanker overturned on black ice and cleaned up three cars. That took almost everyone we had available plus two fire engines and all the ambulances. That road's going to be shut all day. My sergeant and Mr Nash have gone to answer a sudden death call in Garstang Avenue. They were the only ones left. Mr Nash said you'd to join him there to allow my sergeant to return.'

As if to emphasize the point, two phones began to ring. The constable cast a glance heavenward and moved off to answer them.

The fire crew were about to depart, leaving the uniformed officer and two civilians outside the front door. Of Nash there was no sign.

Clara nodded to the sergeant, 'What's happened?'

The sergeant looked harassed. 'Looks like another case of those bloody ancient gas fires. They should be melted down for scrap if you ask me; carbon monoxide poisoning. Your governor came along because there was no one else available. He's given the flat the once-over and there's something he's not happy about. He's outside, round the back.'

The women rounded the building to find Nash crouching by a flower bed, 'Morning, Mike. Taken up gardening?'

Nash looked up and smiled, the warmth of which increased when his gaze took in Zena.

'Come and have a look. Walk on the lawn. Don't disturb the soil.'

They followed the direction of his pointing finger. In the middle of the soft earth about eighteen inches apart were two deep indentations, forming the unmistakeable impression of feet.

'It looks as if someone was standing in the middle of the flower bed.'

'That's what I thought to begin with. But look, there and there.' Nash indicated a series of smaller, shallower impressions on either side of the footprints. 'What do you think those might be?'

Neither of them could make any sense of the marks but Zena said, 'Whoever stood here must be very heavy to make such a deep imprint.'

'That's what I thought. I was about to conduct an experiment when you arrived. Follow me.' He walked ten yards to his right.

'I weigh about fourteen stones, that's about 89 kilos.' He looked down, 'The soil here looks similar to further along so let's see what happens.'

He stepped forward on to the flower bed, waited a few seconds then stepped back on to the lawn. They could just make out the outline of where his feet had been. 'As you said, he must have been very heavy to leave such deep prints, unless …' Nash jumped forward on to the bed.

This time the impression was more pronounced, although still not as deep as the marks further along. 'What are you suggesting?' Zena asked, 'That someone jumped across on to the flower bed?'

'Not across,' Nash corrected her, 'down.' He pointed upwards. 'The window on the first floor was on the latch. That's inside the flat where the body was found. I think someone jumped down from there. I think those smaller marks are where the intruder braced himself from the shock of the fall using his hands.'

'I thought this was an accidental death?' Mironova protested.

'So did I at first. I think we were intended to believe that. Come on, I've more to show you.'

Nash nodded to the two men waiting with the sergeant. 'I think we can let these people go about their business. We'll need a statement from both of you at some stage.'

As he led the way upstairs Nash explained. 'The dead man is a junior doctor at Netherdale General, James Stevens, aged 27. He wasn't supposed to be on duty until after lunch but with the RTA they bleeped him to come in early, got no response. They paged his colleague, the man you saw downstairs. He lives nearby and if they're on the same shift they car-share. He came round and couldn't raise Stevens, knew he was inside because his car's out front. The landlord lives on the ground floor. He also knew Stevens was in because he heard someone moving about in the early hours. He suffers from insomnia and said he thought Stevens might have "had company" because around 5 a.m. he heard a car start. He has a key to all the flats so they opened the door and found Stevens's body. They couldn't resuscitate him so they called us.'

Nash paused to remove his shoes which had soil from the flower bed attached. He pointed to the door. 'Look there. See what you make of that. Concentrate on the lock.'

The brass surface tarnished with age, had three bright scratches across it. 'This lock's been picked,' Clara commented.

'Agreed, but we haven't had reports of a burglary either in this flat or the others. If the motive for the break-in was theft why stop at Stevens's flat; why not try the rest?'

They followed him to the bedroom. The dead man lay on his side in the recovery position. 'They moved him when they were trying to revive him but that can't be helped.'

There was still a strong smell of carbon monoxide in the room. Nash pointed to a small heap of screwed up newspaper on the floor. 'Those had been pushed up the chimney blocking the flue. The firemen said it was carelessness. I don't think so for one minute. Take a close look.'

'It's a fairly common thing to do. People stuff paper up the chimney to stop birds coming down,' Clara objected.

'Maybe, but when would that be? I'd suggest Spring or early Summer when the birds are nesting and there are fledglings about.'

'That's logical.'

'Why do it at this time of the year, when there are few birds about? Those newspapers are only three days old. Not only that, look at the edition. According to his colleague, Stevens has been working all week. Where did he get a copy of a Manchester evening paper? They certainly aren't on sale in this area.'

Nash moved to the wall, closest to the bed and waved them over. 'I noticed that,' he pointed to a small circular hole in the wall. 'I couldn't make out what purpose it served until I got all the other scraps of evidence. Suppose someone fitted a pipe through that hole and fixed a machine to it, one that manufactured carbon monoxide. It wouldn't take much to fill a room as small as this.'

'I've never heard of such a device.' Clara said.

Nash laughed, 'Of course you have. Every internal combustion engine produces carbon monoxide. All you'd need is a small motor. Maybe the landlord was confused when he said he heard a car start. Perhaps what he heard was this motor.'

'Why didn't Dr Stevens hear it?'

'Maybe because he was already unconscious.'

Nash ushered them into the living area. On the wall nearest the bedroom was a sideboard. This had obviously been moved recently and replaced, but not quite in the same position. The indentations made by the legs prior to the move could still be seen. 'They must have had to move that to get to the hole they'd drilled. To get close enough to where Stevens was lying and make sure he ingested a big enough dose to kill him,' he explained.

'Have you ordered SOCO?' Clara asked.

'I was about to do that when you arrived. Attend to it, would you? You haven't said much, Zena. What do you think?'

'I'm puzzled, Mikhail. If someone picked the lock to get in why not walk out the same way?'

'Good question. I believe he wanted to make sure we thought the death was accidental, so he double-locked the door. He hoped we'd overlook his real exit route, which I would have if I hadn't been curious about the paper up the chimney.'

'I think the killer was unlucky you were here. It looks like the work of a professional. So what could the motive be? I'm sure it costs a lot of money to hire a hitman, am I right?'

'As much as £50,000, I believe.'

'Ah Mikhail, such inflated prices in Britain,' Zena teased him. 'The cost of dying in Russia is much lower. So why would someone pay such a huge amount to get rid of a junior doctor?'

Once SOCO arrived, the three returned to the station.

'Okay, Zena,' Nash prompted. 'Tell us about the bear's owner. I suspect this might vary from the rest of the crimes you've talked about.'

Zena nodded. 'It is different. It illustrates the scope of the criminals' depravity. The bear belongs to a girl named Katerina Svetlova. Katerina's background is unlike most of those who fall into the clutches of traffickers.

'Katerina is known as Katya. She's the daughter of Sergei Svetlov, a prominent figure in the Moscow government. His wife Anna is a well-known stage and film actress. By Russian standards, they are affluent. Katya wanted for very little. I'm not suggesting she was spoilt, but shall we say she was indulged.

'Five years ago Katya's parents bought her a computer, one with internet connectivity. I'm awarding no prizes for guessing the outcome. Russian children are innocent when it comes to the dangers of the internet. They know nothing of paedophile tactics of grooming youngsters to corrupt them.

'Katya made acquaintance in a chat room with a boy of similar age. He was very cunning. I have copies of their e-mails. If I'd not been suspicious I'd be convinced he was a young boy. He told Katya all about himself. Of his home in St Petersburg, his family, his school life and friends. Complete fiction, but cleverly put together.

'They'd corresponded for several months when he told Katya he and his parents are coming to Moscow. Something about a business trip his father was making and wouldn't it be wonderful if they could meet. To make it more exciting why not meet secretly?'

Zena's expression grew bleaker. 'Katya agreed. She told him she'd introduce him to her new friend Mitya. This must have alarmed him because Katya got a short message demanding she came alone. This was the only false note in the whole charade. Katya possibly thought he was jealous. It may even have pleased her vanity, because she teased him, telling him Mitya was only a teddy bear.

'She left the house and was never seen again. Despite newspaper and TV coverage, appeals from her parents, there was no trace. Sergei and Anna spent a lot of time and money searching. They had no success until we heard an English detective was making enquiries about Mitya.

'When I'd spoken with you, Mikhail, and knew the circumstances surrounding the discovery of the bear, it confirmed what we suspected; that Katya was dead. Finding the other bodies made me certain Katya had become a victim of sex traffickers.

'My involvement came because "the boy" claimed to come from St Petersburg. Our first task was to see if there was any truth in this. There was none. All of it was a wicked hoax.

'After a great deal of heart-searching I was able to tell Katya's parents the probable reason for her abduction. This was one of the most difficult things I've ever had to do. That's why I believe when Mitya was discovered they were relieved. That may sound strange but they could finally accept that their beloved Katya was dead. That she was no longer suffering.

'I explained to Svetlov the scope of the traffickers' activities. The facts and figures appalled him. He's a big man, both in government and in person. He now understands what other parents suffer after long years with no word from their children. This gave him the incentive to take the problem to the highest level. As a result, our task force was formed.

'This is why I'm here. When we heard of more bodies at the lake, our senior officers and those from your MCU became convinced the sensible action would be to combine the investigations. There was much to be arranged for me to have the necessary authority to visit Britain as a fully authorized police official. I believe it's the first time this has happened apart from anti-terrorist operations with the United States.

'That gave me full power of investigation and arrest. In the same way, if the need arises for any officer in your team to visit Russia you would bear the full authority of a Russian police official.' Zena paused and smiled at Mironova. 'Even Clara would be welcome in Belarus,' she teased, 'despite her parentage.'

There was a long silence before Nash spoke. 'What you've told us underlines the extent of the evil we're fighting. What we need is a strategy to identify those responsible.'

'If we could get just one of them it could cause a domino effect or give the enquiry an organic life,' Clara suggested. 'What about the fourth man from the house where Milla was kept prisoner? He'd make a good starting point.'

'Good idea, Clara. Everything's come thick and fast and we need thinking space. We know nothing about those men. Even the housing application was fake. The supposed occupants: did they exist and, if so, what's happened to them? What did those men do for money? Somewhere, someone knows something.'

They were interrupted by the phone ringing.

'SOCO on the line for you, Sir.'

'Inspector Nash, I'm not sure what's going on, if I didn't know better I'd think someone was playing a practical joke. You're not taking the piss are you?'

'Sorry? You've lost me. What are you talking about?'

'We took prints from Garstang Avenue. Most of them belonged to Stevens. A few were those of the landlord on the outer door and the bedroom door. There was another unidentified set. Given their locations which included the headboard of the bed and the bedside table I'd guess the dead man had a girlfriend,' the officer paused.

'I don't see what the problem is.'

'There's also a single set of prints we lifted from the window frame in the lounge.'

'Go on.'

'We came up with a match.'

'Tell me,' Nash prompted him. As the officer explained Nash listened in disbelief. 'That's impossible.'

'I've been telling myself that. We cross-checked in case someone had fed duff information into the computer or we had a system glitch. I've just got a copy of the originals faxed through to me from CRO and there's no mistake. I'm glad I only collate the information. I'd be fascinated to know the explanation.'

Dacic excused herself. 'I have to report to my director, and also have another call to make. A personal one.'

Nash felt a pang of jealousy. Who to, husband, lover? She plucked her mobile from her pocket. 'Use the landline,' he said generously.

Zena gave him a reproachful look. 'Mikhail, I've heard what a heavy burden British taxpayers have to bear. I wouldn't be able to sleep for the guilt of adding to it.'

Nash was still wrestling with the puzzle set by SOCO when Pearce arrived from Netherdale.

'How's it gone?'

'Nothing positive to report. The dead girls' DNA soup is too mixed to give a clear definition of their origin. The best guess would be just that, merely a guess. If I had to bet I'd go for Ukraine, Latvia, or Belarus, somewhere in that region. Probably Ukraine because it's the largest. It's unfortunate we can't be more specific. Tom wants you to call him when you have a moment. Something to do with a visit tomorrow from the Home Office.'

'Now what?' Nash reached for the phone.

The call took longer than the Superintendent had expected. 'Thanks for calling, Mike. I need you here in the morning. Armistead's bringing some high-powered official from the Home Office and you've been asked,' Nash could almost hear the grin. 'Or more correctly, commanded to attend.'

'Any particular reason?'

'Not one Armistead's prepared to share.'

'I'll be there,' Nash reassured him. 'Whilst we're on the subject of Whitehall, I wonder if you could do me a favour?'

'Fire away.'

'It's in connection with the death of a doctor. At the moment it's little more than a suspicious death but there's a lot I'm not happy with. I'm fairly certain he was murdered. I've just had a report from SOCO and something doesn't add up. I need certain facts checked and the quickest way would be through the Ministry of Defence.'

'What do you need?'

Nash explained. 'If the request comes from someone of more senior rank it might be dealt with quicker.'

'I'll ask Armistead. I know a single suspicious death is hardly MCU's cup of tea but from what you've told me it might tickle his curiosity.'

Nash wandered out of his office. He found Mironova and Pearce sitting with mugs in front of them.

'I'll make you a coffee, Mike,' Viv volunteered.

'Where's Zena?'

'She got a phone call and went off to talk in private,' Clara told him.

'From St Petersburg?'

'No, it was from Moscow,' Clara paused and added thoughtfully. 'I think it was from the Kremlin.'

'Janko, the Soldier is on the line.'

Vatovec picked up the phone at once. 'Yes?' he said cautiously.

Janko's deputy wondered not for the first time about the identity of 'the Soldier'. Vatovec inspired fear within their organization and terror to many outside it. Yet even he seemed afraid when this man called.

The Soldier only contacted Vatovec by phone. Even telephone security was at the highest level. The language used was Serbo-Croat. Guaranteed to fool all but the most learned eavesdropper.

The deputy waited, listening to one half of a one-sided conversation. Janko's part was limited to a series of grunts interspersed with the occasional 'yes' or 'no'. He could tell from his leader's expression the news wasn't good.

Eventually Janko put the phone down. He stared at his second in command. They'd known each other all their lives, hailed from the same village, yet in that short space of time it was as if Vatovec was looking at a complete stranger.

'More problems,' he said bluntly. 'England again. The man who escaped from the house has vanished. If he gets picked up and squeals we're all in deep shit. I've been ordered to England. Get me a ticket on the first available flight. The Soldier has just told me the Snow Woman is in England.'

Next morning Nash drove through to Netherdale for the meeting with Armistead, Pratt and the Home Office official. They were informed that following consultation between the two governments, Katya Svetlova's parents would be visiting England and would be travelling to Yorkshire. Nash was left in no doubt that the onus for ensuring the visit was a success would be down to him. He was surprised to find even Armistead seemed to approve. He was even more surprised at the offer of additional resources should they be required.

An hour later Nash left, carrying the file Pratt had obtained for him. As he left the building Nash turned on his mobile. The only message was curt to the point of rudeness. 'Ramirez. Call me.'

Nash did as instructed.

'Your Doctor Stevens was drugged. He drank a couple of pints of beer and ate a pizza a few hours before he died. The beer was laced with temazepam. Enough to render him unconscious within a couple of hours.'

'Couldn't he have taken sleeping tablets?'

'There were none at the flat and the drug had been dissolved in the beer. It's possible Stevens did that himself. But I think it more likely his drink was spiked, which would suggest he was murdered.'

Nash studied the file from Pratt. Attached to the official records was a newspaper cutting dated four years previously. He picked up the phone. He was making his third call when Zena wandered into his office unannounced and perched on the corner of his desk. She leaned across to see what he'd been reading.

Nash was acutely aware of her closeness, her sensual, slightly musky perfume invading his senses so that he found increasing difficulty in concentrating.

She knew the effect she was having on him. Which she conveyed with an arched eyebrow and a grin of pure mischief overlaid with sexual innuendo. It was with some relief that

Nash was able to ring off. 'Vixen,' he muttered, but Zena appeared not to notice.

She scanned the newspaper cutting. 'Mikhail, why are you reading this?'

Under the headline DISGRACED SOLDIER'S SAD END it described the death of a former army captain, Martin Hill, who'd perished in a fire at his Nottingham home. The article stated, 'Hill was expelled from the army after serving three years imprisonment for abusing prisoners during the Bosnia conflict. Later he'd served as a mercenary in several African countries.' The article concluded, 'Hill was so badly burnt he'd only been identified by dental records. He leaves no relatives.'

'I'm reading it because it puzzles me.'

'Surely this was a straightforward case? Why is it of interest now?'

'I'm trying to figure out how the fingerprints of a man who died four years ago came to be on the window frame of the flat where Dr Stevens was murdered?'

'That's not possible.'

'I agree, but I've had time to think. Let's have the others in.'

'Do you wish me to leave? This isn't my concern?'

Nash looked at her and smiled. Zena felt her face warming. 'No, I don't want you to leave. I've a feeling Stevens's death is connected to our main enquiry but don't ask me how.' He opened the door and signalled to Mironova and Pearce.

'Each of you knows different parts of what I'm about to tell you. Bear with me whilst I bring the others up to speed. We're about to get some important visitors from Russia. Visitors who are here following Zena's investigation and with the blessing of the Home Office.'

Nash explained the significance of Katya's parents' journey. During his account of the meeting Viv's attention was on Nash whilst Clara's gaze switched between her boss and Zena. Clara's expression was one of interested speculation.

Possibly due to the fact that Zena was still perched on the corner of Nash's desk. 'There's also been a development in the case of Doctor Stevens. Something tells me the two are linked.'

Nash repeated what he knew. 'The likeliest explanation; Martin Hill didn't die in the fire. We must assume he's alive. So, who died in the fire? Second, how did they come to be identified as Hill? Third, why did Hill need to disappear? He wasn't wanted by the police or military authorities. Fourth, where and who is he now?'

'That's a shopping list of questions,' Zena commented.

'True, but I think we can take one or two items off the list. I've already made a start.'

He glanced down at the file. 'I rang Nottingham Coroner's office, got his clerk to check their file. He gave me details of the dental practice that treated Hill. I've had a very interesting conversation with their senior partner. He told me about a month before Hill's "death" there was a break-in. The thief only got some petty cash, too small an amount to claim on insurance. I believe the theft was to conceal the real motive, to switch Hill's dental records for those of another patient, someone already selected as a victim. Hill's intention was to kill the other man, set fire to his own house with the dead man inside and disappear. When the dental records matched those of the corpse everyone would believe it was Hill who'd perished.'

'That sounds brilliantly simple.' Clara commented. 'It's cold-blooded but it has a touch of genius.'

'Your choice of words is interesting. I've obtained a copy of Hill's service record. Until he was cashiered and imprisoned, Hill's career was on its way to being distinguished.'

Nash read aloud from the file, 'Hill's leadership is direct, simple and brilliant.' He replaced the sheet. 'I see no reason to think Hill has changed his way of operating. I suggest the simplest, most effective way for Hill to disappear would be to assume the identity of the man he murdered.'

Nobody seemed inclined to challenge this logic. 'There's also a note on his service record to the effect that the motive behind the abuse for which Hill was court-martialled was their refusal to hand over money in exchange for their release. The note goes on to comment that Hill's principal motive seems to have been accumulation of wealth.

'If Hill's become a professional assassin we must consider what's brought him here. A series of crimes have been committed here that are linked to a highly lucrative operation. Surely it doesn't take a gigantic leap of faith to connect the two?'

There was a prolonged silence as they digested what Nash had told them. Then Pearce asked, 'How do you think the doctor's death ties in to this?'

'I said I might be able to provide some answers. I didn't say I could solve all of them.'

'What next?' Mironova asked.

'I'm going to talk to Tom Pratt. I want him to persuade Nottingham CID to re-examine the death at Hill's house. That'll mean checking all the patients registered at the dentists at that time. We need to find a man without close relatives or friends. Someone who disappeared or moved shortly after Hill's "death". Someone of approximately Hill's age although not necessarily similar in appearance. If we identify this man we might discover Hill's new identity and with luck even his current whereabouts. If we can persuade Nottingham to do this, it might be necessary to send someone to help. The dentist told me theirs is a large practice. DCI Fleming and DS Thomas should be back here in a day or two, and that'll free you two to go to Nottingham. Your presence might help persuade them to prioritize this enquiry.'

'Anything we can do in the meantime?' Clara asked.

'Yes, I want a copy of Stevens's phone bills for the last twelve months. I want you go to Netherdale Hospital. Find out if Stevens had a locker and get the contents. Talk to the staff, see if he had any close friends and, in particular, a girl friend. What he did for a social life, that sort of thing. Remember the SOCO team found a woman's fingerprints in Stevens's flat. Talk to his neighbours and have another word with the landlord, hint that we're now treating Stevens's death as suspicious.'

'Right, we'll get going,' Clara nodded to Pearce, 'Leave these two *milaya* [sweethearts] to get on with things.'

Nash glanced at Zena, but she was glaring at Clara. 'That word Clara used, what does it mean?' Nash asked after the others had left.

'She was being silly.' Zena was staring at the door, her face averted. 'Just silly.'

CHAPTER EIGHT

It was early evening when Pearce returned. 'Stevens was well-liked by his colleagues; they all spoke well of him.'

'Find out about his girlfriend?'

Pearce grinned, 'I did better. I talked to her. And it was very interesting.'

Nash raised his eyebrows. 'She's a nurse on A & E; that's how they met. Often their shifts didn't coincide so they talked on their mobiles or sent texts.'

'He didn't have a mobile. All we found was a pager.'

Pearce nodded. 'It gets better. If they had the chance they sent emails. She'd a PC, Stevens a laptop.'

'We didn't find a laptop either.'

'No and I checked his locker; nothing.'

'Did she say if he appeared worried or upset?'

'No, I asked her if she'd noticed any change in him recently. She said he seemed a bit preoccupied, that was all.'

'Any money worries?'

'Just the opposite. She said he seemed flush. Decent restaurants, weekend breaks, that sort of thing.'

'On a junior doctor's salary? I find that hard to believe.'

'That's about it. The only other thing she said was Stevens was ambitious. He wanted to get on to the surgical team but there are no vacancies. He'd set his heart on being an anaesthetist.'

Next morning Pratt got news that DCI Fleming and DS Thomas were en route north. Nottingham police had agreed to re-open the case on Hill; Mironova and Pearce would be welcome to help.

Pratt conveyed the news and mentioned that Katya Svetlova's parents would arrive in London next day. They would spend the night at the Russian Embassy before travelling north.

Nash enlisted Pratt's assistance with a difficulty they'd encountered obtaining Stevens's phone records. The companies wouldn't release them without a warrant.

'I'll see what I can do.'

Zena had taken the day off and gone to York sightseeing.

Nash spent the day helping Mironova and Pearce tidy loose ends on a recent spate of petty crimes.

He finished early. He felt jaded and in need of a break. When he got home he started cooking and uncorked a bottle of Chardonnay. He was half way down the bottle before his meal was ready.

As he ate he refilled his glass whilst mulling over recent events. By 10.30, tired and less than sober, he was ready for a good night's sleep. Unfortunately that wasn't what he got.

He was lying on a long narrow table. Above him large, circular lights burned fiercely, hurting his eyes. He was aware of figures around him. There were four, clad in green gowns with matching caps and gloves. He tried to raise himself. He was drawn backwards, down and down.

He heard a voice echoing, vibrating. 'It is time to begin.' They surrounded him, peering from above their masks. Each one raised their hands high and swung something towards him. The light caught on descending blades. They were scythes. In the same instant he saw beyond the masks. They were eyeless. Empty skulls. Then the scythes hit his naked flesh, his eyes filled with blood.

Nash woke with a start. Knew he'd screamed in terror. His body was wet and slippery. The nightmare was so strong that for a moment he panicked, switched the bedside light on before he knew he was bathed in sweat not blood.

If Nash's sleep was tormented by a nightmare, next morning found him having to cope with another. He'd given up trying to sleep. He was only partly revived by a hot shower and several cups of coffee. The postman delivered the first shock. Nash tore open the envelope and extracted the letter. It took a while for the meaning to sink in. It was from Stella. She'd seen through his subterfuge with the therapist. Stella summed her feelings up with a directness that made Nash wince. He cursed the psychologist whose inept handling of the situation must have caused such anger. Far from helping, the stratagem had resulted in Stella being so enraged she didn't want Nash to go near her.

'I know you're only doing it out of duty,' she ended. 'I've thought so for long enough. Now you've proved it. So don't bother. It's obviously a burden for you and at least I won't have to continue pretending everything's alright when we both know damned well it isn't. So stay clear of this place, my doctors and me.'

Nash felt sick. Sickness turned to anger, anger at Stella's unreasonable attitude. Anger at his helplessness, anger at the evil bastard who'd put Stella in this situation.

The second leg of his nightmare took the form of DS Thomas. Nash walked into his office at 7.40 a.m. to find it already occupied. He was both astonished and infuriated to see DS Thomas standing alongside his desk scrutinizing the files Nash had left there. It took him a moment to grasp the audacity of the invasion. Realization and reaction were quick and angry. 'What the hell do you think you're playing at?'

Thomas looked up and answered coolly. 'I'm bringing myself up to speed on developments. As this is an MCU operation DCI Fleming and I will be taking charge from now on. All activity will be routed through us. That way we'll know exactly what's going on and we'll be able to give the investigation the professional attention it merits.'

Nash blinked in astonishment at the man's nerve. Sleep deprivation had shortened his temper, 'Really? Is that so?' He drawled. His tone was deceptively mild. 'I'm afraid that doesn't tally with my reading of the situation.'

He crossed the room as he spoke, reaching and skirting his desk in a couple of strides. Thomas was leaning on the desk, his left hand braced on the surface. Without breaking stride Nash seized the sergeant's wrist and jerked his arm up and behind the astonished officer's back. As Thomas straightened willy-nilly, Nash's right arm encircled his neck. He frog-marched Thomas to the door, where he pitched the hapless detective out into the CID room. As the evicted man stumbled across the room Nash looked up to see Dacic watching from the doorway in disbelief.

'Have you got a problem?'

'I found him in there when I arrived, going through my paperwork. I'll just ensure this piece of shit's off the premises before I have it out with the head turd.'

Nash got through to Armistead. The conversation was brief and brutal. 'You can save time and money by recalling Fleming and Thomas,' he told the MCU chief. 'I'm issuing instructions banning them from this building. Understood?'

Zena heard an agitated squawking from the phone. Whatever Armistead was saying wasn't anywhere near complete when Nash put the receiver down.

'When I arrived in England I had an unpleasant meeting with Thomas,' Zena said. 'He insisted MCU would be leading the investigation. He demanded sight of all the evidence. He said I should pay no attention to local officers: "They're country bumpkins who'll only be useful for running errands and making coffee." Tell me, what's this word bumpkin? It's one I've never heard. At first I thought he said pumpkin.'

'A bumpkin is a peasant, one of low intelligence.'

'Mikhail, you look terrible this morning. Are you ill? Or has something bad happened?'

'I had a poor night's sleep, that's all,' Nash told her, unwilling to travel down that route.

The expression 'saved by the bell' came to mind when the phone rang. 'Morning, Mike,' Pratt's voice was cheerful and contained a hint of excitement. 'I've had the Home Office on the phone to say Mr and Mrs Svetlov will arrive round lunchtime. They also stressed you're to take overall charge of the enquiry with Commander Dacic in support. They said that way you could cope with the British and Russian ends of the investigation between you. In recognition of this you'll have the rank of Acting Superintendent.'

Any hopes Nash might have entertained that the altered circumstances would act as a deterrent were short-lived. DCI Fleming obviously felt that what Thomas had failed to obtain by direct assault could be achieved by stealthier methods. She was waiting in the CID room. 'I'd like a word in private, Inspector Nash,' Fleming stated flatly.

'My office,' Nash told her curtly. 'And I think you should know its Acting Superintendent.' The glint in her eyes told him Fleming was already aware of the fact.

'I want to start by apologizing. I'd no idea Thomas was going to do that. I'd have forbidden it. The only excuse is that we're desperately keen to see this case progress. The crime we're all working on is the most hideous imaginable. Can you blame him for being a bit overeager?'

Fleming was standing in front of Nash. She put one hand on his arm as she continued. 'I know one isn't supposed to become emotionally involved. But when you think of the terrible ordeal of those victims how can you fail to become angry? How can you not want to catch and punish those responsible? Please, Mike, put it down to overenthusiasm and let's start again. What do you say?'

'Very well,' Nash agreed.

Fleming looked immensely relieved, her hand moving slightly on his arm. 'Thank you.'

The cracks were papered over by the time Sergei and Anna Svetlov arrived. Before that, Armistead and Tom Pratt reached Helmsdale. Armistead took Fleming and Thomas off to a café in the High Street. Nash told Pratt and Dacic about Fleming's apology.

'Do you trust her?' Zena asked.

'About as far as I'd trust a fox in a hen house. That "diligent officer determined to punish evil men" crap was pure flannel. Fleming is out for number one. She's prepared to use any means to get her own way, even feminine wiles.'

'You're resistant to those, naturally?' There might have been an edge to Zena's question, but if there was Nash didn't notice it.

Pratt laughed aloud. 'That'll be a first; Mike's favourite dance is the horizontal tango.'

'That's slanderous,' Nash protested. 'Anyway, Jackie Fleming's not my type.'

'It can't be slander if it's true,' Pratt told him.

'What is your type of woman, Mikhail?' Zena asked lightly.

Nash had endured a poor night, a bad start to the day and the teasing was beginning to get to him. 'I prefer stroppy, red-haired Russian women.'

Dacic's face went as red as her hair. Pratt laughed again. 'You'd better watch him, Zena. Remember, it was Mike who mentioned foxes in hen houses.'

Katya's parents were younger than Nash expected. Probably in their early forties, he judged. Sergei was tall and distinguished, his air of distinction enhanced by greying hair. He held his wife's arm protectively as they entered Helmsdale Police Station. Anna Svetlova was tiny by comparison. She was attractive, elegant in both dress and movement, with dark hair and large eyes of so deep a brown they might have been mistaken for black.

Zena performed the introductions. Nash apologized for the absence of Mironova and Pearce. 'My two junior officers are following a line of enquiry I believe has a connection to the case. I'm anxious to bring it to a conclusion as swiftly as possible. More than that, I'm determined to trap all those involved, not just the small fish.'

Svetlov nodded, a gesture of agreement and approval. 'The leaders are the ones I am most anxious to see behind bars. My only regret is there is no longer capital punishment in Britain. Anna and I have come to terms with the belief that our beloved Katya is dead. Commander Dacic has prepared us for this. The discovery of the bear was sufficient to put to rest any lingering doubts or hopes,' he added with deep sadness. 'We now have three desires. The first being the recovery of Katya's remains so she can be buried near to us in Moscow. The second is the punishment of those who caused her suffering. The third is to ensure no more parents have to endure the torment we've been through.'

Nash nodded soberly. 'It must be done, whatever the cost. I'm not referring to monetary cost. I mean time and resources. I can't think of a price too high to pay for success.'

Svetlov requested that they be allowed to visit Cauldmoor. He said simply, 'We wish to see the place where Mitya was found.'

Nash sat in front, directing the chauffeur through the tangled skein of country lanes whilst Zena accompanied the Svetlovs in the back.

Anna Svetlova shivered as she looked out from the bothy over the dark waters of the tarn. 'Yes,' she said, her voice tight with emotion. 'I feel sure this is the place. It is well named, this lake. Lamentation means great sadness. That is correct, is it not?' Nash nodded. 'There is a feeling of such here. So powerful one can almost touch it,' her voice was soft, barely above a murmur, her attention so distant she might have been talking to herself. 'I feel close to Katya here.'

She looked at Nash with piercing directness. 'I sense you are the one to help us,' she told him, her voice stronger as she explained. 'You're able to perceive what others cannot. I am correct, am I not?'

Nash bowed his head. 'Sometimes,' he muttered.

Her eyes remained fixed on his, 'Tell me, please,' she pleaded.

Nash glanced wildly round. Zena nodded encouragement and spoke in Russian to Katya's mother, 'You're correct. Mikhail has an unusual ability. He told me things that prove it. Things he couldn't have known.' She switched to English. 'If you tell her, Mikhail, you have our promise it won't go further.'

Slowly, hesitantly, Nash began to recount his dream. By the end Anna was weeping gently whilst Sergei was looking at him with a mixture of doubt and awe. 'Describe the girl as you dreamed her.' Sergei demanded. 'Can you remember anything about her appearance?' Nash shook his head.

Anna smiled through her tears. 'She loved Mitya and her doll. I hope she had them both with her.'

Nash looked puzzled. 'We found the teddy bear.'

'You do not understand, Mr Nash. I mean a Russian doll, not a plaything. It is like a brooch. A large pin with three tiny dolls threaded on to it. They have another and another inside them.'

'They're called Matrioshka,' Zena explained.

Anna looked wistful. 'We bought her that brooch for her birthday. She treasured it as she loved Mitya. It was beautiful, so many colours but such a bright red.'

'Red. I thought that was—' Nash stopped short.

Anna went pale, 'You were going to say blood?' She took hold of her husband's hand. 'Please, could we be alone for a moment?'

Nash escorted Zena away from the bothy. 'Let me know when they're ready to leave. I need to walk to clear my brain. That was bloody awful.'

'Okay, Mikhail,' she agreed. 'I'm sorry if this has been a strain for you. It's never easy dealing with bereaved relatives.'

Zena watched Nash striding up the slope. She saw him pause when he reached the crest, turn and look back towards the lake. A fine drizzle was obscuring the top of Stark Ghyll in mist. Zena shuddered; this really was a most inhospitable place.

Nash looked about him for a long time before he began slowly retracing his steps towards the bothy. His mind was in turmoil. He needed time to think. The riddle was like the Matrioshka dolls, each containing another mystery within.

Nash noticed Zena looking at him with a slightly puzzled expression, a look that was to be repeated several times during the afternoon.

Nash said farewell to the Russians on their return to Helmsdale. All three were to have dinner with Armistead and Pratt. Anna Svetlova's expression said she would have preferred not to lose contact with the man who'd conjured up the last image of her daughter.

Nash felt drained, tired, stale and ill. The emotional roller coaster had left his mind so weary he was unable to think straight. He stared at the papers on his desk, the characters swimming incomprehensibly before his eyes. Suddenly he felt nausea rising. He dashed from the room, reached the toilet and was violently sick. As the cubicle began to see-saw in his vision he sank to the floor.

The nausea passed. Nash splashed his face with cold water and returned to his office. He put the papers from his desk into the filing cabinet, locked it and removed the key before locking his office door. Despite her protestations, Nash did not trust DCI Fleming any further than he'd thrown DS Thomas.

He was leaving the CID room when the phone rang. It was Dacic. 'Are you alright, Mikhail?'

'Not really,' he told her. 'I was on my way home when you rang. Why do you ask?'

'I wanted to talk to you about what happened at the lake. But it will wait.'

'How do you mean "what happened at the lake"?'

'When you returned from walking, you looked ill. I couldn't see what happened because of the mist but I thought you'd discovered something.'

'Let's leave it until tomorrow, shall we?' Nash knew he must sound ungracious. 'I need to get home.'

Next morning Nash felt better than for some while. The previous evening he'd only eaten some soup, foregoing the temptation of a takeaway. Contrary to his fears and expectations, his night's sleep was unbroken, untroubled by dreams.

Dacic arrived in Helmsdale shortly before 8.30 a.m. in company with Armistead, Fleming and Thomas. It appeared the MCU team had decided on some bridge-building. Nash emerged from the meeting with the elite squad members doubly grateful. Armistead began by telling him he wanted Fleming and Thomas to concentrate their efforts on discovering how the girls had been smuggled into the country. He informed Nash that MCU had one or two ideas on the subject, leads they felt worth following up.

Nash noticed the new bridge-building policy didn't extend to sharing this information. Perhaps the bridge was only being built from one side. He found their sycophantic attitude more nauseating than the previous air of superiority.

Nash watched them depart without regret. Dacic smiled at his relief. 'Now you've rid yourself of one distraction, I've another for you,' Zena told him. 'Sergei and Anna wish to meet Milla. Anna Svetlova is also from Moldavia. They wish to see if they can do anything to help Milla.'

'I can't see a problem with that,' Nash told her. 'In the UK, a girl in Milla's situation is offered as much help as possible. This process would have started already but for the language difficulty. The only people who've been able to communicate directly with her have been Clara and you. She needs someone to represent her legal interests. If you can persuade Svetlov to use his influence it would help. The case against her will have to proceed at some point, but not until she has legal representation. I'm not keen to prosecute. I think she's been through enough, but that's not my decision. I'll speak to the custody officials and make the arrangements.'

'Thank you. It's as Anna Svetlova said, "Nash will help because he's that sort of man",' Dacic grinned. 'I think Superintendent Pratt is right,' she teased him. 'I think you've made another conquest.'

Nash spent the next few hours making and receiving phone calls, including a call from Mironova. She and Pearce had finished their trawl through the dental files, yielding forty-three names. Their next task would be to examine voters' rolls, council lists and phone books to narrow down their search for Hill's victim.

He also secured permission for the visit to Milla. Sergei and Anna could go that afternoon. Zena rang The Golden Bear and relayed the information. Svetlov told her he'd send the car to collect Dacic.

Alone, Nash sat deep in thought. Eventually he reached a decision. He picked up the phone. 'Tom, I want you to authorize some extra expenditure. The Home Office said they'd sanction any reasonable request.'

'What is it?'

'I want authorization for The Rubber Johnnies to go back to Cauldmoor.'

'Saunders was emphatic there were no more bodies in the Tarn.'

'I know. I'm not talking about Lamentation Tarn. I want them to search Desolation Tarn. I think that's where Katya Svetlova's body is.'

CHAPTER NINE

'The meeting was difficult,' Dacic told Nash the following day. 'Milla was overawed and would say little. Who wouldn't be, in her situation? She's probably from a poor family with a simple upbringing. People in regions such as Milla comes from are naive in the ways of the modern world. Things such as happened to Milla are beyond their understanding. They don't teach children of those dangers. She's had a dreadful ordeal and this must seem like an unending nightmare. She knows her actions can't go unpunished and believes she'll spend the rest of her life in prison.'

Zena sipped at her coffee. 'To add to her distress, she's in a strange land. She can't speak the language, doesn't know the laws or customs. Her only kindness has been at the hands of the police. This must confuse her. Where she comes from, the police generate hatred and fear, not respect.

'Now two rich Muscovites come to see her. She's told one is an important man in the government. It took a long time to get past the barriers Milla had put up. In the end, Anna Svetlova told Sergei to leave us. Then she sat with Milla and took hold of her hand. This was good. Milla wouldn't have said half the things she did if a man had been there.'

Zena considered matters a moment, 'I know what she told you was harrowing. What she told us was indescribable. It took a long time to draw the story out. I think it helped with Anna being Moldavian. When she told Milla of her home life I saw tears in Milla's eyes. I'm sure the story brought back memories of a time when she was happier, or maybe painful memories of what she's lost.

'Milla began to talk but Anna had to prompt her to tell some of the more lurid details. These shocked Anna beyond measure. To be honest, although I've seen many dreadful crimes, I too was appalled. It was twice as difficult for Anna. As she listened she must have known what Milla was describing was similar to what her own daughter had undergone. Despite this, Anna stuck with it for Milla's sake, which I think was very brave. She was deeply affected by the child. When Milla described what she'd done to those men, quietly and without emotion, I saw the strangest expression on Anna's face. It was a look of admiration and respect.'

Zena sat back. 'When we were ready to leave, Anna told her, "Milla, you mustn't worry about the future. My husband is a good man. He'll do his best to ensure you're taken care of, whatever's necessary to give you the help and protection you need. I don't believe the police are unsympathetic. I've met the policeman who talked with you and he says your sentence should be the lightest possible. I'll enlist Sergei's help. He'll do this both because he wants to and because I tell him to".

'That made Milla laugh. She told Anna, "The policeman was kind. He bought me clothes and ice cream." They started laughing, and I was laughing too. It was nice for the meeting to end this way. Anna commented on the child's resilience. "After all that's happened, she's chattering about Levis and Raspberry Ripple".

'Then she said, "Now I know the worst. I mean all of the worst. I had to listen so I could understand and end the questions in my own mind. Uncertainty just adds to the ordeal." Then she asked me to make a promise. "Swear to me, Zena Dacic, that you'll never reveal a word to Sergei of what Milla said. He's a sensitive man, a devoted father. This knowledge may cause me agonies but it would destroy him".

'Anna told Sergei straightaway she wanted him to put the full weight of the Russian government to look after Milla.'

'If that's so,' Nash said thoughtfully. 'It's without doubt the most positive thing to come out of this mess,' he corrected himself. 'The only positive thing.'

Many residents of Westlea council estate were known to the police. The run-down estate had one pub. Closing time was variable, usually when there were no customers to serve. At 2 a.m. one of their best customers was weaving his way erratically home when he passed close by a car parked on waste ground. It hadn't been there earlier. He saw a man pouring petrol over it from a can. 'Hey,' said the reveller, 'what are you doing?'

The reply was short, sharp and to the point. It took the form of a large-calibre bullet that pierced the drinker's chest, killing him instantly. Within seconds the corpse was illuminated by the fierce blaze from the burning car. The killer jogged in leisurely fashion into the night.

The persistent ringing of the phone roused Nash. The bedside clock read 2.30 a.m. Muttering something slanderous about the caller's parents, he reached for the receiver. He was fully awake within the first sentence.

'Mike, it's Tom. There's been a car burned out at Westlea estate with a corpse inside and another close by. They haven't been able to get near enough to establish cause for the stiff inside but the one outside was shot.'

'Oh shit!' Nash sat upright. 'What do you reckon? Drugs war on the Westlea?'

'I don't think so. The car's plates survived legibly enough for a DVLA check. The car's registered to the house where those men were topped by Milla. Can you get there ASAP and find out what's going on? Shout if you need me.'

Damping down was still in progress when Nash arrived. The waste ground, brightly illuminated by the fire brigade arc lights, looked like a film set. He had to remove his skid lid and produce his warrant card before the uniformed officer would let him through. Nash pointed to the Road Rocket. 'Watch that like a hawk,' he looked at the crowd. 'It's worth a couple of year's benefit for this lot. If I find a scratch on it you'll be singing treble the rest of your life. What have we got here?'

'Nothing about the one inside. When I arrived he was doing a good impression of an extra from *Towering Inferno*. The one outside is known to us, though.'

'Who isn't round here? Tell me more.'

'One of the residents recognized him. He's got form for every bit of petty villainy you can think of. Apparently he was drinking in the Coach and Horses until closing time. That's a moveable feast, but they reckon he left about 2 a.m. My guess would be he saw something he shouldn't and paid for it.'

'Curiosity killed the cat burglar?'

Mexican Pete had been caustic at having his night's sleep disturbed and vented most of his spleen in Nash's direction. After a brief examination he told Nash, 'Two corpses. One male, one toast. Both definitely dead. One shot, the other uncertain. Although I think we can rule out drowning.'

'Thank you, Professor. That was really worth staying up for. Have you any other brilliant thoughts you'd like to share?'

'Only to warn you that if matters continue like this, I'll need an extension to the mortuary. Couldn't you transfer to Traffic Division and give us some peace?'

'You're joking. I'd be bored to death within a week.'

'That's about the only diagnosis you haven't provided yet. But don't regard that as a challenge.'

It was late morning before Nash arrived at Helmsdale station. He'd eventually got back to sleep well after 5 a.m. leaving him jaded and short tempered. In the CID room he got two surprises, one welcome, the other less so. Mironova and Pearce were back from Nottingham. Less cheering was

Pearce's announcement that Armistead wanted him. 'There's either a panic on or he's in love with you,' Viv grinned. 'He's called three times already.'

At that moment Nash's phone rang again. Nash scowled at Pearce, whose grin grew broader as he blew Nash a kiss. Nash grimaced comically as he heard Armistead's voice, 'You'll have to be a bit more discreet,' he told the MCU officer. 'People are beginning to talk.'

The remark went right over Armistead's head, fuelling Nash's suspicion that the man had undergone a sense of humour bypass. 'I understand there have been developments?'

How did he know so quickly? Nash wondered. 'If you mean the bodies in and around the burnt-out car, then yes, the car's registered to the address where the other men were found. One of the bodies is that of a local man, the other's burned beyond recognition, at least for the present. I'd guess him to be the fourth occupant who vanished from the building. Proving it could be another matter. Have you anything to report?'

Armistead was obviously more accustomed to receiving reports than giving them. He hemmed and hawed for a few seconds before saying with considerable reluctance, 'There's been pressure exerted on behalf of the Moldavian girl. The Russian authorities are keen that we should deal sympathetically with her.'

'I've no problem with that. I assume the Home Office will handle it.'

'I've no doubt they will. Perhaps you would keep me up to date with any future developments as and when they occur?'

There was the faintest emphasis on the latter part of the sentence but it was enough to rile Nash. 'Of course,' he replied easily. 'And possibly you might reciprocate now and then?'

Armistead may have possessed little in the way of a sense of humour but he wasn't immune to sarcasm. 'What do you mean?' he demanded.

'It might be helpful if you could regard the passage of information as an exchange process rather than a one-way street.' Nash made no attempt to disguise his irritation.

'You'd better explain.' Armistead was now overtly threatening.

'You've taken Fleming and Thomas off to deal with part of the enquiry about which I know absolutely nothing,' Nash answered the hectoring tone with coolness. 'As the officer with overall responsibility for this investigation I'd have thought I should have at least an outline of what they're up to?'

'I'll tell you precisely what I need to, when I deem it necessary.' Armistead was shouting now. 'Furthermore, I take great exception to your offensive attitude.'

Armistead was about to continue but all he heard was the dialling tone.

Nash vented the anger Armistead had caused. 'That arrogant, supercilious twat isn't capable of detecting one of his own farts.'

'It isn't love then?' Pearce asked.

Nash gave a reluctant grin. 'Not quite. How did you go on in Nottingham?'

Clara answered, 'They were very helpful. I knew Nottingham has a bad crime record but I didn't realize how bad until we got there. Helmsdale's idyllic by comparison.'

'You wouldn't say that if you'd been dragged out of bed at some ungodly hour to go to Westlea.'

'What happened?'

'Somebody torched a car and shot one of the local celebrities into the bargain. One of our regulars. There was someone else in the car, doing an impersonation of an overcooked pork joint.'

Clara tutted, 'That's one off our Christmas card list. It's always sad to lose a good customer.'

'It won't improve the detection statistics either,' Pearce pointed out.

'Christ! You're a cynical pair of bastards.' Nash found their brash humour cheering. 'Right, going back to Nottingham?'

'I'd rather not, if you don't mind,' Mironova told him.

'I don't know, it did have its good points,' Pearce objected.

'You're only saying that because you pulled that DC from Vice the first night we were there. The one with dreadlocks and big future in front of her.'

'Now, now children, no squabbling. Think of the good example I set you.'

Pearce and Mironova chorused, 'Yes Superintendent Nash Sir.'

Nash grinned sheepishly and shook his head. 'Okay, okay. Nottingham?' he prompted.

'We narrowed the possibles down to seven. That isn't bad considering the size of that dental practice. They've a list of over 10,000.'

'Fair enough. I'd like you to collate all this info into our system. If you need any paperwork, it's locked in the filing cabinet in my room.' Nash passed Mironova his keys. She stared at them.

'Why do I need these?'

Nash explained about Thomas's incursion. 'Sounds as if we missed all the fun,' Pearce raised his eyebrows.

'Not if what Clara said about the DC from Vice is correct.'

Nash's phone was ringing again. 'That'll be Tom with a complaint about me hanging up on Armistead.'

'Hello, Tom.'

'How did you know it was me?'

'ESP. I'll go one further; you've just had a complaint from MCU about my conduct.'

'Not just a complaint, Mike, the man's gone mental. Told me you were rude, hung up on him and that a couple of days ago you assaulted DS Thomas and threatened DCI Fleming. He's really got it in for you. He wants you suspended from duty pending an enquiry.'

Nash hadn't attempted an explanation nor had Pratt requested one. Pratt merely said, 'I told Armistead if he thought I was going to suspend the best detective in the north of England just because he said so, he could think again. I told him the allegation of assault was totally out of character. He may believe his officers' version but he should be careful about throwing his weight about on my patch. Any such an incident, had it taken place, would only have been as a result of severe provocation.

'That's about the extent of the good news. He was adamant the affair should be taken further. When he'd finished ranting, he said his next call was going to be to the Chief Constable. All we can do is wait to see which way the CC wants to play it.'

Nash forewarned Mironova and Pearce of the possible outcome of the row. The dismay on their faces was heartening. 'If I'm not able to continue, take instructions from Tom and no one else. If Armistead and his crew give you an order or request information, tell them to put it in writing. Without being insubordinate, make life as difficult for the buggers as possible. Concentrate on Dr Stevens's death. MCU don't believe it's connected to the main enquiry. I don't think they'll waste time on my half-baked theories. Liaise with Dacic, though, but wherever possible keep MCU out of the loop.'

'How do you think she'll react?'

'I've no idea.'

'It seemed to me, you and Commander Dacic had established a close relationship.'

Nash looked at her with sharp suspicion. Clara's face was a mask of innocence. As he looked from her to Pearce, Nash saw the DC was inspecting his fingernails with exaggerated interest.

Nash ignored the innuendo. 'Only time will tell. Meanwhile, I'd like a word with you, Clara.'

When they'd gone through to his office, Nash showed Clara the letter from Stella. She stared at it in dismay. 'That psychologist must be worse than bloody useless.'

'Maybe, but I've had time to think about it. Perhaps we're doing her an injustice. She might be cleverer than we think. What strikes you most about the letter?'

'Apart from the fact that Stella's bloody angry?'

'That's the point. The fact that she's angry is the best thing to come out of this. A few weeks ago she'd have sat there and taken it. Her reaction is the nearest thing to a genuine show of emotion I've seen for months.'

'So you think it's good news?'

'I wouldn't go that far, but it could be worse.'

It was mid afternoon when Pratt rang back. 'The CC's decided not to go for full suspension, not in the first instance. She's away for three days at a conference. She's leaving matters until her return. Then she'll want statements from Armistead, Fleming, Thomas and you. Plus any witnesses. In the meantime she's insisted you take three days leave. Oh, there's some good news.'

'What's that?'

'The three days won't be deducted from your leave.'

'Big deal!'

'Funny, I told the CC you'd say that.'

If Nash didn't storm out of the building, a professional walker would have had difficulty keeping up. He strode along, anger fuelling every step. He reached the Market Square before he began to think rationally. Facing three days enforced inactivity, time would lie heavily on him. He'd need some form of distraction. He arrived home weighed down with several carrier bags. The butcher's and greengrocer's takings for the day had been considerably boosted.

Nash set about unpacking his purchases and preparing a meal. He poured a glass of wine and began making a list of the dishes he planned to prepare the following day and was surprised to find that when he'd finished his glass was empty. He refilled it before taking his food from the oven.

By 9 p.m. he was restless and unable to settle. Never a great TV watcher, there was nothing in the evening's programmes to interest him. He was pondering his chances of getting a good night's sleep when the doorbell rang.

He stared at the caller in surprise, 'What are you doing here?'

Zena Dacic stared at him coldly, 'Is that what passes for welcome round here?'

'Sorry, you took me by surprise. You were the last person I expected. Come in,' he opened the door wide. She walked down the hallway into the lounge and looked round approvingly. 'I was in the kitchen. Would you like a glass of wine?' If he wasn't exactly drunk his inhibitions had certainly been loosened.

She gave him a searching stare, 'That would be nice.'

They sat opposite one another at the table. Nash toyed with the stem of his wine glass. 'Let me start again. How did you find out where I live?'

Zena grinned, 'I'm a detective; I asked questions. I spoke to Clara this afternoon and she told me what happened. I'd have come sooner, but Sergei and Anna wished to meet for dinner. As soon as I could get away I found a taxi and here I am. So tell me what's going on?'

Nash was struck by a stray thought. 'Your English is excellent. I mean as a second language. Where did you learn to speak it so well?'

'At university. I had a very good tutor; from Berkshire. And you're wrong. English is my third language, Russian's my second. So now, tell me.'

Nash related the day's events. He'd been concerned how she'd react. Zena's words and the vehemence of her tone swept all doubts aside. 'I don't trust Armistead; he reminds me of many of the old guard in Russia. Ones still clinging to the power they had under the old regime. They've no ability themselves but rely on fear and bullying to get others to do their work. Then they claim the credit. As for the Fleming woman, she is a *suka yobanaja* who wants a good sorting out. We must make a plan to outwit them.'

'What does *suka yobanaja* mean?'

'Fucking bitch,' Zena grinned.

He leaned forward and put his hand on hers. 'Thank you, Zena. I couldn't begin to hope you'd support me in this.'

'Why not? You're the only one working to solve this crime. I believe you're the only one capable of finding these evil men. Of course I'll stand by you.'

Nash became aware he was still holding Zena's hand. It seemed she did too, for he felt it tremble slightly. 'Mikhail,' her voice was low and husky, 'we have three days. We don't have to rush to make plans tonight.'

Their journey to the bedroom took seconds. Clothing and underwear was scattered. Their first encounter was a savage, tempestuous mating, a rape of mutual consent, that left them spent, exhausted and gasping as they clutched one another, their sweat mingling.

Some hours later Zena stroked him to waken him. He came out of a deep dreamless sleep laughing at the manner of his waking, of where she'd chosen to stroke him. He was roused and aroused simultaneously. As he began to caress her she said, 'Now, Mikhail, this time let us not merely have sex. This time I want you to make love to me.'

As he was nuzzling her ear Nash was struck by a random memory. 'What does *milaya* mean?' He whispered. 'Clara used the word.'

'It means sweetheart.'

When Nash woke again he was alone; it was 8 a.m. His senses focussed and he could smell her sensual perfume overlaid with the animal scent of their lovemaking. He could see the small indentation on the pillow, the single strand of dark hair across the white of the sheet. He laid his head where hers had been, revelling in the memory. His clothes had been folded and stacked neatly on the chair. He certainly hadn't done that. In the kitchen he found a note on the worktop. 'Mikhail, I've gone to a breakfast meeting with Svetlov. Phase one of the plan. Trust me. I'll speak to you later, Z.'

He brewed some coffee. A long, empty day lay ahead. He thought about the previous day and the sequel. What was it Clara had said once? 'You could try saying "no" for a change.' Well he could have done, but he'd been a little bit pissed and Zena was bloody attractive. Saying no wasn't an option that had occurred to him until now; far too late.

Now he'd broken his own rule. Embarked on a relationship with a fellow officer, albeit one from another country. The morning regret was tinged with something else, a feeling Nash failed to recognize immediately. It came to him when he caught sight of the envelope containing Stella's letter. The emotion was guilt.

Time dragged on the first day. Nash wasn't bothered about the outcome of the witch-hunt. Whilst Thomas could claim Nash had assaulted him, the circumstances leading to Nash evicting Thomas from his office constituted gross professional misconduct.

What concerned Nash was the interruption. The bodies pulled from the tarn, their identity still a mystery. Who was left to defend them, to stand up for their rights? That was what Nash understood by police work. That was what he stood for. He'd little time for 'prisoner's rights', to him prisoners were in gaol because they'd offended. Their rights weren't his concern. Let politicians and penal reformers look after them. Nash was concerned for the rights of the victims.

For the first time since the enquiry began Nash had the opportunity to reflect on those pitiful girls. During his career he'd witnessed many violent and depraved deeds. None had caused such helpless rage as he'd felt watching the divers unzipping the body bags containing the pathetic bundles. Remains of young lives, snuffed out with as little feeling as dousing a candle.

Their investigation had been slow to gather momentum; Nash felt they were now starting to make progress. He resented the fact he couldn't continue. It wasn't that Nash didn't trust those about him; indeed he knew his team was good. Despite this, Nash was angry. He was a 'hands on' policeman, thrived on personal involvement. Being forcibly removed from the enquiry irked him beyond endurance.

He bought and read the morning papers then, as planned, prepared meals for the freezer. Boredom was taking control but his mind was still full of the enquiry. He began considering different aspects of the case.

Motive was obvious; greed. Getting to grips with who and how was another matter. What they needed was a break. He was confident one would come, but allied to the who and how was the where and when. Gradually his mind began to wander, his eyelids drooped and he fell asleep.

He woke up to find his body was stiff and he had an uncomfortable ache in his back. He was trying to decide how to spend the evening when the doorbell rang.

He found Zena standing on the doorstep clutching a bottle of red wine, smiling a trifle nervously. He stood aside to let her enter. As she preceded him she said, 'I've told Svetlov to inform your Home Office that I'll only work with you.'

'That was kind of you, Zena. Do you know, you're the first person I've spoken to all day, apart from buying newspapers. Have you eaten?'

'No, I came here first. I have news of some importance.'

'Then share my meal, we can talk as we eat. Why not open that bottle you're clutching and we can have a drink while I cook.'

She filled a couple of glasses and perched on a stool watching Nash work. 'Was that the only reason you came,' he asked suddenly, catching her unawares.

She smiled, 'That wasn't the reason, Mikhail. That was the excuse.'

'Good,' he looked up from the onion he was chopping. 'So why not tell me the reason and get that out of the way.'

It may have been the wine that brought an extra tinge of colour to her cheeks; alternatively, it could have been the look in Nash's eyes. 'I have an informant who's a close assistant to one of the crime bosses in my country. He warned me a short time ago of an attempt on my life. We were able to trap the assassin, who is now our guest in St Petersburg. Today I received a text from my informant, telling me his boss has travelled to England.'

'That's interesting, who is this "boss"?'

'His name is Janko Vatovec. He has a long career in crime but has never been caught. He began as an arms dealer in the Bosnia conflict. When the war ended he changed to supplying prostitutes for IFOR troops. That way he not only made a great deal of money but also obtained protection. We believe Vatovec conspired with the army to eliminate his opposition. Certain other criminal leaders disappeared, leaving Vatovec with a monopoly.

'We know he's involved in cross-border trafficking of women. He also has a chain of brothels. We've closed three so far, despite corrupt police officials tipping Vatovec off. These won't re-open.'

'How can you be sure?'

'Because I had them burned down.'

Nash raised his eyebrows.

'It's a policy decision that came from the highest level. It's a demonstration of how serious the problem has become and how desperate we are to control the spread of this evil.'

'Is there any evidence linking Vatovec to child prostitution?'

'I have no knowledge of such, but it seems to me Vatovec would have no scruples in entering this business.'

'It's strange he should come here when so much is happening if he isn't involved.'

'It's natural to make such a connection. I don't think he came here on holiday.'

'I'm not a great believer in coincidence. I think we should take this seriously. I'll follow it up when I get back.'

Zena topped up their wine glasses. 'How have you spent your day?'

'Sleeping a lot of the time,' he admitted. 'I got myself wound up at being unable to be involved in the enquiry.'

Zena took a sip of her wine, 'That's good.'

'What do you mean?'

'I mean,' she studied her glass. 'It's good that you're not in need of much sleep tonight. Perhaps I can find a cure for your frustrations.'

During the meal Zena told him, 'I too am going to be idle tomorrow. Svetlov must return to Moscow for meetings and Anna is to visit Milla at her detention centre.'

'That's kind of her.'

'She's a good woman. She told me she's doing this for Milla, for herself and for Katya. She thinks it's something Katya would have wanted.'

'I'm glad, because Milla deserves all the support she can get.'

'It's also true that Anna admires Milla for her courage and strength.'

'If it's a nice day tomorrow would you like to take a tour of the countryside? We could take my bike out.'

'You have a bicycle?'

'Motor bike. Come on, I'll show you.'

He took her hand and led her to the garage. Zena stared at the machine, taking in the smooth lines, the gleaming silver of the coachwork. 'Mikhail, are you a Hell's Angel?'

Nash laughed, 'Not exactly.'

'Beautiful,' Zena ran her hand lightly over the saddle. 'Is it an old machine?'

'It's a BSA Road Rocket, built fifty years ago for the racing season.'

'I think I'll enjoy riding with you.'

Nash grinned at the double entendre. 'I certainly hope so.'

CHAPTER TEN

The young offenders' remand centre on the outskirts of York was a newly constructed unit. Milla had been taken there whilst it was decided what charges should be brought against her.

Murder was the obvious choice. The act had been premeditated, but a good defence lawyer would argue Milla's actions represented her only chance to escape. Moreover he would be able to present this argument with every chance of securing an acquittal.

There were problems with a charge of manslaughter, generally considered to be an impromptu act. Milla's offences were clearly planned over a long period.

Then again, three men had died violently, and Milla made no secret of the fact that she'd administered the poison, and that she'd hacked off the parts they'd kept far from private.

No matter how much sympathy Milla attracted, no matter how dreadful the abuse she'd suffered, there had to be some retribution for her actions.

Whilst this was being debated, Milla was brought to York. She spent her days watching TV, which she enjoyed but didn't understand, or listening to pop music on the radio, which she did understand. She ate regular meals and exercised in the gymnasium or took walks in the enclosed garden area. Once the full horror of her suffering became known, the attitude of officialdom became positively paternal.

When Anna Svetlova was granted permission to visit Milla for a second time the youngster's natural resilience had begun to surface. She showed a cheerfulness of character in spite of her restricted liberty and the uncertainty over her future.

Their only companion was a middle-aged woman detailed to watch over Milla during the visit. Regulations stipulated that unsupervised visits were forbidden.

Anna commented sadly. 'I understand. I come from a country weighed down with such regulations. Most of these begin with "it is forbidden". It is comforting to feel so much at home.'

The meeting began in the lounge but the presence of other inmates inhibited their conversation. Although no one understood what was being said the atmosphere was stilted and unnatural.

It was a clear, cold winter's day. Anna asked their chaperone if they could continue the visit outside. The centre's location had been selected for security and the desire to make it accessible to visitors. The site was semi-rural, just beyond the outer ring road to the north-west of the city. The high perimeter wall was enough to deter all but the most determined escapee. It also protected inmates from prying eyes. The only place they could be overlooked was from a hill a quarter of a mile to the north. The hill, topped with trees, was encircled by arable land, too remote to concern the designer.

As they walked they talked about Milla's future. 'I don't suppose you've considered what to do?'

'How can I when I don't know what they'll do to me?' Milla objected.

'It isn't easy, but I don't think you'll be punished very hard. The British seem sympathetic. A lot of people are working on your behalf. Even if you've to be detained, you must think about what happens afterwards.'

'I don't know. People here seem kind, although I don't understand them. I suppose I could learn, but would I be allowed to stay? Would I want to? I can't return home, that's for certain. I'd die of shame.'

Anna saw tears glistening in the young girl's eyes. She put her arm around Milla's shoulders for comfort, drawing her to her side. As she did so they heard a noise, a soft thud, followed by another, then a half-gasping, half-choking sound.

They froze in horror as their chaperone staggered, clawing at her chest, the blood spurting from two ragged wounds. The woman collapsed in an untidy heap and realization came to Anna. She pushed Milla to the ground, shouting urgently, 'Crawl Milla. Don't lift your head. Someone's shooting at us. Crawl to that wall! As fast as you can! Go! Go now!'

As they crawled towards the sanctuary of the wall Anna saw gravel spurting up close to Milla's head. 'Faster Milla! Faster!'

She heard the young girl cry out, saw she'd stopped moving. 'Milla,' she called, urgency and panic mingling. 'Milla, move! For God's sake, move!'

Nash supplied Zena with leathers. She wondered why he kept a set that were obviously too small for him. Zena slipped her leg athletically over the bike and put her arms round Nash's waist. 'Carry me away, Mikhail.'

Nash couldn't hear her through his helmet, but he took the squeeze of her arms as encouragement. Zena found the ride exhilarating, the vintage machine reaching speeds that surprised her. They travelled east, reaching the ancient fishing port of Whitby. Nash showed her the Abbey. 'Do you know what Whitby's main claim to fame is?' Nash asked her as they sat over a coffee.

'I've no idea?'

'This is where Bram Stoker wrote *Dracula*.'

'Ah, the Transylvanian, Count Vlad the Impaler,' Zena nodded. 'I've visited his castle.'

'A medieval serial killer,' Nash suggested.

They went inland for lunch before heading back to Helmsdale. It was mid afternoon when they arrived. 'I'm cold,' Zena admitted, 'May I take a shower?'

Nash felt a twinge of guilt, remembering the first time he'd brought Stella to the flat on the bike when she too had wanted a shower. 'Of course, go ahead.'

He noticed the flashing light on the phone. There were three messages from Clara, each reflecting a rising tide of urgency. He was about to call her when the doorbell summoned him.

Clara pushed past him and marched in. 'Where the hell have you been? I've been trying to get hold of you for hours.'

'What's the panic?'

Clara took a deep breath. 'The Rubber Johnnies started work at Desolation Tarn this morning. I've had a message from Saunders. They've already recovered two bodies and when they suspended work for the day they'd located a third which they'll bring up tomorrow.'

'Hellfire, how many more?'

'There's worse. I got a call from Pratt,' Clara gulped. 'You've to get back to work immediately. Milla's been shot.'

'For God's sake! When?'

'This morning. She was with Mrs Svetlova in the grounds of the detention centre when a sniper opened fire. The guard was killed; Milla was rushed to York Hospital. She's in intensive care. Tom said it's too early to tell whether she's going to make it.'

'What about Anna?'

'She's being treated for shock but she's okay. The CC spoke to Tom, your suspension's lifted. I've been trying to get hold of Zena; I hoped she could contact Svetlov before he leaves for Moscow. I couldn't raise her so I phoned the Embassy. They're trying to stop him before his plane takes off. I don't suppose you know where she is?'

The door alongside her opened and Zena stepped into the lounge. If the sight of the Russian officer didn't surprise

Clara, the fact that she was clad only in a bath towel certainly did. 'Oh!' was all Clara could manage.

'Hello, Clara, is something wrong?'

Nash explained before Clara's sarcasm could be unloosed. 'I'll get dressed,' Zena hurried from the room.

Clara eyed Nash. 'It's good to see you doing your bit for East–West détente.'

'I'm glad you approve.'

'I wouldn't go that far,' Clara muttered.

'Do you know if Milla's being guarded?'

'Yes. The CC's ordered an armed officer at the entrance to the ICU. There's another at her bedside.'

'There's nothing to be done on that front then. Has Mexican Pete been to the tarn?'

'No, he's at a conference in Paris, flew out this morning. I managed a word with him on his mobile. Apart from accusing you of necrophilia, the rest of it was unrepeatable even if you understand Spanish.'

'It would have been useful if we could have got an opinion from him.'

Pearce answered the phone then held the handset out to Nash, 'Tom Pratt. He's been ringing every half hour.'

'Yes, Tom, I've been told. Any news on Milla?'

He listened then sighed. 'That's something, I suppose. She's young and resilient.'

'No, we'll set off straight away. Yes, she's here.'

He put the phone down. 'The CC's chairing a meeting at Netherdale in half an hour. She's ordered everyone to attend. Armistead, Fleming and Thomas are already there.'

The Chief Constable asked them to report progress. Zena, encouraged by a nod from Nash, stood up. 'I received a text message from an informant,' she gave them the gist, adding a short biography of Vatovec, finishing with details of his activities. 'Superintendent Nash agrees it's suspicious that Vatovec is in England now.'

They discussed details required for an operation to capture Vatovec. 'I've ordered photographs of Vatovec from my office,' she told the meeting. 'They'll be faxed through.'

DCI Fleming reported next. 'I went to the detention centre. The forensics team established the shots were fired from a small copse a quarter of a mile away. They searched the woodland but there was no trace of the sniper. Significantly, there were no spent shells. There were two bullets in the dead woman, two in Milla. Until we analyse the bullets we must assume the weapon to be a high-powered rifle with a telescopic sight.'

Nash was silent, envisaging the scene. He saw Milla walking round the gardens with Anna Svetlova alongside, chatting as they walked. He pictured the guard, discreetly behind them. He pictured the copse, the sniper waiting.

For how long? Had he a back-up plan? How could he be sure Milla would come outside? 'When prisoners are taken from the centre where do they get picked up?' He asked, noticing a few puzzled looks.

'The transport pulls through the electronic gates at the entrance. For security everything comes in and out there.'

'So the assassin wasn't specifically targeting Milla at that moment. He was prepared to wait until she came out to be transferred. Or he had a back-up plan.'

'You'd better explain that,' Pratt prompted.

'The object was to prevent Milla identifying the traffickers. To ensure she couldn't pick them out of a line-up. Shooting her would be his preferred option, but if that failed he'd have devised another way of getting at Milla. That means they're worried.'

'It sounds chancy taking shots at such a long range,' the Chief Constable suggested.

Nash thought about what she'd said. It was a shrewd point. It was an extreme distance. Even a trained marksman would have preferred to get closer. The fact that the assassin was prepared to take it on reflected what? Desperation? If so, it suggested Milla had evidence of overwhelming importance.

Was the idea to kill the girl or scare her into silence? Nash discounted the latter. The people behind this were too ruthless to leave it to chance. Who could take on a challenge like this? With the ability to pick off someone at that range? Then, after shooting her, quietly tidy up and leave no trace?

Nash's reverie was interrupted by a question from Armistead. Clara, aware of Nash's preoccupation, frowned with annoyance. She knew what Nash had been attempting and resented the MCU officer's blundering intrusion. It wasn't as if the question was particularly important.

Nash answered easily enough, conveying no hint of annoyance at the disturbance of his thought process.

'Moving now to the bodies recovered from the second tarn.' The Chief Constable glanced down at her pad. 'Desolation Tarn, I believe it's called. It seems we now have eight murders to investigate, nine if we include the prison officer.'

Into the silence that followed there came one word. 'Twelve.'

Everyone looked round, puzzled as to who'd spoken. Their attention homed in on Nash. 'What did you say, Mike?' Tom Pratt asked.

'I said twelve. There are twelve murders to investigate. Five bodies from Lamentation Tarn, three from Desolation Tarn, the prison officer, the two men shot dead on Westlea Estate and Dr Stevens.'

'You can't be sure the last three are connected with the bodies in the tarns,' Armistead protested.

'No?' There was a world of contempt in Nash's voice. 'The burnt-out car on the Westlea was registered to the address where Milla's victims were found. Incidentally, if we include them, the count goes up to fifteen and—'

'I give you that. But you can't include Dr Stevens,' Armistead interrupted.

'He was suffocated with carbon monoxide, having been drugged. There were signs of forced entry. Signs of an attempt to make it look like an accident. Signs that the intruder tried to disguise his presence. Add to that the fingerprint of a former soldier turned mercenary, supposed to have been killed several years ago. What was this character doing in Helmsdale? He wouldn't turn out unless there was money involved, big money. What do you think he was here for, the North Yorkshire snakes and ladders tournament?'

'You still haven't connected him to the other crimes.' There was a mulish stubbornness about Armistead's refusal to accept the obvious.

'I thought I'd said enough to convince you, but obviously not.'

Clara thought Nash's tone was gentle, too gentle. She almost felt sorry for Armistead. But remembering his unpleasant attitude and his attempt to get Nash shafted, she sat back to enjoy the show.

'Perhaps you weren't listening when Commander Dacic made her presentation.'

Here we go, Clara thought.

'Let me refresh your memory. She told us Vatovec had been supplying prostitutes for IFOR troops during the Bosnia conflict and advanced to human trafficking. She also mentioned that Vatovec is currently in Britain. Martin Hill served with IFOR in Bosnia. He was in Helmsdale a few days ago. If you can't add those facts together and make the connection then you shouldn't be at this meeting. You shouldn't be involved in this enquiry. All you've done from the beginning is behave obstructively towards me and my colleagues and prevent the real detectives getting on with solving the case.' Nash saw the Chief Constable about to intercede and held up a hand. 'A moment, Ma'am,' he begged. 'Not only that. You've consistently failed to provide information that could be vital to the enquiry. Information such as the method by which the girls were smuggled into Britain. Methods which your officers were sent to investigate. No report of that has been given to me or my colleagues.'

Armistead was red in the face at this humiliation. Before he had chance to reply the Chief Constable said quietly, 'What do you have to say about that, Superintendent Armistead? Have you denied vital information to my officers?'

'I'm not answerable to Nash.'

'Answer this carefully. Who are you answerable to?'

'The Home Office,' he snapped angrily, 'And to them alone.'

The Chief Constable's measured, quiet delivery was in direct contrast to Armistead's hectoring tone. 'Wrong! When you set foot on my territory you and your officers became answerable to me. Those are the terms of reference under which MCU was set up. I should know. I was one of the working party that wrote them. So from now on you'll cease to ride roughshod over this enquiry. You and your officers will share all the evidence at your disposal.'

Nash's attention was caught by Fleming. As the Chief Constable laid down the law to Armistead he saw a glint in Fleming's eyes; it was approval.

The Chief Constable continued as if nothing untoward had happened. 'We need to make a policy decision as to whether to involve the media.' She smiled warmly at Nash, leaving the others in no doubt where her sympathies lay. 'In the light of the discovery of further victims, Mike, what's your opinion?'

'I'd rather leave them out of it. It'll be a few days before we can get the post-mortem results with Mexican Pete, I mean Professor Ramirez, being away. I'd rather get them before we say anything.'

'Very well, we'll take that as read. Now I'd like a word with you in Superintendent Pratt's office, Mike. Is that okay, Tom?'

She closed the door of Tom's office. 'I'm well aware Ramirez is known to everyone as Mexican Pete. I've three brothers who played rugby. That wasn't why I wanted a word.' Her tone became serious. 'It's obvious you and Armistead can't work together. What about his officers?'

'I wouldn't trust DS Thomas, but I think I could work with DCI Fleming.'

'Then I suggest you liaise with her.' The grin reappeared, 'But don't take liaison too far.'

'No, Ma'am.'

Zena had left to visit Anna Svetlova and check on Milla, leaving word she would ring later. Clara told Nash when he emerged from Pratt's office. 'She had a call from the embassy, Svetlov's on his way back. Zena said he'd spoken to the Kremlin, deferred the meetings he was due to attend.' She inclined her head towards the office. 'What went on in there?'

'The Chief wanted to know who I could work with at MCU in view of Armistead's attitude.'

'And?'

'I suggested Fleming. So she told me to liaise with her.'

'I hope that doesn't mean—'

'Don't you start. It's bad enough the Chief Constable making innuendos.'

'Okay, okay. If you don't need me any more I've got something to do.'

'No, that's fine. There's not much we can do tonight. See you in the morning.'

During the drive back, Nash was thinking. He felt sure there was something significant he'd missed. Somewhere, someone had said something he'd failed to pick up on. The others on the task force seemed to accept the fact that Vatovec and Martin Hill were the ringleaders of the trafficking operation but Nash was less than convinced. There was more to it than that, but what?

DS Thomas had been smarting since the humiliation of his ejection from Nash's office. His mortification was only offset by the knowledge that he could hear everything inside. The bugging device he'd planted was working perfectly.

Although DCI Fleming was notionally Thomas's superior, he didn't recognize her as such. Thomas had been with the organization since its inception, felt aggrieved at the interloper. Her presence baulked his chances of promotion;

and she was a woman. Thomas saw no reason to trouble her with this operational detail. He'd applied directly to Armistead for approval, who'd no hesitation in giving it.

Armistead had the case file open on his knee. The two sat in Thomas's car a discreet distance from Helmsdale Police Station, well within transmitting range of the device secreted under Nash's desk. As they listened to Nash reviewing the progress of the enquiry with his DS and Dacic, Armistead scanned the paperwork.

'I'm still trying to work out how the death of Dr Stevens ties into this case,' they heard Nash say. 'I'm absolutely convinced it does. But until we can get hold of his phone records there's little we can do.'

'How long is this going to take?' They recognized Dacic's voice.

'I'd hoped to have them by now but the mobile phone company's been uncooperative. Waiting for a warrant didn't help.'

'In Russia we'd have demanded the records. They'd have given them without question. We don't need a warrant.'

'Viv's gone back to the phone company,' Clara told them. 'He was pissed off by their attitude. The woman who's dealing with it wasn't available. The receptionist seemed to think we'd already got them.'

'Good for him. He's starting to use his initiative. Without them, we must concentrate our efforts on locating Vatovec and Hill. It would have been helpful if MCU had come across with their information about how the girls were smuggled in, but after yesterday's fiasco I can't see Armistead popping in with his case notes.'

'You're dead right there, sunbeam,' Armistead muttered.

'What do you want me to do next?' Thomas asked in a low tone.

'Trace some of the numbers on here,' Armistead gestured to Stevens's phone logs, which lay uppermost on his paperwork. 'Concentrate on those he called frequently and pay them a visit. We can steal a march on the yokels.'

'Should I let Fleming in on what we're doing?'

'No, let's keep the credit for ourselves. When I'm head of MCU I'll reward those I trust. Fleming can go back where she came from. You'll be my right hand. Pulling off a high-profile case like this will go a long way to achieving what we're after.'

CHAPTER ELEVEN

'I need to go to Cauldmoor, find out how the Rubber Johnnies are doing. Want to come along?'

'I might as well.'

The sun was shining as they left Helmsdale.

'How was your evening off?'

'It was very interesting,' she said without marked enthusiasm.

'What did you do?'

'I went to visit a friend in Netherdale.'

'Anyone I know?'

There was no dodging the issue. 'I went to visit Stella.'

Nash was surprised but not shocked. 'She didn't throw you out, then?'

'No, she seemed pleased to see me.'

'How is she?'

'She had a bit of a setback when you had that row, but I think she's looking better than last time I saw her.'

'Hang on, we didn't have a row. She told me to "f" off.'

'Whatever, she's certainly more cheerful and she's started taking an interest again.'

'How do you mean?'

'Before your spat she wasn't concerned about anything, even what was happening to her body. Now she's putting herself through some rigorous exercise sessions. Calls her trainer a physioterrorist. I spoke to the woman and she told me Stella was pushing her constantly to extend the regimen. Pushing herself to the limit to get fit again.'

'That's good news.'

'That's not all. She's also taking an interest in her surroundings. She was telling me about the clinic, her routines.' Clara laughed. 'She even knows how many security guards there are. Thinks they must have some very privileged patients to need so many. Or doing highly secret research.'

'That's even more promising. She's right, too. I wonder why?'

'Perhaps they've been plagued with intruders or scared of thefts. Maybe they've got some mentally ill patients. The point I was trying to make is if Stella's started to spot things like that it's a good sign.'

'Did she mention the letter?'

'What you mean is did she mention you.'

'Yes, I suppose so.'

'What else do you think we talked about?'

'You'd better tell me the worst.'

'You can't get Stella off your mind. You may be kidding yourself carrying on with Zena but you're not fooling anyone. It isn't fair on Zena, it isn't fair on Stella and it isn't doing you any good.'

'You're getting to sound like an agony aunt.'

'Stella wrote that letter because she's convinced you were only visiting her out of sympathy.'

'That's not true.'

'I told her that. I told her how upset you were, getting the letter when you'd so much else to worry about. I told her how you'd reacted. And I told her about Zena.'

'Oh thanks. That's blown me right out of the water.'

Clara laughed. 'That proves you don't know Stella half as well as she knows you. I didn't need to tell her about

Zena. She'd already guessed there'd be someone. She said you wouldn't be interested in her because she's crippled.'

'That's a load of bloody rubbish.'

'Don't tell me. Tell her.'

Nash caught on. 'Does that mean she'll see me?'

Clara grinned. 'I thought that'd cheer you up. You owe me a pint.'

'It's worth it. Thanks, Clara.'

They were three-quarters of the way towards Cauldmoor when Nash overtook a coroner's van. Nash's lips tightened. The implication hadn't escaped Clara either. 'That doesn't look good,' she commented.

Nash was normally easy-going. She'd never seen him demonstrate such impotent rage as he showed then. 'The lousy stinking bastards,' he banged his fist on the steering wheel. 'I'll kill them if I ever get hold of them. I'll cut their bollocks off and feed them to the cats, I'll—'

Clara put her hand on his arm. 'Cool it, Mike,' she urged. 'It won't do any good. We all feel that way. We all want justice for those kids. Revenge isn't our business. We don't do revenge.'

Nash cooled down, the fire dying as quickly as it had flared. 'You're right; sorry, Clara. Just keep me at arms length when we get them.'

'That could be difficult,' she attempted to lighten the moment. 'You've got longer arms than me.'

When they reached the moor, Stark Ghyll was invisible behind a curtain of fine drizzle. The windscreen wipers had been on for the last few miles, dragging their way to and fro with a rubbery screech as they removed the fine droplets of rain. 'You know something Clara, since this thing started I've had a feeling that I've missed something that should have rung alarm bells but I'm damned if I can figure out what it was.'

'Maybe being back here will help.'

'I hope so. It's beginning to bug me.'

They started to climb the ridge separating the lakes. It got steeper as they neared the top. Both of them were fit but they needed to pause for breath when they reached the summit. Nash looked back towards Lamentation Tarn, still searching his mind for that elusive memory. Before them, the mist writhed and swirled, hiding Desolation Tarn from view until it cleared fractionally. Clara looked down to where the diving team was working.

She clutched Nash's arm. 'Mike!' Her voice was filled with horror, 'Look!'

Alongside the tarn were four unmistakeable black shapes. Body bags.

They half stumbled down the treacherous slope. They slipped and slid over moss-covered rocks rendered dangerous by the rain, tripping once or twice as their ankles caught in clumps of heather and bracken roots.

Saunders, the head of the diving team, looked weary. His normally cheerful face lined and etched with the grey pallor of distress. 'This is the worst job I've ever had.' He kicked savagely at some unoffending reeds.

'What's the score?' Nash winced internally at the unintended double meaning.

'We've finished, thank God. There are no more down there. For God's sake catch these evil sods, Mike. When you've done that lock them up and throw the key in the middle of that bloody lake where the bastards put those kids.' He turned away and Clara saw tears welling up at the corner of his eyes.

She put a consoling hand on his arm. 'Come on, Johnnie. You know if anyone can catch them, Mike will. He'll make sure they go down for so long they'll never be able to harm youngsters again.'

Saunders braced himself, 'I hope so.' Nash had taken a couple of paces towards the body bags. 'Don't go there, Mike!'

Nash looked back, more at the tone of Saunders's voice than the words. 'Don't open those bags. Leave it for Mexican Pete. You don't want to see what's in those bags.'

His tone changed, became more urgent, appealing. 'Believe me, Mike, you really don't want to look. What's in there, it's ... it's an obscenity. I had to see it; my lads had to. You don't. I'll never forget what I've seen here. I'll want to, desperately want to, but I know I won't be able to.'

There was a short silence. Nash walked back to where Clara was still holding the diver's arm. 'I'm sorry we put you through this, Johnnie,' he said quietly.

'Not your fault, Mike,' Saunders said wearily. 'At least the job's over. We can guarantee there's nothing more down there. I just hope I never have to come to this bloody hell hole ever again. Now leave us to clear up and move these poor creatures out of here.'

The detectives turned and walked in sombre silence back up the ridge. Eventually Clara spoke. 'It's unlike Johnnie to take things so hard.'

'When they first started, it was just another recovery. But Johnnie's read the case notes, he knows what those kids suffered. His imagination got to work and did the rest.'

They sat on the steps of the bothy whilst the diving team carried the body bags one by one to the waiting vehicle. Nash felt the weight of depression heavier than on his previous visits. The burden of responsibility was his, he knew it. Knew he had to get justice for the victims. Whoever drove them out to this dreadful spot and cold-bloodedly executed them showed callousness beyond his comprehension.

Clara turned her coat collar up and gave an involuntary shiver as she felt the bone-numbing cold strike through her jacket. She burrowed her hands deep into the pockets.

Her words broke so exactly across Nash's thoughts that for a second he believed he'd given voice to them. 'What sort of monsters are these? To bring those girls here to this desolate spot, kill them and dump them in the lake with no more feeling than if they were tipping rubbish? It's inhuman.'

'I don't know Clara. It's beyond me how these kids finished up in such a godforsaken place as this—'

His voice trailed off as his words and Clara's collided in his brain. The conjunction of ideas yielded a thought he should have had long ago. He leapt to his feet so suddenly he cracked his head on the veranda lintel. 'Shit!'

'You alright, Mike?'

He rubbed his head as he began pacing to and fro across the veranda floor. 'Why didn't I think of this before,' he muttered.

'Think of what?'

'I knew there was something.' Clara looked bemused. 'I should have twigged it long ago. You were right when you said being here might cause me to remember. I've asked myself the question, not once but several times, without realizing the relevance. How did they end up here?'

'Presumably because Vatovec and Hill brought them.'

'How?'

'Sorry, Mike, I must be missing the point.'

'Don't worry about it; I've missed it for ages. We suspect Vatovec and Hill of running this paedophile ring, right?'

'Yes.'

'There has to be someone else. Look at it this way. Vatovec hails from the other side of Europe. Hill was born and raised in Nottingham. Neither of them would have a clue this place existed. There has to be someone who did know. They had to know the area well enough to be confident of it being a safe dumping ground.'

'Of course,' Clara breathed. 'It's been staring us in the face all along and we never twigged. But who the hell is it?'

Nash had a flashback to their first day at the tarn, his interview with the angling club secretary, the man's extreme agitation. He remembered everything he'd said.

Like collapsing dominoes one thought collided with the next, then the next.

They returned to Helmsdale in sombre silence, following the coroner's van and the diving team's Land Rovers slowly down the narrow lanes in what seemed like a cortege.

They peeled off at the relief road back to the police station. 'I need a hot drink,' Clara said. 'Want me to bring you one?'

'Thanks, Clara,' Nash's tone was as muted as hers, the experience of Cauldmoor still sitting heavily with both of them. 'I've a couple of phone calls to make.'

He located his Filofax and searched for a number. 'Long time no see. I need some background information, and if it tells me what I suspect, it'll shorten a major enquiry no end. Yes, I understand it might be difficult, but given the circumstances I hoped you could pull a few strings.'

Nash explained what he needed. 'I appreciate it may take a bit of arm twisting, but this is more than a bit urgent. Yes, if you could call me here or at Netherdale,' Nash reeled of the phone numbers. 'I'm very grateful.'

Clara caught the tail end of the conversation as she brought his drink, 'Mexican Pete's just phoned. All Paris airports are fogbound and likely to remain shut for at least twenty-four hours. He won't be able to fly back tomorrow. The post-mortems on the Desolation Tarn victims won't get done until the day after next at the earliest. That's if the fog lifts.'

*

Nash was interrupted by a knock on his office door. He looked up and saw DCI Fleming standing in the doorway. She looked nervous. 'I'm not disturbing you, am I? I want a word, if you don't mind.'

'Come in,' his tone was wary, his expression guarded. 'What can I do for you?'

Fleming was dressed informally. A pair of skin-tight slacks and a low-cut top.

'It's about you and Armistead. If I'd said my piece at the meeting yesterday it would have made matters worse. Armistead would have excluded me from the enquiry.' She paused and sighed. 'The thing is, I suspect Armistead and Thomas are cooking something nasty up between them.'

145

'Why are you telling me? How do I know this isn't one of Armistead's little tricks?'

'Look, I've been trying to pluck up courage to come here. If Armistead knew we were talking he'd go through the roof. I'll tell you what I suspect. Then it's up to you.

'I'm fairly sure they've got hold of some evidence they're keeping to themselves. Don't ask me how because I don't think they could detect their way out of a paper bag. I think they're going to keep this information the same way as they kept the evidence about how the girls were smuggled into the country.'

'I thought you were involved in that?'

'That's what Armistead told you. I was sent to London to liaise with the Home Office and the Russian Embassy. I thought at the time any middle-ranking officer could have done it. I didn't realize Armistead had his own agenda. He's got a track record for grabbing the kudos for other people's work. It was Armistead and Thomas who went to check up at the ports.'

Fleming sat a little straighter in her chair. 'Those two are as thick as thieves and I'm beginning to discover how devious they are. They were appointed to MCU when it was set up and I hear Armistead did a lot of arm twisting to get the job. Anyone who came in after them was seen as an intruder. As if that wasn't enough, I had the disadvantage of being a woman.'

'I'd say that was an asset.'

'In their book, women are only good for shagging, having children and housework.'

'That's bullshit. I don't believe there are still people who think that way.'

Fleming smiled sadly. 'There are plenty in other forces who think just like Armistead and Thomas. You don't know them, Mike,' she shook her head. 'About the only thing I've got going for me is that I'm not black.'

'Idiots,' Nash said dismissively. 'No wonder they don't take us seriously. We're a team of three, one white, one black and one female. Is that why you came here, to warn me?'

'Yes, Mike.' She leaned forward. The action brought the low-cut top she was wearing into the centre of Nash's vision. 'I couldn't stand by without warning you.'

Nash looked her in the eye, no mean feat given the distraction. 'Why do you think they're plotting something?'

'They're acting secretively and now Thomas has disappeared. Armistead won't tell me where he's gone. I've a right to know. I pulled the chain of command as hard as I could and got nowhere. Armistead just blanked me.'

'I appreciate you coming to tell me, but unless I know what they're up to I can't see a way of counteracting it.'

'I wondered if you might get some clue from the way your enquiries are going.' Fleming sighed, 'I don't even know if you're making any headway or not. I get no feedback from Armistead or you.' She raised a hand to still his protest. 'I don't blame you,' she leaned forward again. 'I'd do exactly the same. I feel as if I'm getting shafted from both sides.'

'Not pleasant.'

'I wondered, could I work with you? I'll keep quiet about what we're doing. Seeing the way you, Clara and Viv work together made me realize what I'm missing. I detest Armistead. He uses people then discards them. I've had it up to here with him.' She lifted her hand to her throat and Nash saw the red tinge of anger in her cheeks.

'Let me think about it. I'll give you my decision tomorrow.'

Fleming stood up and stretched, the action displayed her figure to great advantage. 'Thanks for sparing the time.' She turned and placed both hands on the desk, bending forward to emphasize her point. 'I promise I won't let you down, Mike,' her voice was low and husky. 'I'll never give you cause to be disappointed.'

Nash whistled soundlessly as the door closed behind her. Was Jackie Fleming genuine? If so, just how far did that cooperation extend? The implication seemed to be that it was absolute. Perhaps even beyond the line of duty.

'Is the black widow looking for another mate?' Clara had entered the room.

'I may have a dodgy reputation round here,' Nash protested, 'but I think that's too high a price to pay for getting my leg over.'

'I bow to your expert opinion. So what did Spiderwoman want?'

Nash told her what Fleming had said.

'Hell's bells! What the hell's going on? Do you believe her or is it another of Armistead's pranks. Because I wouldn't trust that bastard as far as I could throw him.'

'Who knows? It may be part of some internal power struggle. Only time will tell.'

Time in this instance was short. It was 9 p.m. when Nash's doorbell rang. DCI Fleming was standing outside. Her eyes red-rimmed from crying. 'What's wrong?'

'Can … can I come in?' She seemed lost, oblivious to everything apart from her distress. Nash followed her down the hallway, the rhythmic movement of her buttocks in the tight slacks doing nothing to reduce his blood pressure.

'Have you told anyone what we discussed?'

Nash shook his head. 'Only Clara, why?'

'Armistead rang me an hour after I left you. He was furious, demanded I went to see him immediately. He went spare. Shouting and bawling, swearing and waving his fists about. Mike, he knew all about me coming to see you, knew what we discussed. He told me I was disloyal, untrustworthy, unfit to be working in MCU. He said he could have me suspended and sent for disciplinary action. He said if I wanted to work for you so desperately he could arrange it. He no longer wanted me on this investigation. As soon as he'd selected a replacement, I'd be sent back to my own force with a note on my file regarding insubordination.'

She burst into tears. 'It's not fair. I've worked bloody hard for this. I don't understand why he's so upset or how he found out.'

It was a question Nash was already asking himself. Her weeping became fiercer. He put an arm round her shoulders to comfort her. She clung to him, her lithe body trembled. Gradually, her sobbing lessened. Nash held her at arms length. 'Better now?' Nash led her to the couch. 'Sit there whilst I get you a drink. Tea or coffee, or would you prefer something stronger?'

'I'd better stick to coffee, seeing I'm driving. It'd be the last straw to get breathalysed between here and Netherdale.'

In the kitchen Nash pondered this development. He remembered DS Thomas in his office rifling through his paperwork. Was there a deeper significance behind Thomas being there? Something more sinister?

'Jackie, when you had this confrontation with Armistead, what exactly did he say about our meeting? Try to remember his exact words.'

She repeated what Armistead had said.

Nash thought for a moment. 'That's almost word for word what we discussed.'

'I know. That's what I can't understand. If you or Clara didn't tell him, how come he found out, and so quickly.'

'I think I know. Drink your coffee. We're going to my office.'

Nash paused before opening the door of the dark CID room. 'We'll check the CID room first then have a look in mine. We'll have to make sure we keep quiet, or at most speak only in a whisper, okay?'

'Yes,' she breathed. Her tears forgotten, her eyes glowed with excitement.

They found nothing suspicious in the outer office. They moved into his room and began searching. Nash whispered, 'Under the desk.' Jackie felt his breath against her cheek as he spoke; it felt vaguely erotic. She forced herself to concentrate.

He watched appreciatively as she wriggled into the gap below the middle drawer. Seconds later her hand reappeared, waving excitedly. Nash got down and looked at where she was pointing. The device taped to the underside of the desk was certainly not part of the furniture. He went to remove it, then stopped. He beckoned to her to come out and led her from the room. He locked his office then made straight for the outer door. Only when they were back in the corridor did he speak.

'We'll leave the device in place. It will come in handy as evidence at an internal enquiry should it come to that.'

'What about the CID room,' Jackie asked. 'I know we didn't find anything, but we can't be sure that isn't bugged.'

'Good point. I know someone who can do an electronic sweep tomorrow.'

Her face had lost the glow of excitement as she realized her position hadn't altered. 'I'm still off the investigation.'

'No, you're not. As of now you're co-opted on to our team. We're under strength. Armistead won't miss you and you'll be useful and involved.'

'Thank you, Mike,' her voice was husky with emotion. She leaned forward. He was unprepared for even a peck on the cheek let alone the passionate kiss she gave him. He felt the almost irresistible urge to respond as her questing tongue explored his mouth, but managed to fight it. 'Steady on, Jackie.'

'Now you know how grateful I am.' Then added, 'and how cooperative I can be.'

'This number was one Dr Stevens had never rung until a few weeks ago. Then he rang it no less than a dozen times. The only one he rang more frequently was his girlfriend's.'

Armistead looked at Thomas. 'Got a name and address to go with it?'

Thomas nodded, 'I have.' He passed him a slip of paper. 'What's more, I checked those details against the information we got from the ports.'

'And?'

Thomas smiled, 'It appears as consignee for several pieces of cargo that could have been used to smuggle the kids in. So what do we do next?'

Armistead thought it over. 'At present, we only have circumstantial evidence.'

'You don't think we've got enough to justify a raid?'

'We'd never get a warrant.'

'What about involving the locals?'

Armistead sneered. 'And let them grab the glory? No chance. Let the yokels stew in their own juice. And that bitch Fleming. I never trusted her and she's proved me right. I bet Nash is shagging her. He's got a bit of a reputation that way. From what I hear, one sniff and he's off like shit off a shiny shovel. Rumour has it he's already screwing the Russian.'

Thomas whistled, 'Jammy bastard. I wouldn't mind slipping that one a length myself.'

'No, she's quite a looker.' Armistead returned to business, 'Anyway, let Nash continue his womanizing. You go have a look round this place, get the lie of the land, see if you can spot anyone we're interested in. Then report back. Don't tell anyone what you're up to, especially not Fleming. Even if she didn't report direct to Nash, she may talk in her sleep.'

CHAPTER TWELVE

A message and a visitor awaited Nash next morning. He'd been expecting the visitor from a security business in the town. Nash asked the man to sweep the CID office, then looked at the note Clara had left. *'Gone to investigate ringing burglar alarm in the Market Place. Meeting with Tom and Home Office, Netherdale, this morning.'*

The search was negative. Nash was thanking the security man as Clara returned. 'No problem,' she reported. 'The shopkeeper forgot to exclude the zone where his cat sleeps. The animal must have set it off when he returned from visiting his lady friends. The shopkeeper was most apologetic but I told him round here, all the males behave like tom cats.'

'Thank you, Clara, and good morning to you. What about this message? What do they want me for?'

'Us,' Clara corrected him. 'I'm wanted too and the Russians will be there. It's to determine what to do about Milla.'

'Have you heard how she is?'

'I spoke to the hospital. She's out of danger, although her condition's still described as serious.'

'Where's Viv?'

'I sent him to Good Buys. We're out of coffee.'

'Bad planning, Sergeant. You know this office can't function without coffee.'

Clara made a rude and insubordinate gesture. Fortunately, Pearce returned at that moment. 'Clara's going to make us a brew. Then I want a word with you both.'

They sat in the CID room. 'For the time being, my office is out of bounds. Go in there to get files, but don't hold any conversations and on no account answer the phone or make a call in there.'

They stared at him puzzled. Nash explained about the bug.

'That Armistead's a nasty piece of work,' Clara exclaimed angrily. 'He's a shifty bastard and Thomas is a greasy little sod.'

'Brown tongued as well,' Viv muttered.

'Armistead made the mistake of confronting Jackie about our meeting, that's how we knew. He's kicked her off his team so now she's on ours, but she works alongside us.' Nash looked at Clara. 'You don't take orders from her. Okay?'

Clara nodded.

'I don't think she'll try to give you any, to be fair. I reckon she's alright, just suffered by association with Armistead and Thomas.'

'You don't think it's part of some elaborate plan of Armistead's to get someone on the inside?'

'No, I don't. The thought crossed my mind but by what Jackie said I reckon Armistead's already one jump ahead of us. He's never volunteered that information about how the girls were smuggled into the country, despite the Chief Constable demanding it.'

Right on cue DCI Fleming walked in. She smiled at them nervously. 'Sorry I'm late boss,' she greeted Nash. 'What do you want me to do?'

'You could make a start by brewing fresh coffee. We run a democratic system here.'

When she'd rejoined them Nash told her of his and Clara's impending meeting. 'After that I've a call to make and I want to arrange the post-mortems on the latest victims from the tarn, unless Mexican Pete's still ogling the girls in the Moulin Rouge.'

'Mexican Pete?'

'Professor Ramirez, our local pathologist.'

'What do you want me to do?'

'Go with Viv to the phone company offices again and demand Dr Stevens's records. They've dragged their feet long enough. They keep fobbing Viv off, so I think it needs a senior officer to bang the table.'

Jackie stared at them. 'Surely you've had them already?' She saw the blank stares and explained. 'Armistead got a copy the day before yesterday. I thought they'd come from here.'

Nash was exasperated, 'No wonder they wouldn't let Viv have them. They must have thought he was mad.'

'That bastard Armistead,' Clara burst out, 'he wants a good seeing to.'

'Don't worry, he'll get his comeuppance,' Nash pointed to his office. 'I want that door kept locked. Nobody but the four of us gets access. I don't want that evidence disappearing.'

'What's the score with Mike?' Jackie asked as she and Viv drove towards the phone company offices. 'Armistead seemed to imply Mike spent all his time chasing women. Is there any truth in that? I know Mike's very attractive but he doesn't strike me as a lecher.'

'Maybe that's part of his charm,' Viv suggested. Clara's going to love this, he thought. 'You have to bear in mind Mike's only been back in Yorkshire a year or so. He came back from working in The Met.'

'Yes, they still talk about him at Scotland Yard as if he's some kind of hero.'

'There's been a lot of women he's befriended. I can think of at least half a dozen without trying.'

'You mean he's slept with all those women?'

'I don't think sleep had much to do with it,' Viv grinned. 'Not judging by the look of him some mornings.

To be honest, we don't think any of them mean very much. To him, it's just fun.'

'By "we" I suppose you mean you and Clara?'

Viv nodded. 'We think he's only seriously interested in Stella.'

'Who's Stella?'

'Actually her name's Samantha, but everyone calls her Stella after her favourite drink. Mike met her last year. He fell for her big style and I think she fell for him. It was rather sad the way things worked out. Stella was kidnapped. Mike rescued her but she almost died. When she did recover they found she was paralyzed. We reckon Mike feels guilty, although there's no reason why he should. The problem is there's no saying whether she'll ever be able to walk again.'

'That's terrible, the poor girl. Poor Mike, too. Still, it sounds as if he's found some consolation.'

They pulled into the phone company's car park. 'Do you mind if I take the lead?'

'Not a bit,' Pearce smiled ruefully. 'You can't do any worse than I have.'

'Have you told Tom about the bug in your office or about Armistead sacking Jackie?' Clara asked as they drove towards Netherdale.

'Not yet. I'm concerned Tom would want to play it by the book and call for an enquiry. I think we've enough on our plate. We don't need another distraction.'

'When will you tell him?'

'When this is over. Unless Armistead tells him about Jackie first.'

'What's the plan after the meeting?'

'I want to go see how Stella's getting on. That'll give you time to see Mexican Pete. He was coming to Netherdale this morning according to the university. See what arrangements he's made for the post-mortems. Don't let him try to talk you into a knee trembler against the cabinets, though. Remember those are corpses behind you.'

Clara snorted. 'Don't judge everyone by your own standards. Some of us can say no, even to such an alluring offer. Anyway, there's probably more life in the contents of the drawers than Mexican Pete can muster.'

'Probably more stiffness too.'

The Home Office representative opened the meeting. 'I should explain that the Crown Prosecution Service can only make a decision on whether to institute proceedings on the evidence provided. If they believe that to be insufficient to secure a conviction, they will not move on the matter. The rules are particularly strong where the case involves a minor, such as in this instance. Superintendent Nash, I'd be grateful if you'd give us your opinion.'

'There's evidence connecting Milla to the house where three men died violently,' he began. 'There's also overwhelming evidence of her being systematically ill-treated, physically and sexually abused.'

Then realization dawned. Christ, Nash thought, he wants me to give him a bloody escape route. He wants me to come up with something that will avoid us having to press charges. What does the man think I am; a bloody conjuror?

Nash thought hard as he looked round for inspiration. As his eyes met Zena's, it came. He held her with his gaze, 'Commander,' he asked. 'Have you been able to establish Milla's true identity?'

Zena stared back at him trying to guess the motive behind a question he already knew the answer to. 'Regrettably not,' she replied guardedly.

Nash smiled. 'Then I see one major stumbling block to prosecution. Unless we can establish the child's identity,' he placed just the tiniest emphasis on the word 'child', 'we're unable to judge whether she's old enough to have responsibility for a criminal act.'

'Then that would seem to be a show-stopper. I'm sure an officer as diligent as Superintendent Nash has used all the means at his disposal to determine the child's age. Without it, I'm afraid I can't see how any action can be taken. It's most regrettable but there it is.'

He didn't seem particularly upset, Nash thought, nor had he asked the one embarrassing question. Had anyone thought to ask Milla how old she was? Nash concealed a smile and sat back to enjoy the charade.

'The question remains what to do about the child. I've been instructed by the Home Secretary to offer Milla permanent residential status in the United Kingdom if no other alternative is available. Such a decision can only be made when she's well enough to be told and to understand the implications. Obviously, she'd be entitled to all the benefits and protection of any other British citizen and would receive all the care and assistance Social Services can provide. Has anyone any alternative suggestion?'

There was a moment's silence before Svetlov cleared his throat. 'I have an idea,' he said cautiously. He glanced at his wife. Anna squeezed his arm encouragingly. 'I wish to propose that my wife and I be given custody of the child. You are aware we have lost our own daughter. We feel Katya would have wanted this. Milla would come to Moscow with us, we would ensure she gets the best education we can provide and give her a home.'

This whole meeting's a sham, Nash thought. It's all been set up beforehand. They were all there to witness that the game was being played by the rules. He felt sure there were other gambits available had Nash not provided an excuse not to charge Milla.

When the meeting broke up the civil servant sought out Nash. 'I'm most grateful for your cooperation and advice, Superintendent. Now you must make every effort to catch the men behind this evil business.'

'I'm confident we're starting to make progress. Once the post-mortem results on the latest victims are available I think we'll be able to start making arrests.'

Clara, who'd been listening to the exchange, blinked with surprise. Nash sounded so positive, yet she couldn't see why.

Zena and Anna joined them, 'This is the best for Milla,' Zena said. 'She'll have a good future now.'

Nash nodded, 'There is a condition. When we arrest the men behind this I'll want Milla to give evidence against them. Her identity will be protected, of course.'

'I am sure Milla will want to do that,' Anna Svetlova confirmed. 'It will be a small price to pay and from what I know of Milla she will want to do this to stop other girls going through the same ordeal.'

Anna paused, her voice quivered. She appeared on the brink of tears. 'Commander Dacic tells me more bodies have been discovered. Do you think one of these might be Katya?'

'I'll know more once the post-mortem examinations have been conducted. Our pathologist is one of the finest. He'll do everything he can to identify the victims. Your help will be needed,' he saw alarm in Anna's eyes. 'Don't worry. I wasn't speaking of identification. I'm sure you want to remember Katya as you knew her. I need saliva swabs from you and Sergei for DNA comparison.'

As Clara eased their car through the streets she asked Nash, 'Did you really mean that about making arrests? Because unless there's something you haven't told me I can't see how.'

'There is something but I'm waiting for confirmation. At the moment it's just a string of ideas. I'll tell you once I know for sure.'

'Where's this information coming from?'

'An old friend in London. Then we'll have the full story.'

Neither of them was aware that Mexican Pete was about to add a whole new chapter.

Clara dropped Nash at the entrance to the CB Clinic and set off for Netherdale General. Nash made his way to Stella's room, noting a considerable number of men wearing the uniform of a security company.

Stella had just returned from a gruelling physiotherapy session. 'Hello, Michael. This is a nice surprise.'

He relaxed at the warmth of her greeting. 'I didn't ring beforehand because things are fairly hectic and I didn't want to promise anything then have to renege.'

He perched on the edge of the bed alongside her wheelchair. 'How are you?'

'Bloody knackered, thanks to the physio. She knows more ways of torturing a woman than you do. So what have you come to tell me?'

Nash saw his opportunity. 'I came to tell you you're a bloody idiot. How many times have I asked you to come and live with me? Do you think I'm bothered whether you're in that damned chair or not? Stop being so bloody pig-headed and say yes, for God's sake.'

'Michael, I'm no use to you in this state. You need a woman who can love you properly. Not one who can't feel anything from the waist down. If I'd been fit and well, you know I'd have jumped at the chance; any woman with an ounce of sense would,' she paused and her eyes flickered with some emotion he couldn't guess, 'whatever her nationality.'

'Ouch,' he said as he took her hand in his. 'That only happened because I was lonely, because you'd told me you didn't want to see me again. If I had you I wouldn't go looking elsewhere.'

He reached across and hauled her from the bed on to his knee and began to kiss her, 'Michael,' she protested after a moment, 'Michael, you're hurting me.'

'Where?' He asked glancing down. Her left thigh was pressed hard against the arm rail of the wheelchair. 'There,' she pointed to it.

Nash's smile broadened. 'Really? Stella, that's brilliant!'

It took a moment before she realized. 'I can feel it,' she began to laugh. 'I can feel pain in my thigh, I can feel pain!'

'Have you had any feeling there before?'

'No, never!'

159

'This is bloody great. Let me call your physiotherapist. She's got to hear this.'

The telephone rang insistently, 'Butler speaking. Yes Mr Martin, what can I do for you?'

Both of them knew this was a rhetorical question. There could be only one reason for the call.

'I have a package for you, Doc.'

'I see. When would you be delivering?'

'Tomorrow evening?'

'I think we can cope with that. I'll make the arrangements.'

Nash was standing near the entrance staring at the building with a puzzled frown when Clara arrived.

'Everything alright? Stella okay?'

'Yes, everything's fine, couldn't be better. I was just wondering about what you said the other day. There does seem to be a lot of security men hanging around. I was puzzling out why they need so many. Anyway, that's not important. I've some terrific news. Stella's beginning to get some feeling back in her left leg.'

He described how they'd discovered the returning sensation. 'I spent the last twenty minutes watching the neurologist playing darts on her legs. He says she's now got fifteen per cent nerve reaction. Not much, I know, but it's fifteen per cent she didn't have before.'

'That's wonderful.'

'It's early days. The doctor told her she mustn't get her hopes up. It may be a long time before there's any improvement, and there's still no guarantees. He said this might be all she gets.'

'How did Stella react?'

'She wasn't listening; or she wasn't prepared to accept it.'

'That's good, surely. If she went along meekly she wouldn't put the effort in. What we need is the old feisty Stella who'll fight all the way.'

'You're right. I left her making plans to increase her daily regimen. What worries me is her confidence is too fragile to stand setbacks.'

'Let's hope there aren't too many then,' Clara glanced at Nash. Whatever the effect had been on Stella, the development had obviously been good for him. He was looking better than she'd seen him for a long time.

'What did Mexican Pete have to say?'

'You mean when he wasn't busy telling me about the girls in Paris or trying to feel my tits? Tell me, are all pathologists perverts?'

'There's nothing perverted about wanting to touch you up. I guess you're right, though. All the pathologists I've ever dealt with have been weirdos. Goes with the job.'

'He reckons you're on commission from somebody called Sharon, whoever she is.'

Nash laughed. 'He's trying to impress you with his classical education. In Greek mythology, Charon was the ferryman who transported the dead across the River Styx to the underworld.'

'He's had a preliminary look at the bodies from Desolation Tarn. They're much more recent than the ones from Lamentation. He's also noticed something unusual. He wouldn't tell me what, but he says we've to prepare ourselves for some shocks. He's set the first post-mortem for 9 a.m. tomorrow. But he wants you there before that, say about 8.45.'

Nash fell silent. What would provide a shock? He considered the possibilities. He remembered Saunders's insistence they avoid looking at the corpses when they were at the lake.

Jackie and Viv greeted them with the news that they'd got the phone records. 'Jackie was brilliant,' Viv enthused. 'She told the woman she'd given the records to an impostor! That the search warrant he used was a forgery. When she named the villain as Tom Pratt I nearly gave the game away. She said he was the leader of a gang responsible for defrauding grieving relatives. Then she threatened to arrest her for obstruction if she didn't hand them over. By that time the poor woman was nearly peeing herself in her eagerness to help. She was so frightened she'd dropped a clanger that would cost the company millions.'

'Well done, the pair of you,' Nash said. 'I'm going to call Tom. I think it's time to consider issuing warrants, but I'm curious to know what Mexican Pete's found. I want a meeting tomorrow afternoon in Netherdale. Jackie, I want you and Viv there tomorrow morning. Start putting some names and addresses to those phone numbers. We'll come along when we've finished at the mortuary.

'Clara, as I've got to be there early, would you bring Zena. You can drop me first then go and pick her up. I don't suppose what Ramirez wants will take long.'

That night Nash almost forgot his medication again. He swallowed the tablets with the last of the whisky he'd treated himself to as a nightcap. His deep sleep was disturbed.

Again he was lying on a table. Again he was naked, bathed in a fierce, white light. The figures in gowns crowded round. Void of distinguishing features, their eyes empty, empty but hungry. Nash wanted to cry out. To ask why, but he was unable to speak. He couldn't move. Couldn't escape. His limbs failed to respond.

The silence was more terrifying than any sound he could imagine. They lifted their skeletal hands and placed masks over their faces. Only those dreadful eyeless sockets remained visible. He knew what was to come. They lifted their arms and Nash saw the glittering blades of the scythes. They paused until the agony of waiting was almost beyond endurance before they brought the blades plunging down towards him. Hacking, hacking, hacking, until his eyes ceased to reflect the light of the lamps above.

Nash was up early. Up, but hardly up and about. His limbs were stiff. His body ached as if he'd been used as a punch bag. He crept into the bathroom and took a long, hot shower in the hope that it might help. It didn't.

Drying himself was laborious and uncomfortable. He shuffled back to the bedroom. A few gentle exercises might reduce the aches and pains. They didn't. He tried arm and leg exercises from a standing position. He tried, and failed, to do some press ups, sit ups, side bends in the hope this routine might help. It didn't.

He dressed slowly, much as he imagined an extremely elderly person would do, then went through to the kitchen. His walk was suggestive of someone with a severe arthritic condition. He sat with a mug of coffee. He finished his drink and shuffled across the kitchen to put some toast on. After he'd eaten he thought a second mug of coffee might help. It didn't.

He studied his tablets and was wondering if one might help get him through the morning when he heard Clara pulling up. He shoved the container in his pocket. Clara watched as Nash locked the door and shuffled slowly across the pavement. His movement was a bit like Clara imagined a crab with a hangover might walk. She watched him lower himself gingerly into the passenger seat and reach with obvious discomfort for the seat belt. 'Are you okay, Mike?'

'Been better.'

'What's the problem?'

'Bad night,' he grunted, settling back in the seat with a sigh of relief.

'Bad dreams?'

'Bad nightmares. How did you guess?'

'You mean apart from the black circles under your eyes. The fact that you're walking like someone with a hangover or a bowel problem and you got into the car like a man who'd forgotten his Preparation H. Apart from that how did I guess? What was the nightmare this time?'

'I've had it before. It's horrendous. I wish I knew what it meant.' He recounted the details.

Clara speculated his pending visit to the hospital could be an explanation and watched with concern as he walked slowly across the car park to the mortuary.

Zena was waiting outside The Golden Bear. As they drove, Zena enquired about Nash. The Russian listened sombrely whilst Clara recounted his nightmare. 'It's strange this should keep happening to him. Does Mikhail tell you everything?'

'Pretty much, I guess, except about his love life,' Clara grinned. 'He leaves some of the more intimate details to my imagination, thank God.'

Zena studied Clara for a moment. 'Have you ever danced with Mikhail?'

Clara took her eyes off the road for a second, 'Danced with him?' She asked. 'That's a strange question. Why do you ask that?'

'Superintendent Pratt said Mikhail is a keen dancer. He said Nash's favourite dance is the horizontal tango. I don't understand.'

Zena was surprised by Clara's outburst of laughter. 'Have I said something funny or stupid?'

'Not really. Superintendent Pratt was being rude. He was referring to Mike's love life. Horizontal means lying down,' she explained.

'Ah, so perhaps that's not a good question to ask, but you and Mikhail are so close perhaps it's natural to think this way.'

Clara's cheeks were slightly redder than normal. 'I suppose it is natural, but the answer's no. I've never danced with Mike.'

'Perhaps this is something you wished for?'

Clara shook her head. 'You've seen our office. Far too small for dancing.'

Zena caught the allusion. 'I understand. When you're together working it's a bad thing?' Clara nodded. 'But perhaps forbidden fruit tastes the sweetest?'

'That's something we'll never know,' Clara said firmly. Perhaps a touch too firmly, Zena thought.

CHAPTER THIRTEEN

Nash had lost count of the number of post-mortems he'd attended. He shivered; it wasn't the cold, more a physical expression of his emotions. Morbidity and depression, anger and impotent rage. He could never rid himself of the dread that accompanied these visits. It didn't help that he'd barely slept. Mexican Pete looked unusually grave, 'I wanted a private word before the others arrive. During my preliminary examination I noticed several, shall we say unusual signs. I found them extremely disturbing for reasons which will become apparent. I'm speaking of all but two of these corpses. These other two are completely different.'

'In what way?'

'All but one were completely naked. That victim was fully clothed. She was shot in the back of the head like the bodies from Lamentation Tarn. One I'm not sure about, but the rest were killed in a totally different way. I think I should warn you what you're about to see is disturbing.' Ramirez paused and added, 'Very disturbing. I think it'd be better to show you rather than attempt to explain.'

Once Nash was gowned up, Ramirez asked, 'Are you ready for this?' He moved to the nearest of a line of mortuary tables and gently pulled back the sheet.

Nash felt vaguely sick as he looked at the pathetic remains. The bloated, unrecognizable features of what had once been a child. Ramirez pointed, directing Nash's attention to a small coloured object on the victim's clothing. He recognized the tiny row of small, rounded figures secured on a brooch pin. He'd been expecting this; it was the reason the search of the tarn had been organized. Nash felt an overwhelming surge of sadness for Sergei and Anna Svetlov. 'Matrioshka,' he murmured. 'We'll be able to confirm the identity of this child by DNA matching. I think it's safe to assume her to be Katerina Svetlova. Her parents are here in Netherdale. They came to search for their daughter.'

Ramirez eyed the detective sympathetically. 'This abuse of children is very distressing, but I'm afraid you must brace yourself for worse; much worse.' He turned to the next table and removed the sheet.

Nash looked down at the naked corpse; then recoiled in horror. 'Oh God,' he cried. 'Oh dear God.' He gagged as vomit threatened to choke him. Despite his exhaustion he turned and ran. He ran from the room, down the corridor, into the toilets.

It was five minutes later when he emerged white faced and shaking, having taken one of his tablets to try to calm down. Ramirez took his arm and led him to his office. 'Are you alright, my friend?'

'I'm not alright,' Nash said violently. 'How could I be alright after seeing that? I don't think I'll ever be alright again. What the hell was that?'

Ramirez's voice was drenched with sadness as he explained.

'Dear God,' Nash said. 'I don't believe it. I can't believe anyone could be so evil.'

'That's because you've a normal, law abiding mind. I'd ask you to think carefully before exposing the others to what you've just seen.'

'I don't need to think. I know already.' Nash gestured to the mortuary room, 'Nobody should see what's in there, unless there's absolutely no alternative.'

'I agree. However, as you know, I cannot conduct a post-mortem without a police officer present.'

'In that case I'll have to remain. At least I'm prepared. I can't expose anyone else to that.'

Ramirez nodded towards the doorway. 'I'll leave you to explain. They're arriving now.'

Nash braced himself for an argument as he walked towards them. 'There's been a change of plan,' he told them bluntly. 'Professor Ramirez asked me here early to show me the condition of the bodies. I don't want anyone else to see what's in there.'

He raised his hand to quell the protest. 'Believe me, what lies inside that room is too dreadful. I wouldn't want either of you saddled with that memory. You wouldn't want to live with the horror.'

Any doubts they had were pushed aside not only by Nash's words but by his face. He looked old, old and ill, his normally healthy tan replaced by a grey pallor. Both women accepted his ruling without question.

It was mid afternoon before the planned meeting took place, by which time those waiting at Netherdale Police Station were in a fever of impatience. After the post-mortems, Nash walked back to the station, badly in need of fresh air. He tried to rid himself of the horrors he'd witnessed, grateful that his medication had been in his jacket. He sat down wearily and gratefully accepted the mug of coffee offered by Jackie.

Pratt spoke first. 'Mike, do you want to start?'

He was about to begin when the sergeant came in. 'Sorry to interrupt, Tom. There's an urgent phone call for Mike.'

'Can you put it through here?'

'Yes, hello,' Nash greeted the caller. He listened, then asked, 'When was that?'

He waited again. 'Thanks, that's been a great help. It's exactly what I was expecting.' He listened for a moment longer.

'I don't know if it'll be necessary, but if it is I'll be sure to do that.'

He put the phone down and looked round. Clara was glad to see he appeared to have regained some composure. 'Sorry about that. Tom, I must apologize, because throughout this enquiry I've missed the most blatant piece of evidence imaginable. On the day the first bodies were recovered from the lake I was handed clues that should have enabled me to identify who was behind this. It's taken all this time before I realized their significance.'

'Don't beat yourself up, Mike,' Pratt interrupted. 'There wasn't just you investigating this case.'

'I blame myself because I allowed anger to control my thinking.'

He turned to Clara. 'Do you remember that first day at the tarn?' She nodded. 'Remember when we were at the bothy, can you recall what we were talking about? You were there too, Viv.' He glanced across at Pearce.

'Yes,' Pearce said after a moment's thought. 'You worked out that the girls must have been murdered. I was surprised until you explained why.'

'Can you remember what reasons I gave?'

'You said there was no way they could have got there on their own.'

'Exactly, and that was the first massive clue. That area isn't exactly well known. The road goes nowhere, it isn't on a tourist route and the tarns only appear on a few highly detailed maps. What we all failed to pick up on was there had to be someone involved who had local knowledge. So what else do we know about this mysterious person? Quite a bit actually. He has to be someone who's driven by money. Someone ruthlessly cold blooded enough to dispose of the girls when they ceased to be useful. And somebody with contacts in the places where the trafficking originated.'

'So who is this person?' Zena asked.

'Simon Wardle of Howlingales Farm. He's lived in Cauldmoor all his life and was in desperate need of money to rescue his parents' farm. By the time the farm was in trouble, he'd already got involved in the trafficking business.

In fact, I'd guess he'd been running it for years. Ever since he served in Bosnia. He isn't just involved; he's the head of it. If you think the organization is only involved in providing sex workers think again, they're into far more than that.'

There was stunned silence. Nash leaned forward and spoke to Clara. 'Remember what the secretary of the angling club told us? How successful Wardle had been in turning his parents' farm from the verge of bankruptcy into a thriving business? That doesn't happen these days. Not with the state of agriculture in Britain. Then there was that story about being up there alone one night and hearing a noise as if someone had thrown something heavy into the tarn. I bet he was laughing to himself because he would have been the one heaving the body into the water.'

'But you're not making a connection with Vatovec,' Zena objected. 'And where does Martin Hill come into it?'

'Commander Dacic is right,' Pratt agreed. 'It's an interesting theory, but it's all speculation. It isn't even strong enough to be called circumstantial evidence.'

'I realized that, so I did some checking. Wardle never intended to be a farmer. The man from the angling club told us that. He was an army officer. That phone call,' he nodded towards the receiver, 'was from a friend at the MOD. He checked Wardle's record for me. Wardle served in Bosnia during the conflict and was part of the IFOR peacekeeping force after it ended. He was also Martin Hill's commanding officer.'

There was a long silence whilst they took in what Nash had told them. 'So what now?' Pratt asked. 'Do we arrest Wardle and hope we catch Hill and Vatovec into the bargain?'

'We could do,' Nash agreed. 'But it's a bit more complicated than that. There's more to their operation. Far more and, I'm afraid, far worse. There are others involved we haven't even got close to yet.

'I thought this was all about human trafficking and that's bad enough. That was until this morning. I thought these monsters who kidnap children couldn't sink any lower.' His face was grim. 'But I was wrong. I underestimated just how evil they are. They've found more ways of making money from these poor youngsters than selling their bodies to paedophiles.

'One of the bodies was clothed and in a different condition to the others. I believe it to be the remains of Katya Svetlova.' He produced a sealed evidence bag from his pocket and laid it on the table. 'That was found pinned to the coat the victim was wearing.' They stared at the Matrioshka brooch. 'Why she was murdered is as yet unclear, although Ramirez believes she may have been carrying an infection. Further tests will confirm that.' The others looked at him in surprise. 'If Katya had AIDS it would render her useless for what they had planned.

'A couple of the bodies from Desolation Tarn had been put there only recently, so decomposition wasn't advanced. Ramirez managed to separate and identify a quantity of heroin from one of them. A quantity that was too large to have been present in a user. The only conclusion is that the girl was also being used as a drug mule. This suggests some of the victims may have died because the heroin containers burst.'

'Christ, it gets worse and bloody worse,' Pratt muttered.

Nash shot him a glance. 'You think that's bad; the other bodies were mutilated.'

Nash paused, took a drink of water. 'You remember I've said all along that the death of Dr Stevens was connected. Now I know how. Believe me I wish I didn't. I thought I'd seen the full extent of the depravity humans can sink to. But what these monsters did is almost beyond comprehension.'

He sighed, an expression of disgust and sadness. 'These bastards are greedy. They added a subtle refinement to their business. With the exception of Katya and the corpse with traces of drugs, the other bodies had been operated on. Professor Ramirez says great skill was used by whoever carried out the procedure. That means we're looking for a surgeon of exceptional ability. One capable of removing every internal organ. Heart and lungs, liver and kidneys.

'Anyone with sufficient money, anyone desperate enough for a replacement organ would pay enormous sums to find a "donor". The bodies from Desolation Tarn were only empty shells. These children had been ...' Nash paused and uttered the final word as if it was an obscenity, '... harvested.'

He allowed the full horror of what he had told them to sink in before adding. 'Ramirez told me that for these operations to be effective the victims had to be alive at the time. Stevens wanted to specialize in anaesthetics.'

In the ensuing silence Nash looked round. Clara and Jackie Fleming were crying unashamedly. Zena's eyes were lowered, bright with tears. The men were in little better shape.

'The sick bastards,' Clara broke into the long silence.

'How could anyone be so evil?' Pratt agreed.

Zena raised her head, 'I am grateful to you, Mikhail, for stopping me viewing the corpses.'

'Me too,' Clara added.

'We must move on,' Pratt said heavily. 'No matter how distressing we find it, we have a job to do. We must put our feelings to one side. God knows how. We've got to stop these evil bastards before there are any more victims. We've got to raid Wardle's farm as soon as we can; tonight if possible.' He glanced at the clock. 'I'll see if I can get the Chief Constable to obtain a warrant. Clara, you and Pearce go start the paperwork.' He reached for the phone.

The Chief Constable was predictably horrified. 'Leave it with me,' she told Pratt. 'I'll phone you back. Give me quarter of an hour, tops.'

In less than ten minutes the Chief rang back. 'You don't need to take the warrant for signature. I've arranged for someone to come to you. Have it ready in twenty minutes.'

'Mike, how do we handle the raid?' Pratt asked. 'We can't simply expect them to surrender meekly.'

'We need to talk to Clara about the layout. She's the only one who's been there. We also need specialist back-up, ARU as well as uniforms. I think we should also call for help from Catterick. My contact suggested it. He said they'd be happy to lend a hand in a case like this.'

'You're right,' Pratt agreed. 'You lead the force, Mike. You're younger and fitter than me. Who do you want with you?'

'I'd like Fleming and Mironova. I'll split the force and they can each take charge of a party. Clara's the one with local knowledge. She can work alongside me. I don't suppose Zena will want to keep away so we'll include her.'

'What about Viv?' Clara objected. 'He won't want to be left out?'

'I've another job for Viv.' He looked over at Pratt. 'Tom, will you give Pearce all the help he needs? We need information as fast as we can.'

He saw everyone was looking puzzled. 'We must find the place where the operations were conducted. That means trawling through Stevens's phone records to identify who he called and who called him. I guess he assisted in the operations to gain experience as well as for the money. Then perhaps he got cold feet, or a conscience. Either way, I think that's why he was killed.'

Pratt agreed, 'I'll give Pearce a hand. If we find anything I'll ask the Chief for another warrant and start putting a second raid together. In fact, I'll give her another call now.'

Pratt was reaching for the phone when the door crashed open and Armistead burst in. 'What the hell's going on?' He demanded, his voice barely below a shout.

Everyone was stunned into silence, as much by Armistead's appearance as the interruption.

'This is an operational meeting,' Pratt replied. 'One to which you weren't invited.'

'Why?' Armistead raged. 'Why wasn't I invited? I've a right to attend every meeting connected with this case. It's my case. One of my officers,' he spat the word out as he glared venomously at Fleming, 'is in this meeting. Why wasn't I consulted?'

'Correction,' Nash sounded almost bored. 'DCI Fleming is no longer one of "your" officers. Nor is this "your" case. It's an investigation being conducted by North Yorkshire Police in conjunction with the Russian authorities. Your involvement has always been in a consultative capacity. In theory, at least.'

Armistead fought to regain some measure of composure. 'Where's DS Thomas?' He demanded.

He directed the question at Fleming. She looked startled by the unexpected change of subject.

'Why, have you lost him?' The sarcasm in Nash's voice was undeniable. 'Could it be you've sent him off on some enquiry without bothering to inform anyone?'

'I don't answer to you.' Armistead's voice rose again. 'If I choose to send DS Thomas to check something I don't need your permission.'

'You're wrong there,' Tom Pratt retorted. 'You send your officers on to my patch, you consult with me first. Unless you choose to ignore the Chief Constable's orders.'

Nash continued, 'I suppose this is another example of you getting information and refusing to share it?' He paused fractionally. 'Just as you use any means at your disposal to get information from us. That's what really bugs me.'

He was staring hard at Armistead, putting strong emphasis on the word 'bugs'. Clara bit her lip, as she turned away her eyes met those of Fleming who was also trying not to laugh. Armistead picked up on the allusion. His bluster vanished and he seemed to shrink visibly. 'You haven't heard the end of this, any of you,' he said, his voice reduced to barely above a mutter. It sounded like an empty threat.

'Right, let's get on,' Pratt said almost before the door banged shut. 'When I've rung the Chief I'll put a call in for the ARU, then I'll speak to Catterick. I want everyone in body armour. Even then I won't be happy until those bastards are in the cells.'

Clara remembered the sound of baying dogs. 'Before you speak to the ARU, I think you should ask them to bring tranquillizer guns. Wardle has at least two Dobermans running loose.'

CHAPTER FOURTEEN

Besides Nash's team and Zena, the room contained eight ARU members, a similar number of uniforms, plus half a dozen soldiers clustered discreetly at the back.

Nash introduced everyone and began the briefing.

'It's likely we'll face high levels of security. These people are highly organized, with a huge investment to protect. Two at least are former soldiers used to battlefield conditions. They may resort to all sorts of tactics including trip wires and explosives. To emphasize the potential threat let me point out that the army personnel are from the Bomb Disposal Unit at Catterick.

'Logistically, we start with a huge problem. The farm is in an extremely isolated position to the north-east of Bishop's Cross. There's only one approach road unless you're prepared to walk six miles across farmland. I think we can count that out. Now I'm going to hand over to DS Mironova who'll give an outline of the set-up at the Farm. She's the only officer to have visited the premises. She spent twenty minutes in conversation with the owner several months ago. That's all we have to base our assessment on.'

Clara walked across and flicked back the cover sheet on the flip chart. Underneath was an outline sketch of the farm. Using a steel ruler as a pointer, she explained their target. 'This is the approach road. The only entrance is through this set of gates on the right, beyond the house itself. There's a boundary wall running along each perimeter. It's ten feet high and topped with razor wire. We can't get over that wall, but neither can the criminals escape that way.

'The entrance is protected by two sets of double five-barred steel gates, one at the roadside, the second at the entrance to the farmyard.' She pointed to the image again. 'Along the left the high wall continues to the top of the yard where it joins up with the end of one of the outbuildings. There are sheds all along the back of the yard. These are barns and possibly pig units. To the right of the house are open-fronted machinery sheds containing tractors and machinery. The whole yard is totally enclosed by buildings in the form of an oblong.'

Clara allowed a few minutes whilst everyone studied the diagram before opening the flip chart at the next sheet. 'This is a plan of the ground floor of the farmhouse. Unfortunately, this is all we know. The only door we're aware of opens from the farmyard and is controlled by an electronic entry system. This leads to a hallway stretching from front to back. There are two doors on each side of the hall plus a flight of stairs. This room here,' she pointed to the diagram for emphasis, 'is what we need to concentrate on. That's Wardle's office. It contains some sophisticated computer equipment. There's a bank of filing cabinets on the far wall. The files in those cabinets plus the computer hard drive could yield vital evidence about the gang's activities. We need them intact.'

Nash took over. 'We must anticipate them being forewarned. I want silent approach and when we reach the farm I want everyone parked behind the CID car under cover of the outer wall. I think they'll resist, if only to give themselves chance to escape. I want two men to remain at the rear in case they get past us. If so, I want stingers laid across the road to disable their vehicles.

'We'll split our force into two sections. I'll lead the advance party and a second team will be commanded by DCI Fleming. My section will go in with officers from the ARU and bomb disposal. Once we've gained access and secured the farmyard, our next objective will be the house.

'The second team will follow closely. When they reach the yard they'll concentrate on the barns and outbuildings. Danger could come from any direction. We don't know exactly what strength the opposition can muster.

'We know three of the ringleaders, Wardle, Hill and a Serb named Vatovec.' As he spoke he pointed to photographs from the men's service records along with those Zena had supplied. 'All three are ruthless killers. Don't expect them to be alone. With the money at their disposal they're sure to have hired help. There's one additional problem. That's the lack of communication with our base. This place is so remote neither police radios nor mobile phones will be any use.'

'Superintendent Nash,' the interruption came from the leader of the Bomb Disposal Unit. 'We thought that might be a problem so we've brought half a dozen satellite transceivers.'

'Will they work out there?'

The officer smiled dourly. 'If they don't, the Ministry of Defence will have something to say to the manufacturers.'

'Thanks,' Nash turned to Pratt. 'We should have the police helicopter airborne. When we can communicate with the pilot we can call it in when we're ready. Can you arrange it? And can you have at least one ambulance with a paramedic team on standby at Bishop's Cross plus the air ambulance as back-up.'

Pratt nodded as he moved centre stage. 'Detective Superintendent Nash has already emphasized how dangerous these men are. Let me reinforce that by explaining why we need them behind bars. And why we need the evidence that will ensure they receive fitting sentences.

'Not far from here there's a young Moldavian girl in a serious condition, having had two rifle bullets removed. She'll survive, but nine others that we know of didn't. They're the ones whose bodies were recovered from the tarns. In case you think the girl who survived is the lucky one, let me tell you about her ordeal.'

Pratt related Milla's story and Nash saw the growing revulsion on the faces of the listeners. 'In addition to providing children for the gratification of paedophiles, this gang is involved in a major drug importing operation. Think of the percentage of crime we deal with that's drugs related. Think of people you know whose lives have been ruined by drugs. This raid gives us the chance to smash this racket.

'If I haven't convinced you yet, let me explain the most obscene aspect of their activities. Before these children were dumped in the tarn every saleable part of their bodies was removed and sold for transplant.'

Pratt had only just finished when Nash's mobile rang. 'Ramirez,' the caller identified himself.

'Yes, Professor, what can I do for you?'

'I've been catching up on paperwork. Whilst I was in Paris a report came back from the laboratory. Do you remember the foetal bone I found from skeleton B?'

'Only too well.'

'They've extracted a DNA sample. That means they'll soon be able to give us the genetic fingerprint of the foetus. If we have that we'll be able to match it against DNA from the father.'

'Thanks Professor, it might come in useful at some stage.'

Nash watched the men climb into the vans with admiration and anxiety. They were just ordinary coppers, but not one of them had shown the slightest hesitation about tackling the job. Such had been the power of Pratt's remarks.

He wished them good luck before he climbed into the CID car. Clara was driving, Fleming and the leader of the ARU were in the back. The rest of the ARU members were in the vans along with the uniforms. The Bomb Disposal Unit would travel in their vehicles which carried their specialist equipment.

'My original plan to go for stealth might be impractical.' Nash stated. 'We might have more success the opposite way. If we make a hell of a din it might mislead them into thinking there are more of us. That could work to our advantage.'

The journey was conducted in silence, all four officers busy with their own thoughts. As they drew nearer, the tension increased markedly. 'We're there, Mike,' Clara said at last. She let the car coast to a stop. Nash got out and looked back. He could see the headlights of the rest of the raiding party. Their beams sweeping left and right as they negotiated the twisting country lane. He listened. Apart from the hum of engines the only sound was the distant bleating of sheep. The silence convinced Nash he'd been right. 'They don't know we're here,' he thought. What they needed was sound. The more noise they could make the better.

Nash spoke to Fleming and the leader of the ARU. 'I want both teams lined up; you follow us closely Jackie. I want it done with as much noise as possible. Tell the men to talk amongst themselves. Even if they've nothing meaningful to say, to say it loudly! When you get to the farmyard I still want plenty of noise. Before we move, get the chopper here and have it flood the farmyard with light. That should also make plenty of noise.' He was about to continue when he saw the army Commander approaching at speed.

'You mentioned security. So where are the cameras? Maybe they don't need them. I think my men should take a look at those gates.'

'Go for it. As soon as you're clear I want as much noise as possible. We'll come with you.' He signalled to the ARU officer. 'Bring two men.'

Nash hit trouble as soon as they inspected the first set of gates. The Bomb Disposal officer had one of his men check them. In the distance he heard the throbbing beat of the helicopter's engine. The army commander signified there were no explosives fitted. One of the Armed Response men went to unlatch the gates. As his hand touched the metal there was a vivid blue flash that lit up the darkness. His scream was all Nash could have hoped for by way of noise. Another officer dragged him towards the safety of the wall.

'Damn. Electrified, probably a buried wire. Sergeant, neutralize this. Everyone stand back.'

Seconds later there was an even brighter flash accompanied by a deafening explosion. When the dust cleared what remained of the double gates was hanging from the posts. 'What the hell was that?' Nash asked.

'Hand grenade. You said you wanted noise.'

They stood at the second gates; one of the team carried what looked like an oversized mobile phone. 'Heat sensor, it identifies explosive compounds. Ideal for use in temperatures as cold as this. Explosives always give off heat.'

He pointed to the left-hand side of the gates. 'Device here, Sir.'

'Now we've to find the trigger and deactivate the device.'

'We don't have time. They'll know we're here. Can we detonate it from a safe distance?'

'We can,' the officer conceded. 'Get behind the wall. There could be a bit of shrapnel flying.'

There was a vivid orange and white flash, followed instantly by a thunderous explosion. 'You can come out now,' the bomb disposal officer called. 'It was a trip wire. Sorry it took a moment but we were throwing sticks to get it to explode and our first four attempts failed.'

The sound of the helicopter engine grew louder. It appeared from the shadow of the hillside, navigation lights glowing red and green. The vans emptied their load of chattering, door slamming men, each determined to sound like half a dozen.

'How's the man who got the shock?' The army commander asked.

'Okay, I think. We've called for the ambulance.'

The helicopter pilot switched on his searchlight, the beam carving an arc that swept across the ground, illuminating the raiders before settling on the farmyard.

'Come on. Move.' Nash signalled everyone forward. 'Jackie. Maintain contact with the pilot.'

What remained of the gates was a twisted mass of metal, tangled like a skein of wool after five minutes alone with a kitten. Where the gates had met there was a deep crater. 'Nasty!' The army officer observed. He was interrupted by the sound of barking.

'Guard dogs!' Nash warned.

Two members of the ARU ran forward, dart guns at the ready. The helicopter hovered overhead, its searchlight centred on the entrance. A sudden blur of movement across the beam was followed by the sound of gunfire. One of the attack dogs bark turned into a yelp of pain and they saw the muscular liver and black shape topple over on its side.

The other dog continued towards them, not deflected by the loss of its comrade. Another shot. The second dog stopped abruptly, stiffened and began to sway slightly before it too collapsed.

The teams inched their way into the yard, circling the crater and giving the two Dobermans an even wider berth. Nash was about to order his team forward when there was a sudden burst of gunfire. Men dived for cover in all directions, all but one of the uniformed officers. They watched in shock as he walked forward a couple of paces, before collapsing. Shock turned to horror as they saw the top of his head had been blown away.

'Air ambulance.' Nash shouted to Fleming as several more rounds whistled overhead.

Clara spotted the flash and shouted. 'First shed, window to the right of the door!'

Four ARU officers stepped forward. There was an instant cacophony of sound as shot after shot echoed and mingled. Into the silence that followed the last round, the shed door opened and a man fell forward into the open, an

Armalite rifle trailing uselessly behind. Blood was coming from at least four wounds about his chest and stomach.

'Door enforcer.' Nash yelled. He signalled Jackie towards the sheds. Led by a quartet of armed officers, she checked out the building. The only other occupants were a dozen cattle that had survived unscathed. Two uniformed men stepped forward carrying the heavy steel bolt. They stopped in front of the farmhouse. 'Go for it!'

They took a firm grip of the ram and began to swing it backward and forward. They took a step forward in unison. As they did, there was another blinding flash accompanied by the devastating sound of a loud explosion. The sound echoed eerily as if in a steel tube. Nash swallowed hard to equalize the pressure in his ears and as the dust cleared he stared in horror at the scene of carnage.

The blast had blown a huge crater in the concrete yard. It had torn the two officers' bodies into tattered and bloodstained parodies before tossing them aside like discarded rag dolls. What little remained of the door hung drunkenly from the one hinge. 'Oh shit!' Nash exclaimed. His hearing so distorted he barely recognized the sound of his own voice. 'What the hell was that?'

'Land mine,' the commander of the bomb squad replied tersely. 'Pressure pad activated. Those blokes had no chance. They were dead the moment they stepped on it. You were right when you said these bastards are evil.'

There was a crackle on the radios Clara and the bomb squad chief were carrying, followed by a second, then a third, then a rapid succession. They waited, expecting someone to speak but there was no other sound than the repeated static. This stopped and almost immediately they heard the voice of the helicopter pilot, loud and clear with no interference. 'Two vehicles leaving the rear of the shed to the south of the yard. They're headed across country, quad bikes I think. Do you want me to track them?'

Nash realized there was little more the helicopter could do for them. 'Tell him yes, and on no account lose them.'

Clara relayed the message. 'You take over out here. I want Jackie and her team to go through the rest of the outbuildings. I'm going to take four men and go inside. Get on to Tom. Tell him "officers down" and we need SOCO.'

'Who do you want with you?'

'A couple of armed men,' Nash looked at the army officer. 'And a couple of your chaps.'

'I'll come myself.'

They stepped carefully past the rubble then moved slowly down the hallway where thankfully the lights were still on. The commander of the bomb squad and an armed officer led the way warily across the stone flags. Another policeman shoulder to shoulder with another soldier followed. Nash brought up the rear. They reached the door leading to the office. The door and frame was checked carefully before he was satisfied there was no device rigged to it. He eased the handle down, standing to one side as he gently pushed it open. The room was brightly lit. It was also empty. Nash heaved a sigh of relief then froze as the bomb squad leader pointed to the far side.

In the middle of the desk on the blotting pad was a squat, ugly looking black box measuring some six inches by three. On the top of the box were a red light, a rocker switch and a stubby aerial. The light glowed evilly. Coming from one end of the box was a slender two core cable that ran across the desk before disappearing alongside the computer.

'What is it?'

'Radio-controlled detonator,' the officer replied. His tone tense with the anxiety they all shared. He circled the desk carefully. When he was satisfied there were no secondary devices he looked below the computer console where the server was positioned. He gave a long, low whistle of surprise. After a detailed inspection he straightened, reached across and flicked the rocker switch.

Nash saw what the officer was about to do, he closed his eyes, opening them again to see the red light fade. He breathed a gusty, noisy sigh of relief, to find it being echoed by several others.

'If that bloody thing had gone off, it'd have taken the house and us with it. There's a shed-load of explosives under here, all attached to that detonator. Do you know the ironic bit? The men who planted this device were in the army, right?'

Nash nodded. 'They chose the standard service frequency. Their remote trigger sent its signal alright, but it was intercepted on our radios. Remember the crackling sound we heard outside?' Nash nodded. 'That was them trying to blow us up. Our receivers jammed the signal, weakened it. This little aerial failed to pick it up. I bet they're really pissed off.'

'We were bloody lucky.'

'You need all the luck you can get in our job.'

'Can you get your men to make sure they haven't left any other nasty little surprises?'

The inspection took almost twenty minutes, 'It seems this was their last throw,' the commander told him. 'They obviously thought it would be enough. It would have been, too,' he added thoughtfully, 'but for pure chance. Anyway, the rest of the building's clear.'

Nash waved to Clara to join him, 'Any news from the chopper?'

'They're still keeping tabs on the bikes. They said the riders are making slow progress owing to the terrain. The pilot wanted to know if he should put the searchlight on them. I told him no. I thought you'd want to know where they're headed first before we try to stop them.'

'Dead right.'

They heard gunshots outside and dashed from the building. A couple of the armed officers pointed their weapons towards the end building. Fleming stepped out of the open door. She was holding a man who was wriggling and squirming in a desperately futile attempt to escape the handcuffs on his wrist.

The nearest officer stepped forward and took the prisoner. Nash looked at the man. 'What happened?'

'He was hiding in there with another bloke. The pigs were protesting at the company. Those pigs have good taste. One bloke escaped with Zena and a posse of armed officers in pursuit. This one was about to run but I grabbed him. The gunfire you heard was our men firing warning shots, that's all.'

'Will you administer the caution?' Nash peered at the captive closely. 'Charge him under the name of Janko Vatovec; conspiracy to murder. Come on, Clara, let's go see if Zena's safe.'

Zena and a small group of armed officers were coming through the rear door of the pig unit. 'What happened to the other man?' Nash called out. 'Don't tell me he got away?'

Zena grinned. 'No, he's in deep shit.'

Nash looked puzzled. One of the officers explained. 'He was so anxious to escape he didn't watch where he was going. The Commander here gave him a helping hand, pushed him into a slurry pit.'

'What happened?'

'He drowned,' Zena smiled contentedly. 'Nobody would go to his rescue.'

'You didn't ask us,' the officer objected.

'Would you have done it?'

'Probably not.'

Zena shrugged.

They regrouped in the farmhouse, accompanied by the dejected looking Vatovec. Nash left a detail guarding the approaches to the farm, although he anticipated little further trouble. 'Get hold of Tom,' he instructed Clara. 'Tell him what's gone on and that we believe Wardle and Hill have escaped. The chopper's following them but we're going to need more back-up when we know where they're headed.'

Clara told Pratt the situation. She listened, then said, 'Hang on, I'll get Mike.' She held the receiver out. 'Tom wants a word urgently. He knows where they're going and you need to know right now.'

'Tom, what have you got?'

'We've checked Stevens's phone records. We found some calls to Howlingales Farm but there are a lot of calls to a bloke named Butler, Clive Butler. Name mean anything?'

'No, Tom.'

'It didn't to us until we checked. We thought he was one of Stevens's colleagues. Then we checked again. He runs a private hospital and clinic here in Netherdale. The CB Clinic. You know it, I believe?'

Nash didn't respond. A cold shiver of fear ran through him. Stella! He realized Pratt was speaking. 'Mike, Mike, you there?'

'Sorry, Tom. Yes I know the clinic.'

'Pearce phoned Ramirez who told us Butler's ex-military. I got the Chief to pull some strings with the MOD. They checked Butler's file. He served in Bosnia at the same time as Wardle and Hill.' Pratt continued, 'Ramirez also told Viv that Butler's very highly regarded. One of the best in his field.' Nash heard his boss take a deep breath. 'His speciality is organ transplant.'

Nash pictured Stella wheelchair-bound, defenceless. If they knew she was connected to him ... the thought was unbearable. Nash was certain they would know. He'd made no attempt to disguise his identity when he'd visited. Nash's brain cleared. The need to detain Wardle and Hill became insignificant, meaningless almost. All that mattered to him now was protecting Stella.

'We must cordon off that hospital, we must protect the patients. Stella's in there, Tom.'

'I know, Mike,' Nash could hear the sympathy in Pratt's voice. 'Cordoning off the place isn't going to be easy. We've no more uniformed men, there's a match on tonight.'

'Then get me another ARU from York. Try and get someone to the hospital. We're on our way.'

185

He almost flung the phone at Clara. 'Jackie, we know where they're going. Get that chopper away from the bikes and over to the CB Clinic. It's more use to us there. I'm leaving you in charge. Liaise with SOCO when they get here. Clara, with me, NOW! And you two,' he snapped at two constables coming in through the door, 'get as many men as can be spared after us in the van.' He hurried towards the door. 'And send a bunch of the ARU men as well,' he flung over his shoulder.

CHAPTER FIFTEEN

Before they reached Bishop's Cross Nash set the beacons flashing. The sirens sounded their warning, although for the first part of the journey all they did was excite mild curiosity from sheep grazing in the fields.

Clara hardly dared take her eyes off the road. She glanced sideways at Nash. His face was tense, more than concentration would merit. 'Talk to me, Mike,' she urged him. 'Tell me!'

Nash explained in clipped snatches. Clara noticed the speedometer. They'd taken the last bend in excess of 80 mph, a measure of Nash's urgency, or was it panic?

Clara's satellite radio crackled and she heard Pratt's voice. 'Whereabouts are you?'

'Coming up to Helmsdale, any news?'

She glanced at Nash, if anything his anxiety had heightened. 'The chopper lost Wardle and Hill. The pilot had to swing wide of Helmsdale to avoid pylons. If they're heading for the hospital they'll have to change vehicles but we don't know what to. If they've reached Netherdale already, we've a problem. The football match ended half an hour ago. The opposition brought a big contingent of supporters and there's a huge crowd in the streets. If they get amongst that lot we'll never find them.'

'I'll let Mike know.'

'What is it,' Nash's voice was sharp.

Clara explained.

'Shit! They're heading for the clinic. I know they are,' he sent the car surging forward with even greater urgency.

'It won't help Stella if we kill ourselves.' Clara said miserably.

He eased back a fraction. 'Sorry,' he muttered. 'I'm just petrified they know my connection to Stella. How vulnerable do you think she is, stuck in a wheelchair?'

'Is that it?' Clara asked, knowing Mike, knowing there was more.

'No,' he admitted. 'I don't think Wardle and Hill will leave anybody behind who could give evidence. We've seen how ruthless they are. I think they'll destroy everything in their way. They'll take hostages if necessary then kill them when they cease to be useful.'

Stella had been through a tiring day. Her neurologist had insisted she attend an appointment at York.

She'd been taken by ambulance and kept waiting over an hour and a half before she was seen. His examination was thorough, involving a lot of physical manipulation. When it was over, Stella felt mauled and weary.

She returned to the clinic too late for lunch and too tired to eat in her room. She wasn't too late, however, to avoid the physiotherapy session. Her therapist had happily agreed to increase the exercise programme. Stella explained that she'd been put through the mill by the neurologist and pleaded for a twenty-four-hour stay of execution. She might as well have saved her breath for the exercises.

When she reached the sanctuary of her own room Stella used the last dregs of energy to haul herself on to her bed with the intention of a long, recuperative nap, but sleep was denied her by the aches and pains her exertions had brought about. Had the pains been in her legs they would have been welcome.

She felt she'd only been asleep a few minutes when a nurse came in with her medication. The sleeping tablet undoubtedly helped. The sleep was so deep she didn't hear the sound for a long time. As she came round a little she was aware of a faint noise. It was a bell being rung incessantly. It increased in volume, she thought, unaware that it was she who was regaining consciousness.

The sound came from the clinic's alarm system. She recalled it from the numerous occasions she'd heard them testing it.

'Why were they testing the alarm at so late an hour? Or wasn't it a test?' Stella pulled herself to a sitting position. She was glad she'd been too tired to undress. She heard her door open and looked across to see a figure in the doorway.

She was unable to see clearly. The room was in darkness and the corridor lights also appeared to be out. She fumbled for the switch on her console and saw the corridor lights flicker into life, dimmer than usual. 'Who's there? What's happening? Why is the alarm sounding?'

Stella was still groping for the switch when the main light came on. This too, wasn't as bright as usual. She blinked momentarily before she recognized the man. 'Mr Butler,' she said. Was it Mister or Doctor for a surgeon? She wasn't sure and it wasn't important. 'What's happening? Why are the alarms ringing?'

'We have to leave,' he answered obliquely. 'Get into your wheelchair.'

Stella shuffled across the bed. He made no move to help. Stella was about to repeat her question when he grabbed the handles of the chair, pushed her to the door and into the corridor.

There was a smell of smoke. The building was on fire. Butler increased the pace as they rushed past the lifts. They wouldn't be working, Stella realized. Lifts were always shut off when there was a fire. Then the horror of her situation struck her. How would she be able to get out? Butler would have to manhandle her downstairs. There was no one else around. Was she the last? Had everyone else been evacuated?

Butler pushed her beyond the stairwell and through the double doors. 'Where are we going?'

He didn't answer. At the end of the corridor he slewed her chair into a small office and beyond into a larger room. Two men were standing at the far side of a large desk. One was looking towards her. The other was staring out of the window. Both were armed with small machine guns; small but very efficient looking. Her panic was instant, immediate and total.

'Ah, Miss Pearson. Just the person we need. I understand you're a close friend of the policeman, Nash. Is that correct?'

'What's happening?' She gasped.

'This is a hostage situation,' the man's tone was calm, level, cold even. 'You being the hostage. Please don't scream or do anything dramatic. It would serve no purpose but to exercise your lungs and annoy me. You don't want to do that. Believe me.' He repeated, 'You definitely don't want to annoy me.

'Let me explain. We've evacuated everyone else from this floor. The fires you can smell will soon die out. They were set to give us time to negotiate our escape in safety. Safety for us, that is. You are in considerable danger.'

'Why me? Why pick on me?'

'It isn't for your undoubted attraction. More your friendship with Nash. He's become a thorn in our side. We need a bargaining tool, and that's you. Please don't think that makes you invulnerable. All you're here for is to make our escape easier. We will get away, with or without you. I don't mind which. Far from being indispensable, you're highly expendable.'

'Can we avoid the football traffic?' Nash asked. 'Is there a back way through town?'

'I don't think so. I'll check with Tom; he knows Netherdale better than us.'

'Make it sharp. We'll be hitting the ring road soon. When you've spoken to Tom you'd better check our men are behind us. Damn!'

'What's matter?'

'I should have asked Jackie to send some of the Bomb Squad.'

Clara got busy on the radio. 'Tom says there's no easy way to the clinic. He's diverting a patrol car to meet us at the junction. They'll have instructions to clear a way for us.

'Jackie says the Bomb Squad is only five minutes behind. They're in convoy with the ARU.'

'Good.' Nash slackened his foot off the accelerator. 'If we've to wait for the others, there's no point pushing it. If Wardle and Hill have come this way, they'll meet the same problems. The only difference is they won't have anyone to clear a path for them.'

Was Nash trying to convince her or himself?

The patrol car had just negotiated the roundabout and was manoeuvring into position as they approached. The red and blue beacon was flashing. The ring road was solid with traffic.

Nash pulled in behind and turned off the beacon. Clara noticed his fingers drumming on the steering wheel, saw the frown on his normally cheerful face. 'Relax, Mike. We can't do anything until the others get here.'

Time dragged before they pulled in. Nash flicked his siren to signal the patrol car, and the convoy moved forward.

Traffic was blocked solid in both directions. Drivers weren't ignoring the beacons and sirens. They simply had nowhere to go to. It was an agonizing five minutes before they were able to clear the junction.

With less than three miles before they reached the clinic Clara's radio crackled into life. She flicked the switch into the open channel position. Pratt's voice echoed eerily. 'We've just got to the clinic but we can't access it. Looks as if they've got here first.'

'Why can't you get in?'

'They've disabled the electrics. The building's gone on to stand by power. All the doors are electronic and the generator isn't feeding enough power for them to open. The fire doors only open outwards. We're waiting for the fire service. If they're not here in a couple of minutes we're going to have to force our way in.'

'Why the fire service?'

Pratt took a deep breath. 'The building's on fire.'

'What?'

'There are four different fires, two on the ground floor and two on the first. Small, localized blazes. We'd go in now but there's only four of us and we're not armed.'

'SIDs,' they heard another voice.

'What's that?' Nash thought they'd intercepted a stray transmission.

'Small incendiary devices.' Nash recognized the voice as that of the Bomb Disposal team leader. 'Used as a delaying tactic or to create confusion and panic. They'll burn themselves out unless they've been placed near combustible material. They can also be used to distract attention from more lethal devices.'

The calm manner of the army officer soothed Nash's jangled nerves. But only slightly.

'Care to give us an up-date, Martin?' He turned back to Stella briefly. 'That's what our American friends call a "sit. rep.". Succinct, don't you agree?' He might have been chatting to the newsagent as he collected his morning paper.

'Fire engines are just arriving,' the other man spoke for the first time. 'They're taking their time unloading. Now there's a patrol car, a plain car, two blue vans and two camouflaged Land Rovers pulling up. Look like army Land Rovers.'

'That's got to be Nash back from the farm with the armed unit we heard. The other will be a BD unit from Catterick. Clever of Nash to think of them. That'll be why the device under the computer didn't go off, I bet.'

'How long before you contact Nash?'

'Let them stew. The longer they're kept waiting, the more cooperative they'll be. We'll use Nash and Miss Pearson as our exit pass and head for our destination as planned. Just that Martin, nothing complicated. Remember your training. "Simple works, complicated fails". When we're safe we can dispose of our excess baggage.'

Stella was looking at the man called Simon as he spoke. There was no extra inflexion in his voice, nothing to indicate the cold-blooded ruthlessness of what he was proposing. She saw his gaze slide past her to Butler and realized she, Nash and the surgeon were all going to be killed the moment their usefulness ceased.

Nash was out of the car before it stopped. He weaved his way through the emergency vehicles. The helicopter was overhead, its searchlight bathing the clinic in bright light. This was in marked contrast to the interior of the building. The clinic must still be operating on generator power. There was little sign of the fires, proof that the Bomb Disposal officer's assessment was accurate.

'Tom,' he shouted.

Pratt looked round. 'Thank God you're here. They've moved everyone to the ground floor but nobody's come out.'

'They don't need the electronic doors. Why don't they push the bars on the emergency exits?'

'It isn't that simple. I rang to tell them to evacuate. Got through to some bloke who identified himself as Head of Security. He told me they'd orders to keep everyone inside. I told him I was giving the order to evacuate.'

'And?'

'He said "I don't take orders from you", then hung up. I couldn't get through again.'

'They must be Wardle's men. No wonder we didn't meet more opposition at the farm. They were all here, waiting for their boss.'

'Not boss, more like Commanding Officer.' The interruption came from the Bomb Squad leader.

'What do you mean?'

'Wardle would want men he could trust. Men who wouldn't ask questions, wouldn't talk. Who better than the troops he'd commanded? He wouldn't need to train them. He'd already done that.'

'You seem to know a lot about the way Wardle operates.'

The officer shrugged. 'Standard military thinking. Wardle will be after hostages. Not many, that would create logistics problems. Besides which there's the question of disposing of them later. The question is who? I guess he's already made that decision, but you'll have to wait until he contacts you.'

'I already know. Have you any suggestions as to what we can do in the meantime?'

'You have to wait to see what he demands. Whilst you're waiting, someone ought to recce the building. See if there are any vulnerable entry points. Wardle might be good but I doubt he'll have thought of everything. Besides, I don't think he'll have the manpower to cover everywhere, not given the size and design of the building. Want me to take a look? I've got a bit of experience in this sort of situation.'

'I'll bet you have. And how did I know you were about to make that offer?'

The army officer smiled slightly. 'I'll take Sergeant Mironova with me shall I?'

'Do you want some armed officers with you?' Nash asked with deceptive innocence.

'I don't think that'll be necessary.' The officer's right hand went towards his belt in a reflex action.

'Care for a walk?' He asked Clara.

Nash watched them go, his suspicions about the officer intensified.

'We can't be sure Wardle knows about you and Stella.' Pratt attempted to comfort him.

'We must assume he does. With all those guards hanging around, taking note of every visitor, how wouldn't he get to know something of such value? I think our Bomb Squad man was right. I don't suppose we'll have to wait long to find out.'

'We should be thinking about how to react,' Pratt looked round.

'We should, but we've no specialist trained in hostage negotiation.'

'That's the trouble. We don't carry the manpower. Do you want me to handle it?'

'Wardle will probably insist on talking to me. How else is he going to get his threat across effectively?' Nash's impatience was beginning to show.

He reached into his jacket pocket and discreetly tried to take a tablet. Tom looked at him questioningly. 'Headache,' he said as he put the bottle away.

He tried to analyse what little they knew. Wardle was ruthless, without scruples. Interested only in money and preserving his skin. What would the demand be? Safe conduct for himself and Hill, but to where? Not a commercial airport. Wardle would steer clear of anywhere with an official presence. Ferry ports would also be out of the question, so where?

They'd need to be out of the country as fast as they could. The rest of the equation made him sick with apprehension. Wardle must have a venue lined up, with a plane and a pilot waiting. A light aircraft that could get them to the continent, but how was he hoping to escape the attentions of RAF radar or air traffic control?

Surely he'd have worked out that the police would alert forces wherever they tried to land. And what of the hostages, Stella and any others Wardle was planning to take?

Nash was gripped by a cold certainty. Wherever they'd chosen to escape to, those hostages would be dead long before Wardle reached his destination.

'We've spotted where they're holed up,' the Bomb Squad leader had returned with Clara. 'First floor, corner room.'

'I think I saw Hill,' Clara added. 'I couldn't be certain, the light wasn't very strong and the only photo I've seen is years out of date. But it looked like him. He was standing at the window, watching.'

'There were others in the room too,' the officer added. 'We saw at least two more moving about, although not clearly enough to recognize them.'

'Any way of getting into the building without them knowing?'

'There's no way without making a noise. Have you heard from them yet?'

'Not a word.'

'That's a classic move, designed to get you fidgety.'

'It's working,' Nash said with feeling.

'You mustn't let it. You need a game plan. I said there's no way of getting in without making a noise, but we might fool them, so they won't know where we're coming from. In the confusion, we could get lucky.'

'Go on, I'm listening.'

Wardle spoke on his mobile, 'Is everything ready? Good. We'll be there in a couple of hours. I'll phone you when we're en route.'

'Anything happening out there, Martin?'

'Nothing much, couple of vans dropping off more coppers, that's all. They're all standing around as if they're waiting for a bus, just as you predicted.'

'That means Nash knows what's going on. He's guessed we're holding Miss Pearson,' he looked across at Stella. 'No fool, that boyfriend of yours. Pity he chose the police; he'd have made a good officer. Too late now, for him and for you. But as the saying goes, "where there's life, there's hope", but unfortunately for both of you, not much of either.'

'When are you going to phone?' Martin asked.

Wardle glanced at his watch. 'Let them stew. They'll be all the keener to do as we ask.'

'Won't that give them time to bring in reinforcements?'

'You've got them wrong. They're country coppers. They don't think like trained servicemen. They won't try anything rash. Especially if we're holding Miss Pearson and one of their senior officers. They'll be anxious to baby sit us. They'll stay clear of any action that might pose a threat to hostages.'

'Just as well they don't know what you have in mind.'

'That's a different story,' Wardle smiled mirthlessly.

Stella looked at Butler. He hadn't spoken since he'd pushed her into the office. He was cowering in a chair near the door. He'd moved only once, to collect a cup of water from the dispenser. Now he sat with his eyes downcast. Few people would recognize the eminent surgeon. Stella was shocked by the man's rapid decline. In a short time, he'd gone from an immaculately groomed professional to a wreck. His fingers shook and twitched uncontrollably, at odds with his reputation as a precise and skilled surgeon. Butler was unravelling before her eyes. Why, she wondered? She was scared enough, terrified but in control. What was the extra element of fear that had reduced Butler to such a state?

'It'll only work if everyone does as they're ordered and the timing's precise. The kingpin is you. Do you understand?' The army officer had finished outlining his ideas.

'What do you think, Tom?'

Pratt scratched his chin, 'I don't know, Mike. It's a hell of a risk.'

'I know, but I don't think we've any alternative.'

'It depends on what Wardle and Hill have in mind.'

'I reckon we've got to run with it.'

'It's all down to "is the risk justified". I can't answer that for you, Mike. It's you who'll be in danger; you and Stella.'

'Right,' Nash made his mind up. 'Get everyone together and explain the plan. All we can do then is wait for the call.'

The Bomb Squad officer put his hand on Nash's shoulder and looked into his eyes. 'The one thing that will guarantee failure is lack of confidence. You need courage to succeed.'

It was a further twenty minutes before the call came, patched through from the control room to Pratt's mobile. He held the phone out. 'It's Wardle.'

Nash looked round at the officers and soldiers all waiting expectantly. He nodded and they began to disperse.

'Mike Nash,' he said into the phone.

'You know who this is?'

'Yes, Wardle, I know.'

'I'm sure you must have worked out that I'm holding the delectable Miss Pearson and the somewhat less delectable Mr Butler hostage?'

'I worked that out a long time ago, Wardle, but please don't talk to me as if I'm an idiot. Miss Pearson may be a hostage but Butler certainly isn't. I realize you spend a lot of time with cattle but would you cut the bullshit and get to the point.'

Nash's refusal to be cowed obviously irritated Wardle. 'So you know about Butler. That's bad news for him. What else do you know? Not that it matters. We want a safe passage and you're going to provide it.'

'I'm still waiting.'

'Waiting for what?' He could hear Wardle's voice sharpen with annoyance, exactly what Nash wanted.

'Waiting for you to tell me something I don't already know. So why not cut to the next bit? Tell me which door you want me to come in by?'

'You've a high opinion of your own intelligence, haven't you?' Wardle snapped. 'You don't come in via a door at all. You walk to the window directly to the right of the front entrance. You do that in five minutes. You do it alone and unarmed. You knock on the window, climb inside and stay there. When we're sure you're alone, we will unlock the inner door. You'll be met and escorted upstairs. There you can enjoy an emotional reunion with Miss Pearson. And there you'll start making arrangements for our safe departure. Got all that?'

'Yes,' the line disconnected abruptly. Nash handed the phone to Pratt. 'Five minutes, the window to the right of the front entrance.'

'Good luck, Mike, and for God's sake be careful.'

When the allotted time had crawled past he began walking towards the clinic. 'I'm starting towards the building,' he stated loudly and to no one in particular.

He looked from the corner of his eye towards the first-floor room. He could see the outline of a figure watching his progress. 'At least one of them is still in that room,' Nash observed to the night air.

'He's on his way,' Martin turned away from the window. 'He's climbing inside now.'

'Good,' Wardle said. 'Miss Pearson and I will meet him at the top of the stairs. We'll be handy for the lift there. Take that with you,' Wardle gestured towards Butler. 'Switch the main power on and join us by the lifts.'

Nash knocked, the window yielded to his touch. 'I'm climbing in,' he remarked. 'I've to wait inside.' He'd been given no instructions about the window so he left it open. He could hear muffled screams from somewhere inside. 'Can you hear that?'

The door was being unlocked. 'I'm going into the corridor.' He stepped out into the passage. The shouts and yells were louder. Those listening heard a fresh voice on Nash's radio. 'Turn left and keep walking.'

Nash glanced at the speaker, one of the security men armed with a small but lethal-looking pistol. 'Nice of you to walk with me,' he observed in a loud, clear voice. 'I hope that gun isn't loaded.'

'Don't try to find out,' the guard replied curtly.

A confused mass of panicking patients and nursing staff was being herded into the main body of the corridor by more guards, all armed. 'When you get to reception, turn right and head for the stairs.'

Nash could see other patients sitting in chairs or being forced to sit on the floor. The nurses with them were trying to maintain calm despite their own terror. Nash had to walk round them to reach the stairs. He heard one elderly patient defy the nearest guard. 'If I'd been younger—'

The guard leered at him, 'Shut it, granddad. You ain't young enough and if you don't sit still you won't be getting any older.' He pushed the old man none too gently in the shoulder with the butt of his gun.

'What do you intend to do with these people?' Nash asked louder still over the hubbub of voices and crying.

'They'll be quite safe as long as you behave. Now get yourself upstairs.'

'You not coming with me?'

'You're going up. But I'll be watching from the stairwell.'

'Okay, I'm going.' Nash began climbing the steps.

'There are a dozen armed men with the patients and staff,' he said quietly.

Nash reached the halfway landing. As he turned to continue his ascent he looked up and stopped.

'Stella. You alright?' She nodded. He looked to the figure by her side. 'And I assume you're Wardle. Where's your second in command? The man who cheats death by fire. Where's Martin Hill? What's he doing RIGHT NOW?'

The sound of a loud explosion caused Wardle's answer to die in his throat. He turned towards the source of the blast, close to the office he'd just left. He raised his gun as he saw officers coming through the hole where the fire door had been. A second explosion came from the opposite end of the building followed by a third and a fourth from elsewhere.

Wardle swung back towards Nash, finger on the trigger. Suddenly he was pushed violently from behind. He overbalanced and fell down the steps to land at Nash's feet. Nash ducked sideways as the guard in the stairwell fired a shot that whistled past his head.

He looked up to see Stella topple from her wheelchair. The momentum needed to administer the push had thrown the chair over the top step. Stella came crashing down on top of Wardle, hitting her head against the far wall. The wheelchair followed and before Nash could check it, landed on Stella's back.

The guard fired another round; Nash seized the wheelchair and hurled it at the advancing man. Guard and wheelchair crashed down the stairs.

Martin Hill had just pulled the mains power switches when the first charge was detonated. Half dragging Butler behind him, he made to move forward. He felt an unpleasant cold sensation on the back of his neck. Clara took hold of Hill's free hand in an almost affectionate gesture and snapped one link of her handcuffs over his wrist. She disarmed him and secured the second link. She nodded to the army officer and turned to run down the corridor.

Pearce and an ARU officer completed the capture of Butler and Hill. The bomb squad leader hurried after Clara.

Approaching Wardle, she saw him point his gun down the staircase. Saw him stagger then disappear. To her horror she saw Stella's wheelchair topple from sight.

Wardle was unconscious. Nash removed the man's gun and checked to see he was carrying no other weapons. He didn't bother with handcuffs. Wardle wasn't going anywhere. The end of the thigh bone sticking through his bloodstained trousers would ensure that.

Stella was barely conscious. 'Mike,' she whispered, 'Mike?' Her speech sounded slurred.

'I'm okay. What about you?'

'I don't … know.' She attempted to move. Her eyes widened with fear. 'I can't … move. I can't … move my arms, I can't feel them. I can't feel … anything.'

CHAPTER SIXTEEN

Nash's attention was solely on Stella. He placed his hand beneath her head to try to make her comfortable, it was then he saw the blood. Her eyes appeared unfocused. 'Stella, come on. Stay with me, I'll help you.' Nash's voice quivered as he looked at the girl he loved, trying desperately to avoid panic. He wiped the blood from his hand on to his trousers so she wouldn't see. He massaged her arms and shoulders. Each time he touched her he asked if she could feel his hand. Each time she muttered, 'No.' When she realized he was touching her breast she began to cry, silent tears that formed in her eyes, then trickled across her cheeks. When she couldn't raise her hand to brush them away the tears flowed even faster. Tears were all she could manage before she lapsed into unconsciousness.

Nash heard shots from the ground floor followed by shouting. He heard but paid little heed. He saw the Bomb Squad leader leap down the stairs but the urgency left Nash unmoved.

Beneath Stella, Wardle had regained consciousness and was whimpering. Nash looked round. No one was in sight. He leaned over the injured man. He placed his hand on Wardle's thigh and allowed his full weight to bear on the injured limb.

Wardle opened his mouth to scream but pain overtook him, his eyes glazed over and he passed out.

Pratt hurried up the stairs with a team of paramedics, a doctor and a couple of nurses. The army officer had passed the word. The doctor's examination of Stella was brief. Having attended to her head injury he instructed the ambulance men. 'Netherdale General and drive slowly!' He instructed a nurse, 'Go with her, make certain she isn't bumped or jolted. Tell A & E that I recommend she's transferred immediately to Pinderfields.'

He turned to Nash. 'We're not equipped to deal with injuries of that nature. She needs to be where they've specialist staff and equipment. Pinderfields is the best.'

He winced when he saw the gory mess of Wardle's leg. 'I'd better treat this man next. I'll do it as soon as they've got Miss Pearson away.'

'No,' Nash told him. 'See to your other patients.'

'But this man has a badly broken leg. He'll be in severe pain.'

'Good,' Nash told the astonished medic. 'Leave the bastard to rot for all I care.'

He watched anxiously as the paramedics slid Stella gently on to a stretcher with a spinal board. 'I should go with her.'

Clara touched him gently on the arm. 'She'll be okay, Mike.'

He gave Clara a look of such desolation she shivered. 'Clara's right, Mike,' Pratt added. 'There isn't any point. You can't do anything. Let the medics get on with their job. You're needed here.'

Nash looked around as if seeing the place for the first time. 'I suppose you're right,' he muttered.

Pratt called to the doctor. 'Excuse me. I don't know who's in charge but I need all these patients evacuating.'

'You'll need to speak to Mr Butler, I'm afraid. I don't have the authority.'

'That's not possible. You'll have to deal with it. We don't know if there are any other devices in the building.

Apart from that, this is a major crime scene.' At that moment Pearce marched Butler and Hill to the head of the stairs.

'Okay to bring the prisoners down?' The doctor gaped, open mouthed before scurrying off to make the arrangements.

'Put them with the others and let's get them moved. I want them transferred to the cells along with those so called security men.' Pratt pointed to Wardle, 'This one can go across to Netherdale General under guard. We'll get the Bomb Squad to do a sweep of the building whilst they evacuate. That could take a while,' he added thoughtfully. 'Those that didn't have heart attacks probably shit themselves when the charges went off.'

'What happened downstairs?'

Pratt smiled. 'Wardle and Hill were either careless or overconfident. They didn't secure that window you came through. By the time those charges went off I'd six armed officers in that room. When the rest came in through the emergency doors the guards realized the game was up and surrendered.'

'Thank God. If they'd resisted it could have been carnage.' Nash looked at Clara, 'What about upstairs?' He asked, forcing himself to concentrate on mundane details.

'It worked just as the Major promised. We went up one fire escape, Viv and a second team went up the other. The blasts blew the doors off and we walked in, right on cue to grab Hill and Butler. The ARU are up there now checking for strays. We've men posted at every exit.'

Pratt said, 'We'll start as soon as they're clear. I want every member of staff interviewed. Nip and tell our lads to get names and details from everyone in reception before they start moving. I don't want anyone slipping through the net. We'll search the offices when the dust settles.'

Nash felt weary. The adrenalin that had carried him through the siege and rescue had ebbed away. That and worry over Stella's condition left him drained. When Clara returned, Pratt said, 'Go find the kitchen. Take Mike and make him a mug of coffee. I'll look after things here.'

Clara led Nash to the ground floor where staff had succeeded in calming down the patients. Along the corridor Wardle's men were sitting huddled in uncomfortable misery against the wall, their hands cuffed. Three armed police officers were standing guard.

The Bomb Squad leader was entering the front door.

'I'd like a word with you,' Nash said quietly.

'I thought you might.'

'You're a little bit more than a bomb disposal officer.'

'I do have other strings to my bow.'

Nash looked enquiringly.

'When you started asking questions about Wardle and Hill you rang alarm bells. My CO was contacted,' the officer grimaced, 'you know how it works. Anyway the Old Man had orders to do what he could if we were asked, or to volunteer if we weren't. You didn't ask the right questions, Superintendent Nash. If you had, you'd have known that Wardle and Hill were both Sappers, known how dangerous they were. That's what really terrified your contact. He knew if they were cornered they wouldn't hesitate to use explosives. When we got the call from your chief my CO had already asked me to come along.

'When I told him what happened at the farm he gave me the go ahead to become a bit more proactive.'

'So you approached DCI Fleming about following us?'

'Let's say I suggested it.'

'I suppose it's no use asking your name and regiment?'

'You could,' the officer grinned. 'But how would you know I was telling the truth?'

'Or where you got your specialist training in things like charges to open doors and stun grenades? Hereford, perhaps? You said before I went in, "you need courage to succeed". What you really meant was "Who Dares Wins".'

'Not a bad little town, Hereford. And that's not a bad motto for a soldier; or a policeman come to think of it.' He turned to Clara and took her hand. 'Nice meeting you, Detective Sergeant Mironova, or could I call you Clara? Maybe our paths will cross again.'

'Er ... Clara's fine and yes, I er ... hope to see you again sometime.' She smiled, praying that the colour wasn't rising in her cheeks.

He shook hands with Nash. 'I hope things turn out alright for Miss Pearson. Don't blame yourself. Remember, Wardle and Hill would have snuffed her out as you'd swat a fly.'

In the kitchen Nash felt slightly more optimistic. The knowledge of his friend at the MOD's concern and the lengths he'd gone to on his behalf helped lift his spirits.

Clara was waiting for the kettle to boil. 'I wonder how Jackie's getting on at the farm?' she said, trying to give Nash something to think about.

Mention of Fleming stirred something in Nash's memory. He thought about it, but whatever it was remained elusive. 'Call her when you've made coffee. Tell her what's happened and find out how things are there.'

Clara passed him his coffee and received the satellite radio in return. 'These sets are really good,' she enthused. 'Even when you were whispering we could hear you as clear as a bell.'

After a moment's delay Jackie answered. 'Clara, how's it gone? Have you got them? Is everybody safe?'

'Very well, thanks to the army,' Clara responded. 'One or two problems but at least we've got them.' She explained how events at the clinic had unfolded. Skipping too much detail about Stella's injuries. 'What's going on there?'

'We're still searching.'

'Found anything?'

'Not yet, I've been looking through Wardle's files. All that might be significant are some papers referring to imported cattle. I wondered if that might give some clue as to how the children were smuggled in. I reckon the really sensitive information might be stored on Wardle's computer. Why else would they make such a determined effort to destroy it? I daren't touch that in case Wardle's rigged some sort of virus to wipe the hard drive clean.'

'Sensible. Leave that for the experts. What's Zena up to?'

'She's looking through some videos. I think she was planning to watch bits, see if they were relevant. Do you want to speak to her? No, hang on a moment. Zena's found something she wants me to see. I'll call you back.'

It was twenty minutes later when Fleming got back to them. She sounded upset. 'Is Mike there? I need to speak to him.'

Clara passed the set across. 'It's Jackie, sounds as if she's been crying.'

'What's matter?'

'Mike, this video Zena found. It's awful, really awful. Zena reckons it was shot near Sarajevo. It shows street scenes and people firing guns. Then in the middle of the shooting, it shows a woman and child. A soldier follows them into a house. The video follows the man upstairs. When the man with the camera goes upstairs—' her voice faltered then petered out altogether.

'Jackie, are you there, you alright?'

'Mikhail, this is Zena. Jackie is too upset. The tape shows a man dressed in IFOR uniform. He followed a woman and child into a room.' Zena's voice trembled, her perfect English faltered. 'Soldier shoots woman. Then he rapes child. All this is on video. The man shooting video must be in doorway. Scenes are horrible.'

Zena paused and took a deep breath. 'After. The soldier kills the girl. Before the end there are images of the same man setting fire to the house and leaving. Some are shot close to, they show the face and uniform name badge.' Zena paused and took another deep breath. 'The name is Butler.'

It was a couple of hours before they were able to start searching the clinic, a process that would take most of the night. They started with Butler's office, from which his computer and files were removed. Nash took little part in the early stages. His worry over Stella's condition was compounded by the feeling there was something he should have remembered.

'We ought to inspect the operating theatre,' he suggested to Pratt when they finished in Butler's office. 'We need evidence the transplants were conducted here.'

Accompanied by Clara they followed the signs along the empty corridor to the theatre. They stopped by the emergency exit and examined it. 'Our man knew his business,' Pratt observed. He shivered slightly, 'The trouble is it's left the building so cold.'

They turned into the preparation room then on into the theatre itself. They paused in the doorway waiting for the bank of lights to reach full power. The room was bare and sterile. If anything, Nash thought, it felt even colder in there.

Clara spotted a refrigerator and walked over to it. She opened the door. Her cry brought both men running. Nash felt his stomach heave as he recognized what was in there. The clear plastic boxes contained what were undoubtedly body parts, human body parts.

Nash recovered slightly. 'Where the hell have they come from?' He looked at his companions. 'They can't be left over from the bodies recovered from the tarn. These are far too recent.'

He looked round again then walked beyond the operating table to a large stainless steel door. His memory went back to his childhood, to the job he'd had in the school holidays. He'd worked for the village butcher as a delivery boy. When they were busy, he was also given odd jobs around the shop. The door Nash was approaching was just like the heavy steel door to the meat safe. He reached for the big, levered handle half expecting to see the carcase of a pig hanging from a hook inside.

And there it was. Just where it should have been. Then he realized he wasn't a boy any longer. And this wasn't the village butchers. And it wasn't a pig. Naked, eyeless, the body had a series of gaping wounds where organs had been removed. Despite the mutilation Nash recognized it instantly – the remains of what had once been Detective Sergeant Owen Thomas.

CHAPTER SEVENTEEN

Questioning of suspects had to wait until evidence gathering was complete. Hill was charged initially only with the illegal imprisonment of Stella. Butler's charge sheet merely covered the removal of human organs without the donor's consent.

Wardle was formally arrested and charged at Netherdale General Hospital where operations were being carried out to save his shattered leg. His charges were more serious, relating to illegal possession of explosives and unlawful killing of two police officers. Solicitors for all three men were left in no doubt that more charges would follow.

Nash took time out to phone the specialist unit to which Stella had been transferred. The news was not encouraging and Nash was informed she was not allowed visitors. It was two days before Clara was despatched to take a statement from her. On her return, she explained how difficult it had been. 'It was probably shock. The injury to her head has affected her speech and she wasn't able to give me much information other than what we'd already worked out. She did say Wardle had been talking to Hill about the weather. He seemed concerned about wind speed. Just before you came, he spoke to someone on his mobile phone about them.'

'I'll go see her as soon as I can.'

'Give her a few more days, Mike,' Clara said as she turned to leave the room.

All the security men had been interviewed and Nash turned his attention to Vatovec, charged with firearms offences and conspiracy to murder. Janko had relapsed into a feigned ignorance of English and refused to answer any questions.

Zena came up with the solution. As she translated, Nash thought every English word seemed to be matched by a dozen in their language.

It was perhaps as well he didn't know what Zena was saying, but maybe he wouldn't have been bothered. 'Janko,' she began, 'this policeman wants you to talk. If I was you I'd abandon this pretence of not speaking English. Shall I tell you why?

'Because I've applied to Moscow for extradition for crimes committed on Russian soil. When you get there you'll be found guilty. You'll go to prison for a long time. The British might resist such extradition, but only if they have good reason. The British are very keen to protect the welfare of prisoners. Did you know they have special categories of prisoners? For those who have committed sexual crimes, particularly if those crimes are committed against children.

'Of course, we're not quite so enlightened. We don't believe it's worth the effort. Let me explain. There are many prisoners in our gaols. Men who have been inside for a long time without the comfort of a woman. These men are not homosexuals. They are just desperate for somewhere to get rid of their dirty water. Any receptacle will do. As the English say, "any port in a storm".'

Zena laughed merrily. 'Your cell would be better fitted with a revolving door. You'll be in such demand. After a few weeks your arse will be like a paper hanger's paste bucket. Then I shall come. I shall watch you walking bow legged, unable to sit down. Then I'll believe you're experiencing one small part of what those children suffered. Then I shall rejoice.'

She looked at Nash and winked. 'I'm almost sure Janko is prepared to cooperate.' She continued in Russian, 'Especially when I've told him that if he's ever released from prison, I'll ensure every relative of every child he's harmed will be given advance warning of the place, date and time. I shall also pay their bus or train fares, so they can be there to greet him. And I always keep my promises.'

She smiled again. 'I've nearly convinced him I think?' She spoke directly to Janko again. 'All you have to do to prevent this is confess everything and hope to remain in England.'

After Zena's little heart-to-heart, Vatovec became talkative. He became talkative in English, so talkative they had to stop him to change the tape.

'I was in Bosnia during the trouble. I sell arms to anyone willing to pay. It is normal, many are doing this. I was stopped one day by IFOR patrol as I was delivering guns. The leader was Hill. He took me in front of Wardle. They blackmailed me to supply women and girls, first for troops, then for anyone who pays. That is how it starts. Soon demand is too great for legal prostitutes. Still they want more. Then Hill make suggestion I go to the villages and kidnap women.

'We used different ways to trap women. Still there is need for more. Next they come to me with new idea. They tell me of men who will pay much for sex with children. This becomes big business. There are many like this. They pay great sums for children to be sex slaves. Sometimes things go wrong. They get pregnant, they get disease. Then we cannot use them. Then we cannot sell them. That is when Hill is called for. He is,' Vatovec paused, 'executioner.'

'What do you know about other parts of the trade?' Nash asked him.

Vatovec seemed baffled for a moment. 'There are other things they do. They make trade in drugs. I have job of finding cargoes. They send more and more drugs. Also something to do with hospitals. I do not know what this is.'

'You must have been curious? Were you never tempted to ask?'

'For sure I was curious.' Vatovec leaned forward, his hands flat on the table. 'But always it is Hill who is in charge. You do not ask questions of Hill. You do not do anything to make Hill suspicious. Hill is cold, evil monster. Many men will kill if they must. Hill murders because he enjoys.'

Nash walked into Helmsdale CID room to find Pearce looking forlorn. 'I'm sorry if you're feeling a bit left out,' Nash told his DC, 'but that's about to change. I want you to go to Netherdale in the morning. Wardle's computer's there and the IT boys will be arriving to start work on it. Success or failure could be crucial to our ability to press home the most damaging charges against Wardle and Hill. Admittedly we've got statements from Vatovec and the security men, plus what happened at the farm and the clinic, but the rest is circumstantial. So anything we can dig out of those files could be priceless.'

'I'll do my best,' Pearce promised. 'By the way, there was a call for you half an hour or so back. I rang Netherdale but they told me you'd left. They said you were on your way back so I thought it would wait. The details are on a pad in your office.'

'I'll deal with it in a minute.'

Clara walked into Nash's office as he was making the phone call. He signalled to her to sit down and continued to listen. Nash looked older, older and sadder, Clara thought as she studied him. He put the phone down and stared at the desk for a moment before looking up.

'What's next on the agenda?' she asked.

'Give York Hospital a ring, find out what progress Milla's making. I need to know when she'll be fit enough to attend a line-up. If she can pick out any of our suspects it'll give us another charge to pin on them.'

'I'll get on to that,' Clara waited, certain Nash had more to say.

'That was Pinderfields. The news is about as bad as could be. The whole of Stella's upper body's paralyzed now

212

and he's concerned about the knock she took on her head. He's arranging more tests. He wasn't at all hopeful there'll be any improvement. She could remain that way for the rest of her life. I'm going to see her tonight.'

Next morning, Nash and Clara met Pratt to discuss unresolved issues. Before they began, Nash told them about Stella. 'She looks so ill. All I could do was hold her hand to show I was there. She slept most of the time and I could barely understand her when she tried to speak. We'll just have to wait.' Nash sighed. 'Anyway, let's get on with this lot,' he shuffled the papers in front of him. 'It's clear Vatovec knew nothing about the trade in body parts.'

'That's a shame. I know we've plenty of evidence. Still, it would be been nice to get a confession,' Pratt said gloomily. 'I can't for a minute see either Wardle or Hill giving us one.'

Clara had been thinking the case through, 'What I can't understand is how Wardle got the organs out of the country.'

'That's been puzzling me too,' Pratt agreed, 'Any ideas, Mike?'

'None that makes sense. I keep thinking back to what Stella said. Do you remember, Clara? Something to do with Wardle and Hill talking about the weather and Wardle being concerned about wind speed?'

'I don't see the relevance.'

'Maybe, if it was a light aircraft they were going to use, Wardle might have been concerned about it being susceptible to high winds,' Pratt suggested.

'I don't think so,' Nash objected. 'Wardle and Hill were desperate by then. Wardle would have needed the pilot to take off. Besides the wind that night wasn't enough to ground an aircraft. There has to be some other reason, although I can't work out what.'

'Going back to my original question,' Clara asked. 'Do you think a plane was used to ferry the organs abroad?'

'Hang on,' Pratt objected. 'If a plane went across to the Continent, any cargo would be subject to Customs checks.

The same would apply when they brought drugs or children in. How did they avoid their shipments being searched? I know Customs and Excise are stretched but sooner or later one of their cargoes would have been discovered.'

'I agree, always supposing their point of entry was covered by Customs.'

'The best way would be to find their pilot,' Clara suggested.

'Why didn't I twig that? If Wardle rang his pilot the other evening—'

'—the number will be in Wardle's mobile.' Clara finished Nash's sentence for him.

Nash stood up. 'Excuse us, Tom, we've work to do.'

Pearce emerged from an office in front of them. 'How are you getting on with the IT boys?'

'We're making headway. We've got into Wardle's hard drive and started examining some of the files. I think he kept all the records of their activities in there. One of the files we retrieved first was all his contacts. You told me watch for anything to do with transport and aviation, correct?'

'Yes, what have you found?'

'One of Wardle's e-mail addresses is a firm specializing in helicopter flights.'

'Is it local?'

'Only if you live in northern France.'

'That's disappointing. Still it's something, I suppose. Shame it's not round here, though. Anything in this country?'

'Nothing meaningful. I did have one idea, though I'll need your authority to act on it.'

'Go on.'

'I thought it might be worth checking with the Civil Aviation Authority. Give them the names in Wardle's address book and see if any of them holds a pilot's licence.'

'Viv, sometimes you're brilliant. Anything else?'

'Nothing definite, although I did find a couple of addresses on the east coast. I thought they might be worth checking out. Of course, they may be seaside landladies where Wardle stays on holiday.'

'I don't see Wardle as the bucket and spade, knotted handkerchief type. Keep digging.'

'Okay, boss.'

'I don't see how a helicopter company in northern France can have anything to do with the organ transport,' Clara said as they walked on.

'Neither do I at the moment, although I bet it is connected.'

'It has to be the last number he dialled.' Nash pressed a button on the mobile but the screen remained blank.

'Damn, the battery's flat. See if you can scrounge a charger.'

Clara returned five minutes later, Nash scrolled down the menu, opened the call register and recited the number. Clara wrote it down. 'I'll get Viv to check it.'

'Ask him to run the details past the CAA straightaway,' Nash called after her.

When she returned she was waving a piece of paper triumphantly, 'Got it! This guy lives about twenty miles away. He's got one plane, which he operates from a grass strip. He's also a farmer, cattle breeder and dealer. Whilst we were waiting for the CAA to check him out Viv told me he's found out about one of Wardle's east coast contacts. Seemingly, the address is that of a trawler owner.'

Nash thought over what she said. Something was stirring in his brain although he wasn't quite sure what. 'Get hold of Jackie. I've an idea how Wardle worked this.'

Nash sat pondering the emerging evidence. From out of nowhere he began reciting a poem. 'Night Mail' had been one of his favourites. As Auden's verse flowed from his subconscious he wondered why he should think of it. *This is the Night Mail crossing the border, bringing the cheque and the postal order, letters for the rich, letters for the poor, the shop at the corner and the girl next door. Pulling up Beattock a steady climb; the gradient's against her but she's on time.'*

What was he thinking? Why mail trains? Something about a mail train, something relevant. Still the verses rolled from his brain. *'Letters of thanks, letters from banks, letters of joy from the girl and the boy. Receipted bills and invitations, to inspect new stock or visit relations.'*

Something about letters, but what? Suddenly a picture flashed into his mind. The image of a fast-moving mail train thundering through the night, racing alongside a station platform. Collecting the mail without pausing to break its tight schedule. 'Of course,' he breathed, 'the clever sod.'

'What is it, Mike?'

Clara had returned with Fleming. Nash smiled, 'I've worked out how Wardle transported the organs and how he planned to escape. At least I think I have.'

'Go on then.'

'He had to move the organs quickly or they'd be unusable. And he had to ensure they avoided attention from customs.'

'Yes,' Clara agreed. 'But how did he manage both?'

'He loaded the organs on to a light aircraft operating from a private strip. The pilot took the plane out over the North Sea and dropped the container with the organs. The container would be attached to a parachute. The trawler would pick up the container and set off towards the French coast where it would be met by a helicopter. The helicopter would collect the container and return to base. Neither plane nor chopper would touch down on foreign soil so neither would be subject to customs checks. Maybe the trawler did some fishing to lend an air of authenticity, then returned to its home port, landed its catch and sold it. To all intent and purpose everything's above board.'

'Wouldn't it have been risky transferring the containers from the trawler to the helicopter if the weather was rough?' Jackie suggested.

'Not if they used a winch and a net.'

'What made you think of that?'

'I remembered a film I saw once. It showed how the mail train picked up post from beside the track. That gave me the idea.'

'Sounds feasible. Do you think Wardle intended to escape that way? A container with organs inside is one thing but it would have been far riskier for a man.' Clara objected.

'I'm sure that's what he had in mind. Remember Stella's comment about wind speed? We couldn't work out why it was important. Wind speed wouldn't have made much difference to a light aircraft. But it would have been crucial to anyone parachuting from a plane towards a small target such as a fishing boat. You'd have to get that exactly right otherwise you'd finish up miles away. In the North Sea at this time of year you'd be dead from hypothermia before you were picked up.'

'That wouldn't explain how they got the children into the country. Or the drugs for that matter,' Jackie objected.

'One thing at a time. I'm going to have another word with Vatovec.'

'We'll go pick up the pilot. We'll have a look round whilst we're there. We might find something useful.'

'Take a couple of uniforms. We've already seen how dangerous this lot can be.'

'Vatovec, you were in charge of transportation,' Nash accused him. 'So tell me how you got the children into the country?'

'It was easy. Wardle has business with man dealing in cattle. He has wagons bringing animals in, taking animals out of country. We make special compartment. Girls are given drugs so they will sleep all journey. They are hidden in special compartment. Customs have machine that senses body warmth but this will not work because of cattle. Children are small. There is room in compartment for drugs also.'

'Thank you,' Nash told him, 'that's what I wanted to know.'

He returned to the office and rang Clara's mobile. 'See if there are any wagons about. We're talking cattle trucks. Check behind the driver's compartment. You're looking for something like a box bed, where the herdsman sleeps. That's where the children and drugs were concealed.'

As he awaited their return, Nash spent time formulating his strategy for interviewing Butler, Wardle and Hill.

They reported back several hours later, their mission a complete success. The pilot and two henchmen had confessed. This was prompted by the discovery of several containers of heroin with a street value of millions of pounds. The pilot claimed this was being stored for Wardle. They also found three cattle trucks with hidden containers. Nash told them how he wanted to proceed. 'I'm going to take Clara and Viv to the hospital,' he told Fleming. 'Will you take over with the IT people?'

Fleming looked disappointed, but agreed.

'What's your plan?' Clara asked.

'Wardle will be psyched up for this interrogation. He'll have prepared his defences whilst he's been lying there.'

'How will you counter that?'

'By doing what he least expects. He's had no feedback. No contact with anybody.'

Wardle had been placed in a side room. Nash braced himself before opening the door. He banished all thought of Stella.

He marched across to Wardle's bedside. Clara and Pearce followed, wondering what Nash had in mind. He didn't sit down, which was their first surprise. 'I understand you'll be fit to leave in a couple of days. You'll be moved to police cells. You'll be put up at the first opportunity for a custody hearing and then CPS will take over. It's customary at that stage to interview a suspect and take a statement. When that happens you'll be entitled to legal representation.'

'I have absolutely nothing to say,' Wardle replied in a flat, calm voice.

'Suits me,' Nash sounded bored, disinterested. 'I wasn't about to talk to you. I'm too busy. If you change your mind, Detective Constable Pearce,' Nash indicated Viv, 'will conduct the interview. Come on, Sergeant,' he beckoned Clara. 'We've work to do.'

Clara followed him out of the room, mystified. 'Don't you think we should have pushed for a statement?'

'Why waste our time? He's got his guard up. He thinks we need information. He doesn't know we've got Vatovec and the pilot's confessions. He's left wondering how much we know. By seeming unconcerned, we've turned the tables on him. Instead of us wanting information from him, he's desperate for news about our case. He probably thinks all we've got is the business at the farm and some circumstantial evidence, but he's not sure. It's that uncertainty I'm building on.'

'What was the idea of leaving Viv there?'

'Viv's the most junior officer we have, added to which he's black. Wardle's used to army disciplines, the hierarchy and attitudes. He sees a constable as no more than a private. To leave Wardle in the charge of someone he thinks of as a squaddie isn't only an insult, it demonstrates how unimportant we think he is.'

'Mind games,' Clara nodded. 'I like that. Have you something similar planned for Hill?'

'That's going to be different. When Hill's interviewed I won't even be present. I'm going to let you and Jackie have that pleasure. What's more, you'll be going in with a strictly prepared script.'

Clara groaned. 'From mind games to amateur dramatics. Don't tell me you'll be giving acting lessons?'

'Something of the sort,' Nash smiled.

'Let me into a secret. Why Jackie and me?'

'Because you're women. There's nobody more sexist than a professional soldier and Hill would see that as an insult. He'll also be aware how much more personally women take the sort of crimes he's responsible for. If I'd been guilty of half the offences Hill has committed I wouldn't want to be left alone with a couple of women. Didn't you see what Vatovec was like when Zena confronted him?'

'Have you been reading books on psychology or have you been on a course?'

Nash smiled. 'Neither, but I'm willing to have a bet with you. Within forty-eight hours we'll get a visit from Wardle's solicitor demanding to know what evidence we have.'

'Will you give him it?'

'Legally I can't deny him access to it. But I'll go further than that. I'll be so cooperative he'll wonder what I'm up to. Which is exactly what I want. I'll give him chapter and verse about what happened at Howlingales Farm. I'll give him a detailed account of what we found at the clinic. Then I'll hand him copies of the statements from Vatovec and that pilot.

'Here's the brief for your interview with Hill. I want you to tell him it doesn't matter whether he talks or not. We've got him without a confession. You can say I couldn't spare the time to interview him. Quote me as saying "It isn't necessary, so why bother".'

Less than twenty-four hours later Nash would have been able to claim his winnings. Wardle's solicitor arrived ready to argue for what the police had against his client. When he left, he looked shaken and more than a little puzzled. An hour and a half after his departure Nash had a phone call from Pearce. 'Wardle wants to make a statement,' Viv told him. 'What do you want me to do? Shall I wait until you arrive?'

'No Viv; I want you to take a statement, and Viv …'

'Yes, Mike?'

'Continue to act as if it doesn't matter. We've got all the evidence we need against Wardle and Hill. Anything they tell us will be a bonus.'

Hill was a slightly tougher nut to crack. But after two sessions with Jackie and Clara, at the second of which he was shown Wardle's confession, he too made a statement.

220

CHAPTER EIGHTEEN

During their next update Pratt asked, 'What are you intending to do about Butler?'

'I think we should be able to crack him,' Nash assured him. 'Particularly in view of the video. It identifies Butler clearly by the insignia and name on the uniform.'

'We can't be certain that'll give us anything more than Butler's part in the organ trade,' Clara pointed out.

'I'm not so sure,' Nash contradicted her. 'I reckon Butler would be a prime customer for child prostitutes. The video proves he's a paedophile. I can't see the leopard changing his spots.'

'We've still nothing to prove he was involved in underage sex in this country.'

'I realize that and I'm not sure how we can get proof.'

The meeting was interrupted by the phone. Nash picked up the receiver. He listened for a few minutes, his smile widening. 'Really?' He said eventually. 'You're absolutely sure? There's no chance of an error?'

He put the phone down and looked round. He grinned. 'It's not my birthday for several months,' he told them. 'But I've just been given the best possible present.'

Nash explained what he'd been told. 'I vote we act straightaway. We'll talk to Butler. It's just a question of who to take in to that interview.'

'Who do you suggest?'

'Clara and Zena, I think,' Nash replied.

'I'll go along with that,' Pratt agreed.

As the meeting broke up, Fleming stopped Nash. 'Have you heard about Armistead?'

Nash shook his head. 'He's been suspended. I heard from the office an hour ago. An ACC has been drafted in to handle Armistead's work on a temporary basis. An internal enquiry team will be put together over the next few days. They'll want to interview everyone involved,' she took a deep breath. 'Apparently I was scheduled for suspension but the acting chief had a word with Tom Pratt and he blocked it.'

Butler was accompanied by his solicitor, a thin-faced, middle-aged man with a morose expression. It was the lawyer who took control of the start of the interview. He leaned forward and spoke to Nash, ignoring both women. Throughout the lawyer's speech his client avoided eye contact with everyone by staring down at his hands, which were clasped nervously in his lap.

'My client wishes me to place on record,' the lawyer began, 'that he admits having conducted organ removal and transplant operations in contravention of government regulations. He wishes to assure everyone that the operations were his only involvement. Moreover, my client will admit that the reason for his involvement was because he was blackmailed over some alleged minor misdemeanour supposedly committed when he was in Her Majesty's Forces. He wishes to add that his fear of the man Hill, who he knows to be extremely violent, was also responsible for his agreement to conduct the operations.

'My client has no knowledge of the origins of the donors, nor of the circumstances surrounding their decease.

He's prepared to answer questions relating to the operations but will categorically refuse to comment on any other subject.'

The solicitor leaned back and waited for Nash to begin, no doubt having rehearsed the line they would take with his client.

Nash knew he had to drive a wedge between solicitor and client. 'I think we'll start with the video. Zena, as you and Clara have seen this perhaps you wouldn't mind standing behind the TV. There isn't much room in here and I want to be sure Mr Butler and his lawyer can see everything.'

Any doubt as to whether Butler knew what was on the film vanished with the first frame. He took one look then his eyes dropped to the table. 'Watch the TV, Mr Butler,' Nash instructed.

Butler didn't want to watch. That was clear. He'd have given anything rather than have to sit in that room. With Nash's insistence and his solicitor's ever more curious gaze on him he'd no alternative.

Nash didn't watch it. He'd seen it once, and once was more than enough. Instead, he concentrated his attention on Butler and his lawyer. As the video ran its course he saw the growing look of revulsion on the solicitor's face. There was a long and painful silence when the film ended. Nash nodded to Clara, who switched the TV off.

'That was you in the video, Mr Butler?' Nash asked the question ever so gently.

Butler didn't reply. Nash transferred his attention to the lawyer. 'Some minor misdemeanour,' he said, sarcasm crackling in his voice. 'If you class the rape of a child of no more than ten or eleven years old, and the murder of that child and her mother as a minor misdemeanour, I'd be interested to hear what you regard as a serious crime?'

The lawyer shuffled defensively. 'I had no prior knowledge of the contents of that video,' he protested weakly. 'I'd like to consult with my client.'

Nash signalled to Clara, who delivered the interview termination message before switching the recorder off. The detectives filed out.

'I can't believe Butler hadn't told his lawyer about that film,' Clara said as they waited.

'Would you? Butler didn't know we had it. He probably hoped Hill or Wardle had secreted it somewhere safe.'

'That's right,' Zena agreed. 'When you mentioned the video Butler went as white as a sheet.'

'He'll be hearing some fairly unpalatable advice right now.'

Zena realized what Nash was referring to. 'That's why you wanted me in the room, for the benefit of the lawyer. He's probably telling Butler he's likely to be subject to extradition.'

'Will you apply for it?' Clara asked.

'Not my decision. They will only make such a request if they think it's likely to be granted. What are the chances, Mikhail?'

'I'd start preparing the paperwork now. I won't oppose it, and I can't imagine anyone else doing so.'

Butler's solicitor appeared at the door and signalled they were ready. Once the tape was running he told them, 'I've advised my client to answer your questions as truthfully as possible. I warn you, he still maintains he'd no knowledge of anything apart from the transplants. If you intend to ask questions on such subjects, be careful how they're phrased.'

'If Mr Butler is prepared to answer our questions truthfully that's a step in the right direction.'

Zena looked perplexed, and vaguely disappointed. Clara braced herself for the storm that was about to be unleashed. If things had been different Clara might have felt sympathy for Nash's victim, but remembering what was on the video ruled that out. She smiled reassuringly at Zena.

'What your solicitor said implies that what we saw on the film was an aberration, an isolated incident, never to be repeated. Is that so?'

'That's correct,' Butler replied, eager now.

'And you know nothing about the victims,' Nash saw the lawyer's head come up like a striking rattlesnake. 'Sorry, the donors who were brought to your hospital, on to your operating table? Is that also correct?'

'It is. I knew nothing about them.' Zena and Clara could see Butler relaxing as he answered each question easily.

'You've no idea where they came from?'

'None whatsoever.'

'Can you explain how they finished up in those tarns?'

'No. Hill brought them to the hospital. I removed their organs. Then he collected them and that was it. I'd no idea how he disposed of them.'

'You didn't know any of them?'

'No, I've already said that.'

'You have indeed, Mr Butler. I just wanted to be absolutely certain you'd never seen any of them in your life. That they were completely unknown to you. Can you give me such an assurance?'

'I can. I'd never seen or known any of them before.'

'My client has answered that question more than once, Superintendent,' the solicitor frowned. 'I think you should move on.'

'I've a problem with that, to be fair,' Nash scratched his chin reflectively. 'I agree your client has answered the question several times, but a few minutes ago you told me he'd agreed to answer truthfully.'

Nash turned back to Butler. 'So, I'm going to ask you one last time, Mr Butler, did you know or had you met any of those victims before they appeared on your operating table?'

'Absolutely not,' Butler said flatly.

Nash's tone reverted to conversational. 'Tell me something, Mr Butler, do you know what DNA is?'

'Of course,' Butler's confidence had grown so rapidly he could manage some level of scorn. 'I'm a surgeon. DNA is part of my daily life.'

'Oh, I'm sorry, I forgot,' Nash was almost humble. 'Please forgive me for asking but I'm a layman and these complicated medical terms baffle me. Let me ask you this, Mr Butler. Is it possible to determine the parentage of a child from that child's bones?'

'Naturally,' Butler said. 'That's easy to do.'

'Even from an unborn child, a foetus say?'

'Still perfectly possible.'

'That's most interesting, Mr Butler. Thank you for your guidance.' Butler bowed his head gracefully. Nash stood up as if to leave. Then, almost as an afterthought he turned and placed his hands against the edges of the table. He leaned forward until his face was only inches from Butler's and stared remorselessly into the surgeon's eyes.

'One more question, Mr Butler, bearing in mind that you've just informed us not once but several times that all the victims were completely unknown to you. Can you explain how the DNA extracted from a foetal bone removed from one of the corpses indicates that you were the father of the child the victim was carrying?'

Butler began to crumble. Throughout Nash's verbal onslaught, Butler's solicitor sat in uncomfortable silence, aware that he should be raising objections but with little enthusiasm for such an intervention.

'You've lied all the way through. First you lied about being a rapist and a murderer. Then you lied by saying your involvement was limited to the organ removals. Next you lied about not knowing how the victims died. You're a surgeon, Butler. You'd have to know. You'd have to test them to ensure they weren't carrying any infection that would have rendered their organs unusable; or should I say unsaleable? You'd have to keep them on life support whilst you carried out the extractions. So all that business about not knowing how they died was another lie.

'Then there was your last lie. The biggest and worst lie. You lied about knowing the identity of any of the victims. You lied about having met any of them, when all along one of them was carrying your child. Did you know the girl was pregnant? Don't answer; it'll probably be another lie.

'You've portrayed yourself as an upright citizen, a distinguished surgeon, the owner of a prestigious clinic, but that was all a sham. Your whole life is a lie from start to finish, isn't it, Butler? I intend to see those lies exposed. I intend to have your whole facade torn down and expose you for the world to see the putrid, stinking, rottenness within. Your career is over. The distinguished surgeon is a thing of the past. Where you're going you won't even be able to cut your fingernails unsupervised.' Nash paused and stood looking down at the wreck sitting before him.

'Tell me something, Butler, do you like food? You look like a man who enjoys wining and dining. People imprisoned for offences such as yours are protected from other inmates. Unfortunately, that protection doesn't extend to the kitchen. You'll be in for some interesting meals, very interesting I can tell you. They prepare special menus for the likes of you. The prisoners in charge of the cooking take great delight in it, I'm told. Sometimes they piss on your food, sometimes they wank into it. They vary that with other ingredients, like shit, or powdered glass.

'Prisons are fairly secure but we all know security can't be guaranteed. Mistakes happen. They tend to happen when prison officers with young families are on duty. Most of the mistakes are put down to carelessness. The mistake gets a fair amount of publicity, in the tabloids particularly. Usually the headline reads something like sex pervert knifed. People read it. Law abiding people who wouldn't wish harm on anyone. They read it and think, "Oh good. He's got what he deserves."

'These mistakes are rare but they do happen and sooner or later I reckon one will happen to you. They'll take their eyes off you and next thing you know you're in the prison hospital with a knife in your gut. You won't be able to operate on yourself either. You'll have to rely on some underpaid and overworked medic. I doubt you'll get much sympathy from him.

'Face it Butler. Your life is in ruins. You're as good as dead already. What's the term convicts use in America when a condemned man is on his way to the gas chamber? "Dead man walking", that's what they say. That's what you are, Butler. You're a dead man walking. The only difference is your death will be long, slow and, I hope, painful. So how about breaking the habit of a lifetime and telling the truth?'

There was a long silence after Nash finished. He stared at Butler, his expression a pitiless glare. Zena looked at Nash and shuddered. All trace of the gentle compassionate nature that had marked his dealings with Milla, the tenderness that had impressed Zena, had vanished as if it never existed.

Eventually, the lawyer felt the need to break the silence which had become charged and oppressive. He looked at Butler, who was staring at the floor, at his hands, at the table, anything to avoid Nash's gaze. 'I have to advise you, Butler, to cooperate fully and answer Superintendent Nash's questions truthfully,' he told his client.

Even his solicitor had dropped the prefix 'Mister'. It was a measure of how far the surgeon had fallen. In the space of the interview he'd ceased to attract the slightest particle of respect. They might as well have issued him with a prison number already.

Nash sat down again, leaning back on his chair. 'Well?' The question was delivered like a whiplash.

Butler flinched, cleared his throat and licked his lips. When he spoke his voice was barely above a whisper. Even in the confines of the small room his listeners had to strain to catch what he said. 'I'll tell you all I know. But I don't know everything. Only the part that involved me.'

'Very well. But be aware I won't stop until I'm satisfied you've told us everything. No more lies, no more half-truths.'

'I don't own the clinic. My name is on the paperwork but Wardle owns it. He set me up there when we left the army. Originally, all he asked me to do was to treat one or two girls who'd got infected. I was already getting a reputation for transplant surgery, so Wardle paid for an extension to house an operating suite. Then he and Hill started bringing the girls for organ removal. There was a big demand in both Britain and Europe. It was a lucrative market. As soon as the organs had been removed they were despatched as fast as possible; there was only a limited time before they became unusable.'

'How were they transported?'

'I wasn't involved in that. All I can tell you is they were packed carefully in dry ice and put into special containers. Hill collected them. That was the last I saw of them. Some didn't get sent away, though. If they'd been sold within Britain I carried out the transplants at the clinic. Anywhere else and people would ask awkward questions.'

'These transplants. Did Dr Stevens assist?'

'Yes, he acted as my anaesthetist. He started getting cold feet once he realized what he'd got involved in. Wardle ordered Hill to silence him before he could blow the whistle. He was told to make it look like an accident.'

'Well, it didn't. What did they pay you for your services?'

'I was paid part of the fee for the transplants and part of the sale price for organs that were shipped elsewhere. I was also supplied,' Butler paused and looked away, looking, if possible, even more uncomfortable. 'I mean they brought girls for me sometimes.'

Clara felt vomit rise at the back of her throat and clamped her lips together, her hand over her mouth. Nash continued to stare at the prisoner. The solicitor was looking at Nash, shock apparent on his face.

'One more thing and then we'll suspend this interview,' Nash told him. 'I don't know about my colleagues, but I'm sick of the sight and sound of you. Before we switch the tape off can you tell me how Wardle and Hill intended to escape? The other night at the clinic, Wardle obviously had a plan. Do you know how they were going to do that?'

'They planned to go abroad but I've no idea where or how.'

'Is that everything?'

Throughout it all, Butler had spoken in a low monotone, not investing any of his words or phrases with the slightest inflexion. Clara's eyes strayed from time to time to the sound level indicator on the tape recorder. Her concern that Butler might have been speaking too softly for the tape was only marginally relieved by the flickering needle.

There was a long silence before Butler spoke again. If anything his voice was even quieter. 'Yes,' he muttered, 'there is one other thing. I have … that is … at my house … you see there's a girl …'

Nash jumped to his feet, his chair clattered across the floor. 'All the time you've been here in a cell you've had a girl prisoner in your house? You sat there and didn't tell us? Didn't think it was important? Or is it that you're so divorced from decency you didn't think one more girl mattered?'

'She has food and water,' Butler said defensively.

'Sergeant,' Nash turned to Clara. 'Close the tape off. I'm terminating this interview. Then get this piece of shit out of here before I say or do something I'd regret. He disgusts me.' He turned back to Butler, his anger barely under control. 'Where is she?'

Butler's head hung lower. 'Garage,' was his only response.

'Come on, Zena,' Nash urged. 'We'll get Jackie and find this poor child.'

'Why hasn't Butler's house been searched?' Zena asked as they hurried down the corridor.

'That's my fault. We've been concentrating so hard on Wardle and Hill that I forgot about Butler's home. I just hope the kid's alright.'

Butler's house was a large, detached stone building on the moor road out of Netherdale. They directed their attention to the double garage.

They entered by a door in the side wall. The first half of the garage was just that, but there was a dividing wall running down the middle of the building. The only door

230

to the second section was bolted and padlocked. 'This must be it,' Nash muttered angrily as he sorted through Butler's keys.

The inner part was divided into a kitchenette, a shower cubicle and toilet and a bedsitting room. In this room they found the sole occupant. A slender, black haired girl of no more than twelve who was sitting huddled against the wall, her eyes wide and her body trembling with fear.

The child's terror transmuted into bewilderment as she saw the intruders were not who she expected or dreaded. She stared in shocked disbelief as Zena addressed her in Russian. Then she burst into tears, tears Nash guessed were part relief, part shame. The women hurried over to the girl, Zena knelt alongside her, putting an arm around the child's shaking shoulders and smoothing her hair as she talked to her in a whisper.

Nash coughed. 'I'll wait outside.'

As he returned to the first part of the garage Nash kicked savagely at an empty cardboard box. Twenty minutes later Zena and Jackie emerged with the child. Each had a protective arm around her. 'Mikhail, this is Lyuba,' Zena told him, adding, 'perhaps her name is a good omen. It means love.'

Nash smiled and said hello. The little girl stared back with wide, frightened eyes that Nash knew would haunt his dreams for a long time. 'It is alright,' Zena told the child in Russian, 'Mikhail is a good man. He made it possible for you to be set free.'

Nash saw the look of fear lessen and disappear, to be replaced with a sweet, shy smile. Maybe there was hope after all. 'Lyuba was kidnapped from the streets of Kiev two months ago,' Zena continued. 'On her way home after gymnastic class. A van pulled up and the driver asked for directions. As she was telling him another man crept up behind and threw her into the back. He injected her arm and she fell asleep. She awoke in that place,' Zena gestured behind her. 'She has been here ever since. Lyuba is eleven years old.'

231

It was late afternoon when Nash returned to Helmsdale. He left Jackie and Zena to escort Lyuba to the rape suite and to take her statement. Nash told Pearce about the developments and the discovery of the child.

Pearce shook his in head disbelief, 'Poor kid. It makes me want to ...' He found it impossible to give voice to his fury.

A few moments later Clara walked in. 'Zena phoned; she promised to stay with Lyuba tonight. The police surgeon's going to check her. There's a problem with counselling, though. None of our counsellors speaks Russian, so Zena will do the translation. I've promised I'd help when I'm free. That's all we can do until some decision's made about her returning home. Zena's spoken to Lyuba's parents and the police in Kiev. She didn't tell them everything, just that the child was safe and well. They were overjoyed, as you'd expect. One good thing, if you can call it that; Lyuba told them it was only Butler who touched her. She hadn't been hired out like the rest.'

'I suppose that was to come,' Nash said.

Nash took the confessions into a meeting with Tom Pratt, the Chief Constable and Zena plus his own team. He handed out copies of the three statements together with those of Vatovec and the pilot. 'That's the lot. All we have to do is follow the trail of Wardle's contacts as we retrieve them from his computer. It's already shown us names and addresses throughout Britain and the Continent. We should be able to roll up the entire network.'

The Chief Constable beamed with pleasure. 'Well done, everybody. That sounds like game, set and match.'

CHAPTER NINETEEN

Nash reached his flat in a somewhat deflated state of mind. He'd been working on adrenalin for so long that now he felt immeasurably tired. He checked with the hospital on Stella's condition, to be told there was no change. Now all he wanted was sleep, but first he had a call from the leader of the team enquiring into the death of DS Thomas. Nash confirmed he'd be available for interview the following day.

He'd just put the phone down when the doorbell rang. He muttered something vaguely impolite and went to answer it. Zena was standing on the doorstep, a bottle of champagne in her hand. 'I've come to say goodbye. I fly to St Petersburg tomorrow. I'll start mopping up the Russian end of this operation. For me, this is only one battle in the war. I was asked to deliver you this.' She held up the bottle. 'I have a message. It is from Sergei and Anna Svetlov. They asked me to say that it's in gratitude for recovering Katya's body. Now they can take her home, bury her and mourn her. This is something for you to remember them by.'

'Come on in. There's far too much for me to drink.'

Nash went into the kitchen and put the bottle in the freezer to chill. When he returned to the sitting room Zena had removed her coat. Nash stopped in his tracks. Zena was wearing nothing but a smile. 'I also wanted to give you something to remember.'

'From the information we got out of Wardle's computer we've already secured the release of five more youngsters in Britain,' Nash told Pratt. 'A further thirteen men are in custody. We've sent paperwork to seven countries in Western Europe, plus a shipload to Zena's office. There have already been over two hundred arrests.'

'What else is left to do?'

'Not much. I delivered the papers to the CPS. One of their men looked through them whilst I was there. I thought he was going to wet himself with excitement. He told me he'd heard that Wardle's solicitor has approached three top barristers and all three had refused the brief. They pleaded pressure of work, but the word is nobody wants to touch it.'

Pratt smiled, 'Barristers with principles, now there's a first. I've got news for you. They've finished the investigation into Thomas's death but Armistead's disciplinary hearing opens tomorrow. They've booked a hotel in Cheshire, close to Manchester airport. You're to report there tomorrow. You'll be needed for a couple of days. Here are the details.' He passed Nash a fax.

Nash stuffed the paper in his coat pocket.

Back in Helmsdale, he called Clara into his office. 'I'm going away for a couple of days. It's that disciplinary hearing. If you need me urgently I can be contacted at ...' He rummaged in his pocket and unfolded the fax. He gave a low whistle of surprise.

'What is it?'

'Talk about coincidence. The hotel I'm booked into. Lauren works there.'

'Lauren? The girl who used to be receptionist at The Square and Compass? The one you were sha ... I mean seeing.'

'Shagging, was what you were going to say? Yes is the answer to both questions.'

Nash gave evidence the following afternoon but was asked to stay the night in case the enquiry needed further information. His testimony centred on the bugging of his office and the pilfered phone records. He made it clear throughout that he considered both acts to be the work of Armistead and Thomas alone. That there was nothing to suggest DCI Fleming had been involved or had prior knowledge of the irregular conduct.

He decided to dine in his room. It had not been pleasant testifying against a fellow officer, despite his loathing for Armistead. Added to that, there were over a dozen other officers in the hotel. Events at Helmsdale had hit the headlines; the grapevine had done the rest. Nash was well on the way to celebrity status, which was something he didn't particularly relish.

About 9 p.m. there was a knock on his door. 'Room service.' The trolley was set out with his order.

He stood aside to let the woman wheel it in. She pushed the trolley to the middle of the room and turned to face him. She looked at him with amusement and something more. 'Where would you like it, sir?'

'Lauren! I wondered if I might see you. I wasn't sure whether you still worked here.'

'There was I thinking you'd arranged the whole thing just so we could get together. When I saw your name on the reservation sheet I couldn't resist the temptation to surprise you.'

'You certainly did that. I haven't heard from you since you left Helmsdale.'

'I haven't had much time with all the training and I've had a lot to worry about. My father died last month and mother's taken it hard.'

'I'm sorry.'

'What I need is something to cheer me up.' Lauren walked up to him and put her hands on his shoulders. He caught a whiff of her scent, remembered the light fragrance. His pulse began to race. 'And I think you've got the very thing,' she continued. One hand slipped from his shoulder and reached towards his groin. 'I thought so,' she whispered.

He'd removed her blouse and skirt when there was another knock at the door. He zipped up his trousers and padded across the room. 'Whoever it is, send them away. Tell them you're doing something important. Tell them you're doing me.'

From the doorway Jackie Fleming's gaze went straight past him to the sofa. She lowered the champagne bottle. Her face flushed with anger. 'I was going to suggest we celebrate but I see you have company. Of a sort.'

Nash stared after her as she flounced down the corridor. 'Mike?'

He turned. Lauren was standing in the bedroom doorway. 'I'm coming,' he told her.

'Oh I hope not,' Lauren laughed. 'At least, not yet.'

*

The following lunchtime, Clara was alone in the CID suite when Nash returned. She looked up as he walked in. She looked distraught. Her eyes were red with crying. 'Clara! What's wrong?'

'Mike, I'm sorry. I can't … I had a phone call … I don't know how …' Clara gulped and took a deep breath. 'There was a phone call this morning. I'm so sorry, Mike. Stella died last night.'

THE END

AFTERWORD

Christmas was approaching when Nash received an envelope bearing a Russian stamp. The letter expressed the gratitude of the Russian government. It took Nash a few seconds to decipher the signature of the President. He read it before placing it in a drawer. Somehow it all seemed meaningless.

A few days later he received another envelope with a similar stamp. It contained a Christmas card. He studied it in silence. Clara had entered the room. 'What is it, Mike?'

He passed the card to her. Instead of a traditional Christmas scene, it depicted a smiling family group, consisting of a handsome middle-aged man, an attractive woman and a pretty teenager with the joy of life blazing from her eyes. The signatures were Sergei, Anna and Milla. 'About the only Christmas present I could have wished for.'

AUTHOR'S NOTE

All authors approach writing a book differently. Some think up the whole plot before they set a word down. Others sit in front of either a blank screen or sheet of paper. If I had to say which of those is closer to my approach I'd say the latter. *What Lies Beneath* is a fair example of what I mean. I started with only the idea of an angler fishing a skull from a tarn. I even had a stretch of water in mind. But that was all. The rest of the plot was organic, if you'll pardon the pun.

At the beginning of every work of fiction there's a disclaimer about the characters and events being purely fictitious. Well, that's certainly true of the characters in *What Lies Beneath*. Unfortunately, the incidents described reflect real life. Okay, so they didn't happen in Yorkshire; or at least I hope not.

When I was researching *What Lies Beneath* I was horrified to find that every one of the crimes perpetrated by the villains in the book was mirrored by events in real life. In fact, I shrank from portraying worse deeds. Everything is there for anyone to read: the trafficking, the prostitution and the organ removals.

When Zena quotes statistics regarding the scale of human trafficking, those figures came from official reports.

I wish it were otherwise. If that had been so, this book would never have been written. I would have gladly paid that price for the events not to have happened. But they did, and once I'd learned it, I was compelled to continue. If you think that was easy, think again. Whilst I was writing some of the more harrowing passages, particularly those relating to the ordeal of the victims, I found myself unable to sleep. Nash's nightmare about being attacked by scythe wielding surgeons stems from a nightmare I endured.

Bill Kitson 2009

The D.I. Mike Nash Series

Book 1: WHAT LIES BENEATH
Book 2: VANISH WITHOUT TRACE
Book 3: PLAYING WITH FIRE

Please join our mailing list for updates on D. I. Mike Nash, free Kindle crime thriller, detective, mystery books and new releases.

www.joffebooks.com

FREE KINDLE BOOKS

Please join our mailing list for free Kindle books and new releases, including crime thrillers, mysteries, romance and more, as well as news on the next book by Bill Kitson! www.joffebooks.com

Thank you for reading this book. If you enjoyed it please leave feedback on Amazon or Goodreads, and if there is anything we missed or you have a question about then please get in touch. The author and publishing team appreciate your feedback and time reading this book.

We're very grateful to eagle-eyed readers who take the time to contact us. Please send any errors you find to corrections@joffebooks.com